To Char
Enjoy!

Call
Me
Mikki

DANIEL LANCE WRIGHT

Call Me Mikki

Edited by Jake George
www.sagewordservices.com

Printed by Sage Words Publishing
www.sagewordspublishing.com

Cover artwork by Sage Words Services
http://www.sagewordsservices.com

ISBN-13: 978-0997096224
ISBN-10: 0997096225

Contents

CHAPTER 1

"My friends call me Mikki," she said, zooming in on Patrick Daniels, the 45-year-old news anchor. She adjusted the focus from behind studio camera one.

"Okay," he replied, glancing her direction, as if disinterested in the information he requested.

Through the camera's viewfinder, Michaela studied the image. Daniels was a good-looking guy with a full head of neatly combed auburn hair, and just a smattering of gray above the ears. Other than the hint of crow's feet, his skin was smooth and slightly tanned. No doubt, the man was good-looking, but she was convinced he was a player before she ever accepted employment at KBTA TV. Still, she felt an urge to get a better look. She peeked out from behind the camera to get an unframed view of the man sitting behind the desk on the news set as if he was the king of the news business in Comanche Falls. She thought about that for a moment. In a way, he was. At least viewer ratings indicated that he might be. He seemed to be in good physical condition for a middle-aged man. She wondered if he had played college football, or some other physically demanding sport.

Maybe he was currently into some sport—tennis perhaps, or maybe golf.

Daniels' seeming disinterest in her response to his question about her name irked her. He did not seem to care one hoot in hell whether he received an answer or not. Was his inquiry just a conceited attempt at cordiality? Could the man think so little of her that he did not care what the answer would be, or if an answer was forthcoming at all? Could he have been ruder? She thought not. *What a jerk.*

Daniels shuffled through scripts fanned out on the desk in front of him. Harsh halogen lights shining down on the news desk from multiple directions obliterated shadows in every cranny. He scrutinized the teleprompter mounted on the camera lens. "Tell Shawn, the teleprompter operator, in case you don't know him yet, to roll off the cover page. I'll go straight to the headlines." He smirked. "I think after eighteen years of sitting in this chair I can remember my name, what show this is, and what time it is without a script."

Michaela leaned sideways from behind the camera and nodded confirmation. "Sure." His attempt at humor was blatantly sarcastic, maybe pompous, too. It did nothing to change her opinion for the better. *He better not start talking about me that way. I barely know this guy and I already don't like him. I don't care how good-looking he is. I bet the stories I've heard about him are true.* The newly hired young camera operator pulled the small microphone on her headset intimately close to her mouth and repeated the anchorman's order into it. She locked the camera head into position and stepped from behind it out to the side. Flipping the small microphone attached to her headset up and away from her mouth, she announced in a loud voice, "One minute to studio. Get your mike clipped on, Mister Daniels... you, too, Miss Crane."

Danica Crane, Patrick's co-anchor, was just then rushing through one side of the swinging double doors into the expansive studio. "Sorry I'm late," she said, leaping up onto the foot-high platform stage and dropping into her chair on the news set. Although harried, Danica otherwise looked perfectly put together in a blue dress with a modest collar—every golden blonde, shoulder-length hair in place and makeup done to perfection. As quickly as Michaela's opinion of Patrick Daniels deteriorated, her assessment and admiration of Danica Crane skyrocketed. Here was a lady put together in perfect fashion even while under duress of a deadline, probably racing in from a breaking story somewhere.

The young camera operator stepped laterally behind studio camera two and repeated the set-up procedure for the opening two-shot of Patrick and Danica.

Patrick looked at his co-anchor and appeared amused as she fumbled with a small clip-on microphone. "Tell me," he asked, "shall we make a wager on when I'll have to begin the show without you? I would bet a hefty wad of cash that it'll be soon. Even if I lost and had to pay up, I still wouldn't believe that you have it in you to be on time...to anything, anywhere actually." He seemed to enjoy making the point in sarcastic expression and tone.

"Oh, shut up," she mumbled while pulling out a wrinkle on her lapel above and below the microphone. She added, "You may be my boyfriend, but that doesn't make you any less a wiseass. My ability to dismiss your snarky crap is thinning rapidly."

Michaela ground her teeth together as she zoomed in to the co-anchors and then pulled out to a full two-shot. She was a new hire and it certainly was not her place to comment, but she wanted to. She wanted to tell that arrogant ass exactly what she thought.

Grin fixed, Daniels winked at Danica, but otherwise ignored the terse comment by his co-anchor and turned his attention back to Michaela, now standing between the cameras. "So, you're new here, huh?" he asked.

"Sure am... thirty seconds to studio... today's my first day."

"Part-timer?"

"Yep."

"Usually I see new camera operators with a trainer assigned to them and at their side. Where's yours?"

"Not my first rodeo. I came over from the heathens across town. Fifteen seconds..."

"Ah, the fine folks at KFAL. Have some insurmountable problem with them?" he asked, regarding the local CBS affiliate.

"Not at all. Fine bunch of people. Just no room for advancement. Live in five... standby." She held a hand high over her head with fingers spread wide, folding fingers down one at a time.

"Nice to meet you, Mikki."

"Call me Michaela. My *friends* call me Mikki. You're not there yet," she said just as her last finger folded into her palm.

Daniels' head reared back while glancing toward his grinning co-anchor who obviously enjoyed the put-down, never pulling her gaze away from the eye of the camera.

Danica whispered sideways, "She gotcha good. What did you do to get on her bad side already?"

The young technician brought her stiff arm down to point at Patrick for the cue. Red telly lights came on beneath the camera lens. They were on the air.

As Daniels read the first headline while on a two-shot with Danica, Michaela stepped back behind camera one, allowing a private smile to sprout. *He deserved that. Sarcasm tumbled out of his mouth a bit too easily, like it's an everyday, all-the-time thing with him. I bet he's an arrogant dick, just like that idiot FAL anchor.*

The two news anchors topped one another, alternating news teasers in crisp fashion.

Daniels began wrapping up the thirty seconds worth of headlines, "... And, the President responds to criticism of supplying arms to a Muslim country without consensus from Congress. Good evening, everyone. I'm Patrick Daniels..."

"... And I'm Danica Crane ..."

"... And this is News Central 12's *News at Six.*"

The microphones switched off while intro music played over canned montage video of the biggest news stories of the previous year. "We're clear," Michaela said. "Thirty seconds out."

Daniels straightened his script and tapped the bundled ends on the desk to even them. "It's still nice to meet you, *Michaela*," he said, drawing out her name, exaggerating each syllable, as if he had a speech impediment.

"Fifteen seconds," Michaela announced, and then added, "I'm hoping it's nice to meet you, too. Let's wait and see how it goes. Whaddaya say?" Her hand went up. "Five seconds. Standby." She counted down.

It appeared Daniels had been attempting to formulate a comeback but ran out of time before going live. The first news segment underway, Michaela knew it would be about seven minutes of live news before the first commercial break. She had studied the broadcast log and developed a quick understanding of the shows' format, as only an experienced hire could. This allowed time for her mind to wander onto other things, personal things.

Michaela was not at all fond of Walter Peck, the chief news anchor at the other station. He was younger than Daniels, unmarried and a player, always trying to talk Michaela into a date. He was lewd and full of himself. Peck's idea of a date was little more than a euphemism for sex—nothing to do with relationship building or having any kind of a good time outside the bedroom. She took a chance once, but never again. She had to threaten violence to prevent Peck from sexually assaulting her. Thanks to good old Walter, and having glanced into Wally's world, Michaela's opinion of anchormen carried over to this station and Patrick Daniels. This guy had to be a player too, judging by the stories she had heard. As far as she was concerned, Daniels was no different, just older. It may have been a snap opinion, but she believed it sound. Nothing Daniels said or did had thus far shaken it.

The director, a long-time friend, spoke into her headset from behind the glass wall to her left. "Standby camera two, Mikki..."

Michaela stepped from behind camera one and stood between the two electronic eyes mounted on substantial bases. She held her arms spread wide.

"Cue cam two."

She swung an arm away from one over to two.

The voice whispering into her ear from the headset sounded bored, maybe drowsy. Word was that her buddy, Stan Brister, the director and commercial production manager, didn't just drink, but had an alcohol problem. If so, as far as Michaela could tell, he must be a high-functioning alcoholic, because he had a reputation in the business for flawless work. She thought he was the most professional television man in the city, regardless what popular gossip happened to say. And, all that chatter came from peers at KFAL. Since she knew Stan fairly well, she had always assumed they were jealous of his creativity as a production manager. No one in town could produce better commercial spots than Stan Brister.

Since his drinking was no secret, even to the competition, management may have turned a blind eye to it because of his ability. He was about fifty, maybe mid-fifties. She was not sure of that, but his hair was white and he wore a flat-top haircut. He reminded her of a cigar-chomping, aging drill sergeant with a lean and tight body, complete with multiple tattoos on both arms. Never married and the quintessential confirmed bachelor, Stan was not gay but had no desire for a long-term relationship. He was honest about that mindset—vocal, too. He certainly was not a skirt chaser like Walter Peck. She knew Stan socially before coming to work at KBTA, and she liked him. Stan's style of in-your-face, but low-key honesty was rare and refreshing. He happened to be the reason that she sought employment here.

Both local network affiliates tended to congregate at the same bar downtown, a place called the Lazy S, the perfect Texas name for a local watering hole that ballyhooed the state's ranching heritage. That's where she first met Stan. Friends, co-workers, others in the television business and, of course, the staff at the Lazy S were his only family. Although he seemed very happy with that arrangement, Michaela had recently noticed Stan paying particular attention to one specific waitress. On several occasions, Michaela noticed that while she attempted conversation with him, his eyes followed that waitress instead, while offering only one-word answers to whatever Michaela might ask him.

Michaela's daydream evaporated and attention refocused when she detected descending inflection in Danica's voice. The co-anchor had begun wrapping a story. Michaela again stepped from behind the camera.

Danica finished with, "... and both sides of the aisle have not come together on that issue either." She paused. "More news after this break."

The red telly lights beneath the camera lens blinked off. "And, we're clear," Michaela announced. "Ninety seconds out then back to studio."

Michaela had learned much of the story on Patrick and Danica through conversations she was privy to among co-workers and friends she'd had since entering the television business. She called it lazy-ass chatter, a direct reference to the gossip and rumor mill at the Lazy S Bar. Apparently, Patrick and Danica developed a romantic relationship sometime last year, sparking a feud with Patrick's wife, Margaret. She kicked him out of the house and filed for divorce. From what Michaela had gleaned, he did not want to divorce his wife and was stringing Danica along for sexual amusement. Now the relationship—if that's what it should be called—between the co-anchors had become rocky, or so was her understanding of it.

They sniped at one another and were not smiling about whatever it was they now whispered about. Michaela grinned and shook her head when she visualized a caricature of Daniels with a woman dangling from each ear, teeth clamped on the lobes, and him appearing as a clueless, droopy-eyed dog. *Yep, he's a dick all right.* Michaela stepped forward from between the cameras into the circle of light created by the harsh halogen scoop lights. "Fifteen seconds... standby."

Daniels had the last word in the more-or-less private conversation with his co-anchor. Michaela distinctly heard him say, "Okay then, I'll go by myself."

Michaela cued him.

He seemed to have trouble relaxing that knit of annoyance in his brow. As luck would have it, the story was about fatalities from a plane crash northwest of Comanche Falls, about two hundred miles northwest in the panhandle near Amarillo. The look on his face came off, coincidentally, as appropriate—sad concern.

She glanced to Danica who was waiting her turn to introduce a video report by one of the field reporters. She was more than annoyed. She appeared angry—lips clenched, face reddening.

Michaela enjoyed the drama and hoped it continued. If so, it would keep an otherwise menial television job as a studio camera operator less monotonous. It seemed as though she may have come to work at KBTA just in time to see a rift developing in their love life. On second thought, the word "love" might not bookend comfortably between those two. Although workplace romances are common, they hardly ever survive, or last beyond the initial passionate heat. Michaela had no desire to become involved with anyone she worked with, or with anyone else for that matter, not until she achieved her goals. Walter Peck soured her on dating in the workplace anyhow, leaving her convinced that any liaison would be doomed from the beginning, even if it did begin with strong attraction and good chemistry. She felt silly for giving that idiot, Peck, a shot.

The remainder of the news sequence proved uneventful. The two spoke no more off-camera. Patrick went into the wrap nearing the end of the half-hour show; the director went to a two-shot of Patrick and Danica, both smiling as if everything was peachy. The studio lights went out. Backlights came up. A musical outro to the show blared inside the cavernous studio when the co-anchors' microphones were clipped. The two on set kept right on smiling even though silhouetted faces were all that remained for the viewers at home. Music built to a stinger end and then the deep, resonant voice of a popular actor reverberated through the studio, voicing a Dodge Ram truck commercial.

"We're clear," Michaela announced, followed by the perfunctory, "Good show, guys."

"Thanks," Danica mumbled as she stripped the small microphone from her lapel. She sprang to her feet and hurried off the set. Without slowing, she hit the double doors and threw them open with attitude as she left the studio like an angry gunslinger exiting a saloon for a high-noon showdown.

"I apologize for Danica's little outburst earlier," Patrick said.

"Sounded to me like Miss Crane simply gave as good as she got. I heard no outburst, and I certainly don't think you need to be apologizing for *her*."

A smile curled one side of Daniels's mouth, accompanied by a quizzical frown. "Well then... maybe I should be apologizing for me. I'm sorry for her outburst and my lack of attempt to stop it. Better?"

She rolled her eyes. "Not really," she replied as Stan Brister exited the director's booth and approached them.

In a gravelly, cigar and alcohol soaked voice, Stan called out from across the studio, "Another magnificent news show under our belts... eh, Patrick?"

"You bet. We keep settin' 'em up and knockin' 'em down."

"Are you going downtown for a drink or two or three or... you know?" Stan asked.

"Not sure... haven't made up my mind yet."

"Is Danica coming?"

"Nah, she's pissed," Patrick replied.

"What about you, Mikki? Want to meet me there?" Stan asked. "Hey," Daniels blurted. "You called her Mikki and she didn't complain."

Michaela raised her eyebrows, holding a satisfied expression. "Yeah, he did call me Mikki, but he's my buddy."

"So I have to earn the right? Is that what you're saying?"

"Yep." She turned back to Stan. "Sure, I'll have a drink with you."

Stan extended what appeared to be a disciplinary finger. "You have to promise me that you'll sit at the BTA table and not wander off and sit with those yahoos from FAL. You're with us now. Deal?"

"Of course. I wouldn't have it...hey, wait a minute." She flipped a finger toward Patrick. "Will he be with us?"

Stan opened his mouth to speak but didn't have a chance to get a word out before Daniels blurted, "Thank you so much for the invitation. I think I *will* join you for that drink, after all." He pulled a sly half-grin.

She offered a weak smile and turned away. She then grimaced and hissed for no one to hear, "Oh crap."

CHAPTER 2

Patrick Daniels sat alone at a table at the Lazy S Bar. He left Stan and Michaela at the television station. They were finishing about ten minutes of post sequence wrap-up work needed before they could join him. Patrick was not the introspective type, but here he sat, alone, first gin and tonic half finished. He was somewhat happy they were slow about showing up. The quiet decompression time was nice. No distractions and the birth of alcohol-induced mellowness happened to be the perfect combination for thinking about things. Whether he wanted to or not, he needed to. Matters in his life needed sorting and decisions needed to be made. He had been riding the fence long enough on at least two huge issues—his so-called girlfriend, Danica, and his estranged wife, Margaret.

Tossing aside twelve years of marriage to Margaret was an ongoing struggle. He wrestled with the notion of life without her, as he had for some time—the reason for his countless delay tactics regarding signing the divorce papers. The fling with his co-anchor began as just that, a brief encounter. Indulging in it was stupid in the first place. Unfortunately, that stupidity did not subside over time. Instead, it teamed up with procrastination and took on a life of its own, allowing the fling to become a long-term affair, reeling out of control. After a time, there was no way to keep the relationship a secret—not in a television station and certainly not while entrenched in a job that kept him in the public eye—sitting next to the object of his lust night after night. The affair was doomed from the beginning to become a subject of gossip. *Yep. I stepped into a deep pile of crap long ago and have been mired in it since the start.* Patrick gulped his gin and tonic. Even before the glass left his lips, he was signaling the waitress for another. To make matters worse, he did not love Danica; he never did. The problem needed to be fixed. The only way to fix it was to end it, but how could he do that without hurting her and jeopardizing both their careers? Those problems, he thought, would go hand-in-hand. Maybe there was no way to do it delicately, but it did not keep him from searching for a magically perfect solution.

After playing mental badminton with the issue for a time, Patrick finally decided that he did not want to think about these problems anymore right now. It was a headache he did not want— not at the moment anyhow. So, as always, he set the problem aside to worry over another day. What he did want was the next round that the waitress had just delivered to his table. He smiled and glanced up. "Thanks."

"Just wave if you need another," she said as she spun on her heels and was off, responding to another patron.

Slipping into an alcohol haze was inviting. Patrick hoped it would help him set his dilemma aside for a while, but so far, the predicament continued to circle his thoughts. He thumbed condensation from the side of his drink glass and hoisted it to his lips. He was stuck with a sex partner who believed herself his significant other and who, on top of that, was jealous of his wife. Nothing could be more screwed up.

He wondered if he would have strayed if he and Margaret had had children. It was a question he thought about often, but it was impossible to answer. Margaret was incapable of bearing children. As disgusted as he was with himself for acting like a rutting buck, he figured that he would have succumbed to temptation anyhow. Now, he was torn. He did not know whether to fight to repair his marriage or let Margaret go. He still loved her—no doubt about that—but she deserved happiness, not this limbo he imposed on her. Would it be a selfish thing to try and hang onto her at this late stage? Did Margaret even think of him as a spouse anymore? These questions needed answers, and soon, if he planned on retaining even a smidgen of control over a future with or without her.

Regardless of the marriage situation, he had to figure out a way to disengage from Danica without jeopardizing their on-air partnership. Both of their careers depended on ratings they received from their nightly performance as a news team. News Central 12's *News at Six* had a solid number one Nielsen rating in the market, fetching premium advertising dollars. He was convinced that altering the newscast by splitting a duopoly would cause ratings to plummet, followed by advertising income, eventually ending their jobs at KBTA and possibly ruining both of their careers. Viewers were fickle about their favorite news anchors.

He lifted his cradled chin in his palm and watched a small contingent of people from the other television station, KFAL, come through the door laughing—four people led by counterpart Walter Peck.

Patrick smiled and waved amiably, but had no desire to strike up a conversation. Apparently, neither did they, returning the cordiality but veering away and heading for a round booth in the corner some distance away.

Patronage of the Lazy S appeared typical for a Monday night. Aside from the group from the competition, there was only a smattering of customers, mostly individuals sitting at the bar. Patrick knew a couple of the men by name, but only because they were hardcore drinkers who came in every night; most were white-collar, single and attracted to this bar because of its downtown location near the big banks and office buildings. All the cowboys, farmers and oilfield workers usually went to those bars near the outskirts of Comanche Falls. Like him, most regulars, both male and female, searched for a semblance of companionship for a while longer before calling it a day and going home.

Patrick turned up the last swallow of a gin and tonic and waved at the waitress for another. He removed his tie and stuffed it into his blazer pocket.

The waitress delivered the fresh drink moments later. "Is your friend, Stan, coming in tonight?" the waitress asked. She was clearly the oldest of three waitresses working the floor but quite attractive for a fifty-something woman. Patrick glanced toward the door. Stan and Michaela were just then coming in. He flipped a hand their direction. "See for yourself."

The waitress grinned and scurried away.

Walter Peck whistled and waved at Michaela.

She glanced his way without returning the greeting or smiling. A flick of her eyes in Peck's direction was the only indication she even heard it.

Patrick wondered if there was something going on between them. "Okay, guys," he said, "you have to order two drinks apiece. You're already behind by two. But I confess that I'm probably drinking a bit too fast."

"I can't get carried away tonight," Stan said. "I have to be at the station early for a studio commercial shoot in the morning." He politely helped Michaela into a chair. "You're a great camera operator. Can I get you to come in and help me with it, Mikki?"

"Sorry, Stan, but I have class in the morning. You mind if I beg off and come in at the regular time tomorrow afternoon?"

"Nah, I don't mind. It was a shot in the dark anyhow."

"Class, huh? Are you still in school?" Patrick asked. The effects of the gin had begun lightening his head.

The waitress placed coasters in front of them. "Nice to see you again, Mister Brister," the waitress said. Although she addressed him as "Mister Brister," the lilt of her voice was clearly meant to be personal in nature, not businesslike.

He blushed. "Please, call me Stan. In fact, I'm begging you to. 'Mister Brister' is an odd-ass rhyme."

She chuckled. "Sure... Stan. What can I bring you?"

"How about a pitcher of beer and a couple of mugs." He looked to Michaela. "Is that okay with you, Mikki?"

She nodded. "Perfect." She turned back to Patrick. "I have one more year before I can claim a diploma, Mister Daniels."

"It may not rhyme, but it sounds just as awful as 'Mister Brister.' Call me Patrick." He grinned. "Or, 'Hey You,' would be preferable to 'Mister Daniels.' I feel old enough as it is."

Her eyebrows lifted slightly. "Okay, *Patrick*," she said, overemphasizing each syllable just as he had done with her name earlier.

Patrick grinned. "Touché." He took a sip of his gin and tonic. "What's your major?"

"Journalism, with a minor in telecommunications. Actually, that's the reason I left FAL. I want to work in the news department and your news director, Harry Alexander, told me that a news videographer position was opening soon. That, of course, would put me in a good position to accelerate my goal of becoming a reporter and writer... the sooner the better. Life as a studio camera jockey isn't awful, but it won't get me where I want to go. This lateral-move job was offered to get me employed and begin training so I can jump right into the position sooner. While Randy, your current news photog, works off his notice, I'll be going out with him this week on mornings that I don't have class. I went with him this morning and he taught me tricks for getting good shots with a touch of artistry. It was a hoot. He's talented. No wonder that station in Houston hired him away."

As Michaela spoke, Patrick studied her. She was a beautiful creature about half his age—dark auburn hair bound into a ponytail hung to the middle of her back. She was tall, about five-nine or ten, and slender. He wondered if she would be tough enough to be one half of a field reporting team, toting a camera with a mounted shotgun microphone on her shoulder for extended periods of time. Judging by her youth, quick wit and candor, the answer would have to be yes. Having the opportunity to stare back at that beautiful face beside the camera often did not sound like a bad thing either.

"How about you," she asked. "Do you do much field reporting?"

"I wish I could do more... the investigative type. I prefer it to studio work. It's interesting, sleuthing out stories like a detective." He sipped his gin and tonic. "As a matter of fact, I've begun an investigation of Landers Energy Company. A group of homeowners have filed a class action suit against them, charging culpability for fouling a community's water well and for recent earth tremors." He stabbed the air with a stiff finger. "Hey, I have an idea. Maybe I can talk ol' Harry into letting you come along with me on an interview with Robert Landers this Friday. Would your schedule allow it? Or would you even want to?"

She straightened, suddenly more attentive. "Heck, yeah. I have classes Tuesdays and Fridays this semester, but I've been a good girl and it would not hurt a darn thing to miss my Friday class one time, especially for something like this. I bet that since it's a journalism class, I might even convince the prof to allow class credit... if Harry will write a note for me to deliver."

"I'm thinking that he will. I'll talk to him about it, too," Patrick said.

Her demeanor changed, becoming more talkative and cheerier. "I forgot that Landers' home office was here in Comanche Falls. Wasn't it a subsidiary of Landers Energy that spilled fifty thousand tons of arsenic-bearing coal ash on the east coast?"

"One and the same," Patrick said.

"I heard they paid no federal income tax on seven-point-one billion dollars in profits to its shareholders over three tax years, yet claimed four hundred thirty million dollars in tax refunds from various subsidies. True?"

"Hey, that is true. Wow! I'm impressed. A young adult that actually keeps up with current events...go figure."

The glimmer of interest in her eyes faded upon hearing the sarcasm. "There's something else I know...your reputation. Just so you know."

"Reputation? What reputation?"

"This *favor* you'd do for me; what's it going to cost? Should I expect to wake up in a motel room someday in a drugged stupor, next to you, naked?" One eyebrow lifted and her head tilted to a suspicious slant.

Patrick saw that Stan, who had been quietly drinking his beer, now grinned like a chimpanzee at Michaela. She looked at him and nodded, eyebrow remaining high, as if it were a private joke of some kind. "Oh, come on. Do you guys really think that I would try—?"

"Yep," she interrupted. "I do. From everything I've heard, it's not just possible but probable."

Stan clucked his tongue. "Well, buddy, I've known you for some time. So, I'll not say that you will, but I sure can't say that you won't."

Patrick opened his mouth to object, but nothing came out. At a loss for words, he slammed his mouth shut. Although he had no plan to ask for a return favor, and certainly nothing of a sordid nature like that, he was enamored with Michaela. So, he went with it and feigned having been insulted, turning his nose up. "Humph. I can't believe you think so little of me." He tried holding a hurt expression, but it did not last. He smirked, with a wink.

"Aha! I was right," Michaela exclaimed. "You *are* trying to put me in your lecherous cross hairs."

He did not answer. Still grinning, he lifted the gin and tonic to his lips and sipped. Returning it to its resting place on the table, he said, "Settle down. I was kidding."

"No you weren't."

"Look, I have enough drama in my life right now without adding you to the mix."

Michaela added a squint to her distrustful face.

Patrick nodded approval. "Although I have to say, Stan, she's not totally ugly is she?"

Stan laughed. "Oh, hell no. She's fine... really fine."

"Hey, guys, I'm sitting right here. Don't talk about me like I'm a medium-rare, rib eye steak," Michaela responded, rolling her eyes.

Patrick lifted his gin and tonic and gulped the last swallow. "This has been fun, but I'm going home." He rose and shoved his chair under the table. He looked down at her and then leaned over the chair toward her. "What's your last name?"

"Ross."

"Well, Michaela Ross... Friday?"

She drew a deep breath, held it for a moment and then huffed it out. "What the hell! Friday it is."

CHAPTER 3

Margaret Daniels checked the price on a twin pack of steaks in the refrigerated meat case of the grocery store near her home. She tossed it into her cart and began to roll on when the absurdity of what she had done struck her. She jerked the shopping cart to a standstill. Emotion swarmed her, and tears welled in her eyes, rolling uncontrollably down her cheeks. She did not need a twin pack of anything. She was buying for one ever since making the painful decision to force Patrick to leave the home they had shared for twelve years. For Christ's sake, she did not even care much for beef. Patrick did. She backed up two steps and tossed the package of meat back into the case.

Patrick had moved into an apartment a few weeks back, and although she knew where, Margaret struggled against recurring urges to go talk to him. Even now, walking through a grocery store, the desire was strong to do just that. She had to take firmer steps to get on with her life, and dropping by for a visit was no way to get it done. She realized distance and time between them would be the only way to sever the bond. It was the most difficult thing she had ever done.

The supermarket was busy. She stood motionless, head down, trying almost desperately to control her breathing and compose herself before moving on. She did not want to be seen in such a vulnerable state, even by strangers.

After a tense moment, she came to realize that it was futile. She could not stem the flow of tears streaking her cheeks as her emotions took control.

Margaret glimpsed a man approaching from the opposite direction. She dropped her head, trying to hide her tears.

The man casually looked her way and offered a quick smile. He glanced again and the smile vanished. He abruptly pulled his cart to a stop next to her. "Are you okay?" He tried getting a better look at her downturned face.

She attempted to shield her face from view and chuckled nervously, refusing to look up. "Oh, I'm just having one of those girlie days. I can't seem to keep my emotions in check."

"I hope it's not too forward of me to say, but it looks to be a little more than that. I don't want to move on until I'm sure it's not something worse... an illness perhaps."

"Oh, no, nothing like that," she said, and then paused. "Unless you consider a failed marriage a disease. And, if so, then I guess I'm sick." She finally lifted her chin from her chest. "You're very kind but..." She was taken aback when her eyes met his. He was attractive, extremely so—six-two perhaps with a thick head of wavy black hair. He was slender but not skinny. Muscles rippled beneath a red golf shirt conservatively tucked into gray slacks. Her eyes went to his left hand—no ring, nor a pale area where one had been. She found herself quite suddenly without a voice. "I... uh... well—"

"Tell you what," he said. "I have time and, if you do, how about we set aside grocery shopping for a few minutes. I'll buy coffee for us at that little food court at the front of the store. I bet whatever is troubling you won't seem so bad afterwards. What do you say?"

"I've never seen you in here before. Do you live in Comanche Falls?"

"I do now... been in town about a month. I'm Randall Forrester with Baker Mortgage Company, that little gray brick building at the corner of Elm and Tenth. It's a converted old house."

"Sure. I know where that is."

"I was recently transferred from the home office in Dallas to manage the branch office here for a time and work it into a profitable enterprise in this North Texas area. And you?" He extended a friendly hand, placed her hand in his. Throwing caution to the wind, she answered, "I'm Margaret Daniels, former housewife and currently unemployed. Nice to meet you."

"It's certainly nice to meet you, too," he said, shaking her hand. "Can you type, use an adding machine and operate a copier?"

"Sure. Why?"

"I might be able to do something about the unemployed part of that comment."

She released her grip to disengage from his hand. "You're very kind, but—"

"I am starting to interview. This is not a pick-up line...honestly." He did not release her hand, despite Margaret's gentle insistence. "It's nothing you have to decide now, just something we might talk about." He continued holding on to her hand.

Somewhat shocked by his reluctance to release her hand, she blurted, "This is not how I would have chosen to meet someone like you."

"Someone like me?"

"Uh... you know what I mean."

"Not really." He smiled. "I'll assume it's something good."

"You should." She retrieved her hand. "Come on. Let's go get that coffee before I go directly from crying to embarrassment."

They created a two-shopping-cart caravan and headed for the front of the store. On the way, Margaret had second thoughts. *How could I have agreed to coffee with a total stranger so quickly?* Although not yet legally binding, for all intents and purposes she was divorced. Still, years of monogamy had her thinking that somehow she was unfaithful by doing this.

Randall glanced over his shoulder and smiled at her, as if to see whether she still followed.

She returned a fast, nervous smile, her only outward response. On the inside, however, she felt a fluttering tingle in the pit of her stomach, followed by a quick draw of air in response to that gorgeous smile he gave her. She realized then that her reservations had little to do with feelings of disloyalty and everything to do with a physical attraction strong enough to disrupt good judgment.

Randall parked his cart next to a brick partition and helped Margaret pull hers in close behind his. He gestured to a small table with two chairs. "Have a seat. I'll get coffee."

Margaret's eyes followed him, but she kept glancing in another direction, across the many faces coming through the checkout lines. Each time she glimpsed someone looking her way, she felt as though she were being judged. That perception intensified when an elderly man met her analytical gaze with a smile and a wink, as if to say, "You can't fool an old geezer like me.

I know that guy isn't your husband, and I saw you looking at him like you were checking out the flavor selections at an ice cream store."

She fidgeted, believing these long dormant, lustful feelings were on display for all to see. The word "mistake" repeated in her head with machine-gun rapidity.

"Here you go," Randall said as he set the steaming paper cup in front of her. "Can I get you creamer, or sugar perhaps?"

"I take it black, but thanks."

He sat across from her. "I truly don't want to pry, but if it helps to talk, I'm more than willing to listen."

"If you have ice cream in your shopping cart, you don't have time," she joked, and then wondered if he did have ice cream, what flavor it would be.

He snickered. "There's nothing in the cart that ten or fifteen minutes sitting here will ruin. Besides, with a woman as pretty as you, I'd take the chance."

She blushed and sipped her coffee, then sipped again—extra time to think over whether she wanted to share her problems with a stranger. She figured a quick explanation would not harm anything. Heck, once Patrick finally got off his butt and signed the divorce papers it would be common knowledge anyhow. "I recently filed for divorce and am having trouble letting go."

"Sounds like you still love the guy."

She thought about that. "Yeah... I do... but I've got to move on. He essentially moved on with his life last year. As you might have imagined, I knew nothing about it until recently."

"Ah, unfaithful husband, huh?"

She nodded and then sipped her coffee. "Look, I am really uncomfortable talking about this with a man I just met." She grinned and bobbled her head, adding, "It's probably twelve years of monogamous conditioning making me feel this way, but I can't help but think that sitting here with you, a strange man, in a public place, is somehow... wrong."

"Hey, I understand."

She shrugged her shoulders.

"Seriously, I do. A little over five years ago I was where you are right now."

"You're divorced?"

"Yep, single and sober for five years and counting."

"Over a drinking problem, huh?"

"Afraid so. Dumbest thing I ever did. I walked out on her in a drunken rage. Here's the kicker, I don't even remember what I was angry about. It was the gin talking. She was a good woman, a good wife and mother."

"So you have children?"

"We have a fifteen-year-old boy and a seventeen-year-old daughter. Lori will be graduating from high school this year and Scotty is a freshman with raging hormones." He shook his head and pursed his lips. "When I think about it, it still troubles me that I walked away from all that. But the point is, it does get better with time." He paused, and then asked, "Do you mind a little advice from a total stranger?"

"Go for it."

"From this day forward, live life at *your* pace. Let no one dictate a course of action for you. Listen only to your heart and follow those desires, no one else's. And when the day comes that you love yourself above all others then, and only then, can you comfortably allow someone else into your life and consider sharing that love."

The advice went beyond sound. Profound would be a better descriptor. Margaret's head whirled with an abrupt rejuvenation of spirit. That raw sensation of loss that was crushing her just minutes ago, developed a thin callous over it that might grow thick faster if she chose to follow the advice. She pulled a scrap of paper and a pen from her purse. "Randall Forrester, I have to go buy one chicken breast and a single serving of broccoli and then go get on with my life." She scribbled her phone number on the paper and slid it to his side of the table. She rose and, while slipping the long strap of her purse over a shoulder, added, "Call me. Coffee is on me next time."

CHAPTER 4

Danica Crane sat in her car in the KBTA parking lot fingering the rim of a Grande Starbucks paper cup. It was early morning by her standard—a few minutes after eight o'clock. She should be in the television station at an editing bay right now. She was salaried, not an hourly worker, and she did what she needed to do, whenever needed, to get the job done. Since she did not have to clock in, it also allowed her to indulge a weakness: her disdain for punctuality. That alone kept her sitting, staring and thinking. Patrick was right. She was incapable of being on time for anything, but she would never give him the satisfaction of knowing she agreed with him on the matter. Someday, she would have to get therapy and figure out what happened in her past that created such a high disregard for something that should simply be the courteous thing to do.

The anchorwoman façade of last evening was nowhere to be seen. This morning she displayed the opposite side of that coin. The well-put-together, all-business look would have to wait for her regular intensive afternoon grooming and makeup session back at her apartment. She had stuffed unruly blonde hair beneath a black cap emblazoned with an NBC sports logo and a colorful peacock. She wore a tight pair of beltless blue jeans and a baggy sweatshirt that the collar had been hastily cut out of, exposing bra straps and a shirttail hanging haphazardly below her waist. Flip-flops from the Dollar Store were her footwear choice. She kept the bill of her cap pulled low to conceal puffy, sleep-deprived eyes. Although the look was what she intended for the morning, that did not mean she wanted the public to see her this way and possibly recognize her.

She had two fluff news pieces that needed to be written and voiced over, and then a nine o'clock appointment in editing with Randy, the news videographer, to put them together for the six o'clock news. If she continued to linger, that appointment would be late as well. Although a deadline loomed, it added no urgency; she felt no pressure to hurry. The stories were not that important—a disagreement by two retailers before the city council over the placement of signage downtown, both looking for an ordinance modification to satisfy selfish needs. The other story dealt with a young local novelist who had just released her first book. The way she saw it, either story could run today, tomorrow, or next week for that matter. Who would really care, other than those three people and their families? But she promised Harry Alexander, the news director, to stop procrastinating so much. Pleasing her department head was the only reason to be here at all, but even that held little sway.

Danica yawned and gulped the cooling strong coffee. This moment to pull herself together must end—too much work to be done and her workload grew another layer each day. Suddenly, she realized that getting too far behind was her greatest enemy and potential career ender. She sucked in a breath of determination, got out of the car and headed for the front door of the television station.

Walking into the lobby, she tossed the empty coffee cup into a trash can and glanced to the *Today Show*, airing live on a large screen television mounted on the wall and locked onto Channel 12 directly ahead. She wondered briefly if Matt Lauer looked as droopy and bored as she did early in the morning, or always had that camera-ready face. *Damn him.*

Someone waited in one of the visitors' chairs to her left beneath a grouping of anchor portraits on the wall. Portraits of her and Patrick hung alone side-by-side, like a king and queen, topping two more rows of on-air personalities. To the right was the reception desk. "Mornin', Jeanie," she mumbled.

"Good morning, Danica," Jeanie replied with the obligatory cheerful chirp of a good receptionist. The young freckle-faced, redheaded receptionist held out two slips of pink paper. "A couple of messages for you."

Some of the staff teased Jeanie Fromme about her last name and called her "Squeaky," invoking the name of the Charles Manson follower that attempted to assassinate President Gerald Ford. Danica did not see the humor in it and thought it mean-spirited, although Jeanie never seemed to care, even encouraged it. Besides, the story of Squeaky Fromme and the President was long before her time on this earth and meant nothing to her. Jeanie had not even been aware of who the woman was until she was told the story.

"Is one of those calls from Patrick?"

"Afraid not, just an invitation to a Chamber of Commerce banquet and a compliment from an elderly lady; that's all. Sorry."

"Oh, well..." she said as she breezed by the desk snatching the messages from Jeanie's extended hand, heading down the hall toward the newsroom.

"Have a great day, Danica."

"You too."

As she strode the hall toward the newsroom and the editing bays, Stan Brister exited the control room to the left with a production work order in one hand and a sheet of commercial copy in the other. "Early start for you, too?" she asked.

"Not by choice. When our largest commercial client says jump, I'm told that's what I should do." Stan slumped his shoulders and went into a Tim Conway version of an old man shuffle. He pointed to himself. "This is me jumping."

Danica laughed. "Hey, you didn't get Patrick too drunk last night did you?"

"Shoot, girl, he left the bar before dark...disgustingly sober. Or, he seemed sober anyhow. He went home and left Mikki and me to drink alone."

"Mikki?"

"Michaela Ross, that new studio camera operator you guys worked with for the first time during the six o'clock sequence yesterday."

"Oh, yeah, her... cute girl."

"That she is." He let out a breathy whistle. "Patrick thinks so, too." Danica stiffened. "He does?" she asked, and then hesitatingly, "Just how cute does he think she is?"

He grinned. "What's the matter... jealous?"

She backhanded him in the stomach. "Shut up."

"Honestly, Patrick said nothing to me. I saw the way he looked at her. That's all."

"That's worse."

"Aw, don't be concerned. You have nothing to worry about. Mikki was giving him a hard time over almost everything he said. I don't think she likes him much."

"Well... good. Would you ask him if—"

"Stop right there. Whatever this thing is that you and Patrick have going is very entertaining to watch, but I only want to observe from a distance. I don't want to wind up in the middle. Becoming a bit player in y'all's drama doesn't appeal to me at all. So, if you're about to ask if I'll talk to him about Mikki... forget it." Stan turned away to continue his journey to the studio to get production underway for the car commercial. He stopped and spun around. "Hey, want to voice a thirty-second piece of commercial copy for me?"

"You know Harry would go ballistic if I did. Hell, upper management wouldn't let it air anyhow."

He sighed. "I know. Just thought I'd ask. You'd be perfect for this one. Oh well... later... got to get busy." Walking away, he looked over his shoulder and added with a grin, "Good luck with your situation. I'll be watching... from a distance of course." He laughed.

Stan had planted a seed in her head. His comments about Patrick and Michaela may not have started it, but it did nothing to lessen jealousy either. She knew that look of Patrick's well, because it was the way he looked at her, once upon a time. He was a charmer. She figured that if he had designs on a younger woman, he would not give up until he had her on his side—and eventually under him. That's what happened to her; therefore, logical. She hated these possessive feelings and fought them but was drawn to Patrick. Now, she felt as though she had a deepening need to explore his future intentions beyond whatever "this thing" was, as Stan called it.

Patrick said he was getting a divorce but had not yet, blaming his wife for the delay. Was that the truth? Maybe he was no better than a player, toying with her while waiting for the next conquest to come along, like Michaela. She had to know. She had to find out before investing more time and energy in a relationship that might be highballing toward collapse. After all, she loved him and she deserved to know. On second thought, maybe she did not want to know. What if she discovered the worst of all possibilities and that forced a decision? What would be her next move?

She thought about that for a moment, but then tossed her arms into the air, grunted frustration and walked on.

CHAPTER 5

Michaela Ross left her apartment, heading for work with more verve than usual—the spring morning clear and comfortably cool. She chose to put her window down and allow the wind to caress her face. Along the highway heading toward the television station, she noticed bluebonnets and Indian paintbrush flowers—an explosion of blue and orange boasting a dappling of yellow from small wild mustard blossoms. It struck her as odd to notice—even more unusual that she made a point to appreciate its beauty. Most mornings such a view would not pull her from her thoughts or her eyes from the highway. She thought about that and began to smile. Maybe it was not so unusual. Today was certainly not most days. This day promised to be special.

Normally, Fridays did not have the thank-goodness-it's-Friday effect that it did on others. She did not look forward to Fridays, or weekends, usually. Saturdays and Sundays were filled with menial tasks—laundry, grocery shopping, apartment cleaning, dishwashing, class prep work and a myriad of other chores and errands hardly ever finished until Sunday evening, and sometimes not by then. Hardly anything ever happened on weekends worth anticipating joyfully. A busy schedule of classes and work demanded that chores undone in five days had to be taken care of in the final two days of the week, for now.

Today was a different kind of Friday though. She had looked forward to this one day all week—the interview with Robert Landers, founder and C.E.O. of Landers Energy Company. Rumors indicated Landers bought politicians and walked over people to become the monolithic company that he continued to head up today—a huge organization with oil, gas and coal subsidiaries scattered all over the world. Their international ties were substantial, and it all began in the late fifties right here in Comanche Falls, Texas. This is where Robert Landers opted to maintain a home office, a twelve-story building downtown. The structure had a tri-cornered revolving sign atop it, boasting the Landers Energy name—a black teardrop shaped logo with L, C and E sandwiched by the two giant words, Landers and Energy. At night, spotlights mounted on the flat roof focused up at the sign, bathing it in amber light. The man had money, enough to buy any outcome he desired. That was the point of Patrick's planned investigation, to find out how legal some of those purchases had been, or get him to deny it on camera. Landers Energy seemed to be getting away with things that would have been deemed criminal by less endowed companies and those with less political clout.

Michaela breezed through the front door of the television station and rounded the receptionist's desk without slowing. "Mornin', Jeanie."

Jeanie Fromme beamed. "Good morning, Michaela," said the pale, freckled, red-headed receptionist in her usual bubbly way. "I'm sure glad you joined our happy little family here at KBTA."

Michaela stopped, turned back and smiled. "Thank you very much, Jeanie. Why don't you call me Mikki? All my friends do."

"Call me Squeaky."

"Squeaky? Really? Are you sure?"

Jeanie's cheerful demeanor did not waver. "Oh, yes, quite sure. I love the family atmosphere here and nicknames add a cozy closeness. Don't you think?"

"I guess." Michaela shrugged her shoulders. "Okay," she said in a lazy southern drawl, "you are now Squeaky from this point forward." She turned and walked on.

"By the way, uh... Mikki, Patrick wanted me to tell you that he's waiting for you by the news van out the side door of the newsroom. Have a wonderful day." Her voice went higher as Michaela strode down the corridor, putting distance between them.

"Thanks," she said over her shoulder and continued on. *Wow, that girl is bubbly beyond belief. I wish I had a little of that.* Michaela worked hard at taking her career seriously. As a result of such intense focus, she felt as though she might appear dour to people at times. In reality, all she wanted was to avoid distractions on the road to her goals. Pragmatism took her years to cultivate and it ran deep.

She shoved the glass door of the newsroom open and marched down a corridor lined with cubicles furnished with identical desks, chairs and computer terminals— each personalized by reporters with family pictures and souvenirs. They were all enclosed on three sides by four-foot-high paneled partitions topped with a couple more feet of glass, offering the merest hint of privacy. The ambience was old school, right out of the sixties. Clearly, the newsroom had not been remodeled in about half a century, if ever. And, although smoking had not been allowed since some time in the eighties, the smell of smoke still saturated everything. A slight stench lingered to this day, conjuring visions of a cowboy honky tonk bar the morning after a rowdy, smoke-filled night.

At the end of the corridor, standing outside his office, Michaela approached news director Harry Alexander. Old Harry had been at this station since those yellow ceiling tiles were bright white. He stood on the other side of a file cabinet from Stan Brister. A chessboard lay atop it between them. They seemed engrossed. Stan had a finger on his queen, tipping it to and fro, contemplating a move.

"Are you ever going to give up that queen and get it over with?" Harry blurted.

"Who's winning?" Michaela asked.

"We'll never know if Brister doesn't speed it up."

"Aw, shut up, old man," Stan mumbled while chewing on an unlit Swisher Sweet cigar.

"Tell me to shut up again and I'll revoke your cigar-chewing privileges back here. Just because you're not smoking the nasty thing doesn't mean it's okay to have it stuck between those conceited lips of yours while inside the station."

Stan never took his eyes off the board, or ceased chewing, clearly working a strategy. "Yeah...well...shut up anyhow."

The two had been friends for many years. That was clear enough by the banter. "How long have y'all been playing?"

"Since 1978," Harry said.

Michaela laughed. "That's not what I meant. How long have you been playing this morning?"

"Oh, twenty minutes or so," Harry said. "But we're never finished. I've seen games take over a week to wrap up, and then we immediately begin another. We have no problem walking away from a game and getting back to it a day or so later. And God help anyone that screws with our board and a game in progress."

"You're kidding."

"Nope. And as far as this particular game is concerned, we're very close to your buddy Brister here owing me lunch." He looked back to Stan. "Get on it, man. I'm visibly aging waiting for you to move. I don't have all day. I need to get back to work."

Stan pulled the cigar from between his teeth and glanced up at Harry. "I see that telling you to shut up didn't seem to have the desired effect." He poked the cigar back in his mouth and continued perusing the board.

"Just get the move made, Brister."

"Why are you here so early?" she asked Stan, and then added, "I figured Friday mornings you'd be sleeping in a while longer."

Still chewing the slimy end of that cigar, his eyes remained fixed on the chessboard and apparently, so did his attention.

"Hey, Stan..."

"Huh?" He finally looked up and stopped chewing.

She grinned. "I asked why you're here so early."

"Eh, couldn't sleep. Whenever that happens I come see Harry. A few minutes with him is like taking a valium."

Although Harry's eyes were on her, he snapped an accusing finger at his friend. "Ya hear that? That's the kind of abuse I have to put up with from this yahoo."

"Hey," Stan said, "this is the morning of your maiden voyage as a news photog without Randy looking over your shoulder, isn't it?"

She took a breath and blew it through rounded lips. "Yep. I'm excited but a little nervous."

"Don't worry," Harry said. "Randy showed me the work you've been doing. It's more than adequate. It's pretty darn good. Trust me. Your moves are smooth, really smooth, and you seem to have an eye for artsy shots like Randy. You'll do fine." He stroked his chin thoughtfully for a couple of seconds. "Word's gettin' around fast that you're cool to Patrick because he's arrogant." He paused. "And... I guess he is, but lean on him for help and advice. He has been in the business a long time and knows what he's doing. Deep down, he's a good guy."

She had to struggle to remain expressionless and not roll her eyes, although she could not prevent her eyebrows from rising. "I'll take that under advisement."

Stan abandoned the chessboard and turned his back to Harry, offering Michaela his full attention. "Patrick came through a few minutes ago." He flipped a finger toward the side door of the building. "He's waiting for you out back by the news van."

"Yeah, Jeanie filled me in." She began walking away. "Patrick told me we should be back at the station before lunchtime. If not, blame him."

"Admit it, Brister, I've gotcha beat. Just make the doggone move and let's end this game."

Stan pulled the little cigar from between his teeth and flashed a toothy grin. "Not today. I think I'll let it linger and make you wonder if you really do have me beat or not."

Harry sighed. "Oh, all right. I have work to do anyhow." He turned his attention to Michaela heading toward the door. "Bring me something good, kiddo."

"I'll certainly try," she replied as she disappeared through the side door.

When she rounded the news van parked near the door, Patrick stood between the open back doors of the vehicle and seemed to be taking inventory of video and audio equipment. "Hey, I thought that was my job."

He offered her a George W. Bush smirk. "It is, but I thought I'd give you a hand since this is your first news story in the field without a trainer looking on."

"Thanks... I guess," she said as she nudged him to the side and took over."

"Okay, okay, it's all yours, but get a move on. I haven't checked battery charges yet. We don't want to pull a novice mistake and have it all go dead in the middle of the interview," Patrick said. "Our appointment with Landers is at eight-thirty and it's already after eight. This interview took me almost a month to procure. I don't think we'll get another shot at an appointment, so let's not be late."

Michaela checked the meters on the battery chargers—both in the green zone. She then glanced at her watch. "If we're late, it won't be my fault." She slammed the metal case holding the camera and latched it. "Let's go."

On the way downtown, Michaela got her first crack ever at driving a panel truck that looked as though better suited to delivering furniture or appliances, although everyone in the news department called it a van. It was a new experience and quite different than her Volkswagen Passat. She liked it, sitting high with an unobstructed view of the highway beyond the cars in front of her—a welcome feeling of superiority to start the day with, albeit tiny.

"You're sure quiet this morning," Patrick said.

"I'm not much on chitchat," she replied with a purposeful lack of expression.

"Aw, come on, give me this one. You could at least pretend to be cordial."

Michaela rolled out her lower lip. "Okay. Just remember you asked. I noticed Danica has sure been going at you with a serpentine hiss during commercial breaks in the six o'clock news this week. Did she misplace her rose-colored glasses?" She remained focused on the street ahead but could not stop a smile from sprouting.

"That's not fair, and really none of your business."

"I told you I wasn't much on chitchat."

"I apologize for doubting you."

Michaela turned onto Garland Street—the Landers building only a couple of blocks away in the heart of downtown Comanche Falls. It was the tallest building in this modestly-sized northwest Texas city. In New York or Chicago, this building would be lost among true giants of skyscrapers. But here, it happened to be the most imposing structure for miles in any direction. She leaned over the steering wheel of the van and looked up to the rotating sign on the roof. "You can see this building from anywhere in town and I've driven by it a thousand times, but it never meant a thing to me, till now." She wheeled up to the curb into a vacant parallel slot near the front revolving door. "This is a fifteen-minute loading zone. Do you think we'll be in there more than fifteen?"

"Probably, but don't worry about it. The station helps the police department often. They'll let a parking violation slide."

"I'll take you at your word. I sure don't need to be responsible for the station getting a parking ticket my first day out."

"Won't happen."

She killed the engine. "Good. Then let's go do this thing."

Loaded down with gear, she checked the menu board next to the elevator. Landers' office took up the entire twelfth floor. "Of course. He took the entire top floor. Why did I feel compelled to check?"

"Yeah... why?"

She rolled her eyes as the elevator doors parted. "Your sarcasm underwhelms me. Let's go."

The elevator zipped upward. Upon arrival it stopped fast enough to force a readjustment of the equipment she carried. The doors opened and she stepped into a richly paneled outer office with an even dozen metal desks, all occupied by very young, very pretty women. Michaela figured the platinum blond with huge breasts sitting centered at the end of the double row of desks behind a more expensive looking one that matched the paneling behind her had to have been Landers' personal secretary, the gate keeper. Judging by her low-cut top and general appearance, she may have done more than type for him. "That must be where we need to go."

"Yeah, I'd say so," Patrick said as he took the lead.

The blonde was typing. She did not stop or look up. "May I help you?"

"I'm Patrick Daniels with KBTA Television and this is my camera girl, Michaela Ross. We have an eight-thirty appointment with Mister Landers.

Michaela snapped a startled look at Patrick. *Not camera operator or cameraperson or videographer, but camera girl! That's patronizing as hell!*

Clearly unimpressed, the blonde still did not look up and continued typing. "I'll let him know you're here. I must warn you, Mister Landers won't be able to give you much time. I just called his driver to bring the car around. He'll be leaving shortly to go to the airport for a flight to Dubai. His pilot is waiting for him now." She finally wheeled away from the computer terminal and spun to face the phone. She punched a single button. "Yes, Trixie," came a disembodied voice from the phone's speaker. *Trixie? You've got to be kidding. My assumption about this woman must be right with a name like that.*

"Your eight-thirty is here," the secretary said with her face close to the small microphone.

"Send 'em in."

She rose and led them to one side of intricately carved and richly stained oak double-doors, having to put a shoulder into one side to open it for them. As Patrick passed, he eyed the beauty, lingering on the low-cut top suspending ample breasts that appeared poised to spill out. "Thank you, Trixie. It is Trixie, right?"

Michaela shook her head. *For God's sake, could you look any more lascivious?*

The secretary smiled and gestured him through the door.

As Michaela followed him through, she noticed a come-hither smile from the secretary toward Patrick. *You're no better, lady,* she thought as she walked by the woman. Once the door closed behind her, she stopped. The opulence and size of the office was impressive, but not at all garish, as she had expected. The entire wall behind Landers at his desk was smoky glass with an unobstructed view of the western part of Comanche Falls, and the rolling countryside beyond the city limits for many more miles that disappeared in a distant haze. The room was huge and sparsely furnished; although, small decorative pieces adorning tabletops appeared as though any one might have cost more than her annual paycheck at the television station.

The leather of Landers' high-back desk chair squeaked as he rose. "Please come on over." He gestured toward two chairs on their side of his desk.

Patrick stepped lively and shook the man's hand. "Nice to finally meet you, Mister Landers." He sat, and then turned to Michaela and pointed to a specific spot behind him. "Miss Ross, if you would, just do a shoulder-shoot from right there. Don't worry about setting up the tri-pod. We need to be quick about this so Mister Landers can be on his way."

"I do apologize," Landers said as he lowered himself back into his chair. "I know I've put you off for weeks and now must rush, but we've had a bit of a problem with the Dubai fields. It seems terrorists have been blowing the heads off producing oil wells and setting them afire. I'm scheduled to meet Congressman Banks. He has graciously agreed to assess the situation and take recommendations back to Congress for security funding."

As Michaela readied the video equipment, she glanced at Landers. It was a small thing, but obvious. Landers smirked as the word "funding" came out of his mouth. *What a disgusting pig.* She lifted the camera from its case and set it on her shoulder. When she flipped the "on" switch, the viewfinder flickered and a small image of Landers appeared in it. *Congressman Banks must be one of the politicians this man has purchased for personal fun and profit.* The dislike for Landers and all who catered to him came quickly and hardened fast. She had many questions for him, but she could not ask even one. It was not her interview. She was just the videographer, or "camera girl" as Patrick would say. All she could do was make two men she did not care for look good.

She framed a shot over Patrick's shoulder with Landers centered and pressed the button. A red indicator light began flashing next to the viewfinder. "Recording," she announced.

"Mister Landers," Patrick began, "let's start with the problem that surfaced in Dubai."

Landers repeated the security issue with terrorists in that part of the world almost verbatim for the camera.

"You and Congressman Banks seem to work on a number of problems unique to Landers Energy. Is he your go-to person in the government?"

Landers hesitated and appeared somewhat shocked by the way Patrick phrased the question. "Well... he has been helpful because an inexpensive supply of energy is in the country's best interest to maintain. Our job at Landers Energy in friendly areas of the world is to do just that... find it, drill it, and then maintain it."

Michaela kept the camera steady and recording. *Didn't think ol' Patrick would get to the heart of this interview so fast, did you?*

"Rumor has it that a U.S. Congressman was helpful in getting criminal charges dropped against Landers Energy for dumping fifty thousand tons of coal ash loaded with arsenic out on the east coast. Was Banks that congressman?"

Landers sprang to his feet. "Stop the camera!"

Patrick gave Michaela a faint but obvious negative headshake, meaning for her to continue recording.

Landers' face tightened and went rubicund, his anger sudden and substantial. "I see where you're going with this. I'm not going to play this game with you. You lied to me. You said this interview was to be about making it to number five on the list of world energy companies."

"I do plan to ask about that," Patrick said, "but, if that's all we discuss, the end result would be a commercial promotion for Landers Energy, not a news interview. Can I assume by this response that it was indeed Banks? And was he equally helpful in quashing that investigation on sinkholes resulting from gas drilling and fouling water wells from hydraulic fracturing alleged against Landers Energy?"

"Get out!"

"May we also assume that Congressman Banks' trip to Dubai is merely a formality and funding will be forthcoming? Are you anticipating a generous funding bleed-over for other projects?"

Landers hit a button on his desk phone. "Trixie, get security up here! Have them escort this KBTA jackass and his girl out of the building! Leave explicit instructions to never let anyone from that damn station onto our property again!"

"Yes, sir," came the response.

Landers hurried toward an unadorned door at the back corner of his office. Opening it, he took a parting shot, "Lesson learned. My advice, Mister Daniels, is to tread lightly with things you think you know." The door closed behind him.

"Wow. That was much more than I expected. It was great." Michaela stopped the camera, and as she lifted its saddle harness off her shoulder, it snagged her long auburn hair. "Ouch! Damn," she mumbled, as she pulled several strands caught between the harness pad and the frame.

"Problem?"

"Not really. Just need a more appropriate hairstyle for this work, meaning much shorter." As she was returning the camera to its metal case, she added, "I assume Landers has a private elevator back there."

"No doubt. A person doesn't own a building like this and *not* have a private elevator."

"Shall we try to beat him to his car for a couple more quick questions that I'm sure he won't answer?"

"Nah. The video you have is a great way to lead into a story on the class action suit against him." He paused.

In his eyes, Michaela saw an idea coming together.

"You know what? Now that I've lit that man's fuse, the word will be going out to bar access everyplace Landers Energy has control. If our plan includes video of that gas drilling site west of town, which it does, we'd better beat the flow of information out there if we can. Are you game?"

"Sure. This is getting interesting," Michaela replied, squatting down and busily preparing her camera equipment for travel. She suddenly stopped, sighed, and looked up at Patrick. "I have to admit that I'm impressed."

"Oh? With what?"

"You. The man told you nothing, yet you have a story, a good one. His anger will be interpreted by the public as an affirmative nod on all counts."

"Gosh, thanks. And, yeah, I agree with that assessment. It's great circumstantial evidence of guilt. But, this is only the beginning. I can taste national news awards coming out of this one. Cool, huh?" He bounced his eyebrows and grinned like a Cheshire cat—cockiness bubbling up fast.

"Hand to God, you just can't help yourself, can you?"

CHAPTER 6

Patrick and Michaela rushed out of Comanche Falls into the gentle hills of Texas ranch country that began at the city limit sign. The city ended quite abruptly, and rolling pastureland with scrub mesquite, numerous patches of prickly pear cactus and broom weed became the norm on both sides of the highway as they sped out of town. Patrick took pleasure at Michaela's obvious thrill in being at the wheel of the KBTA news van.

Patrick knew all it would take was a phone call from Robert Landers' personal secretary, Trixie, or Landers himself to bar them from property under the purview of Landers Energy. "Could you speed up a little?"

"Okay, but if we get a speeding ticket, I'm telling everyone at the television station that you were driving."

"Fair enough."

"Where, exactly, are we going?" she asked.

"Cattle Trails Ranch, a huge operation about ten miles out of town. Landers Energy drilled a few wells employing hydraulic fracturing on the eastern edge of the ranch near Webber community water supply wells. Folks in that housing development can now, literally, set fire to the water coming from their taps."

"So, that's the basis for the class action suit?"

"Partially. Fingers are pointing at LEC for three different and, alleged, related reasons: earth tremors that began shortly after wells began producing, sinkholes that showed up on the Cattle Trails Ranch that are feared will spread into the Webber community, and of course that other problem... natural gas leaking into the water supply."

"Why can't we just get our shots from the Webber side? Why go onto the ranch? We may not be a welcomed sight, ya know."

"That's good thinking, but I already know it won't work. The wells may be close to the Webber side, but they're out of sight over a hill from there."

"Why can't we walk onto the ranch, and then up and over the hill from the Webber side, a quick in and out thing?"

"Can't do that either. Ol' Ned Barrett, owner of Cattle Trails Ranch, installed a twelve-foot-high wild game fence along that boundary. And, since fences like that are located nowhere else on the ranch, it's obvious that the wildlife he wanted to contain were the residents of the Webber community. The escape, or intrusion, of wild animals was clearly not the goal. He wanted to keep people from freely crossing onto his property from that side."

"Then what makes you think Barrett will give us permission to come onto his property? I'm betting he'd look down on anything that might interrupt royalty checks."

"True, but here's a little secret: The gate at the highway that opens onto the gravel road up to those wells is never locked. It's about a mile this side of Barrett's home. If we're lucky he'll be at home, and we can get the shots and get out of there before anyone notices."

The shock of his statement caused her to jerk the steering wheel. "Trespassing! You plan on trespassing?

You never had any intention of getting permission, did you?"

"Okay, now, calm down. Hold it steady. Everything will be fine." Patrick grinned sideways. "Just drive and turn where I tell you to."

Michaela pulled a deep breath. "Okay," she said, drawing out the word. "You're the boss." Lightning flashed from cloud to ground beneath a gray/green line of clouds not much farther west. It appeared to be an ominous thunderstorm that separated all the world between them and points west of it. "Whatever we do, it'd better be quick...looks like a storm coming."

"I'll call Harry and let him know we may be back at work later than expected." He finished his call and then tossed the phone on the dash. "Why didn't you let Harry know where we were going?"

"Simple, plausible deniability. I don't want to get Harry or the television station in trouble over our antics."

"'*Our* antics!' Oh, yeah, sure...you think it's okay that *I* get into trouble with you, but *not* the television station or the news director? You are a royal putz, ya know that?

"If we get caught, I'll tell them you were my hostage. Now, keep those accusing eyes on the highway. See that lone mesquite tree on the right up ahead?"

"Yeah, so?"

"Turn onto the caliche road next to it. I'll open the gate."

"Why are you so confident that this is the place?"

"Last year, after those wells began producing oil and gas, a couple of sinkholes developed a few hundred yards west of them. Your predecessor, Randy, and I came out and got shots of them. At the time it was simply an interesting story and Ned Barrett didn't mind. At the time, no one associated the sinkholes with the wells. Not only that, it was confined to his property and did no damage, other than eliminating about half an acre of grazing for his cattle. But now, with gas leaching into water wells and earth tremors that are *not* confined to his property, the implications are much broader."

"It is a little scary to contemplate. What if sinkholes begin swallowing houses... worse yet, people?" She turned off the highway onto the gravel road and stopped.

"Exactly. Webber residents feel if they can legally force Landers to accept accountability for the water issue then that will make it easier to force financial responsibility on the company if the more serious problems of sinkholes and earth tremor damage occur later on." Patrick shoved his door open and set foot on the ground, looking back at Michaela. "Those poor folks in the Webber community don't need houses dropping into holes to go along with a gassy water problem." He jogged to the gate and lifted the circled chain from it. The gate swung open on its own. He looked back at Michaela in the driver's seat of the van and waggled the short length of chain at her. He shouted, "Told ya so."

The bumpy, rutted road was a little wider but no better than a cattle trail. It meandered one way then the other, up hills and down. "It would seem you have a gift for finding every hole and rock in the road," Patrick quipped as a front wheel dropped into one. He bounced off the seat.

"Quit your yammerin'. I'm doing the best I can."

He snickered. "Yeah, that's what I'm afraid of."

"Shut up," she mumbled.

Patrick noticed a subtle shift in Michaela's expression, from snarky too apprehensive, causing him to wonder if he would, indeed, get this young girl into trouble. A nagging little voice in the back of his head had already set up a one-word mantra: maybe. He considered heeding the self-induced warning and have her turn around and leave, but the investigative reporter in him buried the concern beneath layers of desire for a network worthy news story.

Going was slow. Dust boiled up from beneath the van, coming off the white caliche graveled roadbed, a good sign that the coming rain would be a welcome relief from drought conditions that plagued this part of Texas for over five years. It was all uninhabited and mostly open ranch land with occasional clusters of scrub oaks in the low areas, prickly pear cactus and mesquite bushes. It appeared that the land had been cleared at some point in the past. Rotting logs and piles of brush dotted a large area, but mesquite had regrown and covered the rolling hills with a uniform covering of brush, all the same height and girth. The only structure within view was an abandoned house with a swayed roof, rotting lap siding and most of the windows broken out. Frayed curtains that had sucked outward through a glassless window waved in the breeze, eerily beckoning. A wooden windmill with rotting cross braces, some disengaged and dangling, stood behind it. The rotor blades turned with a breeze that was becoming gusty with the approaching thunderstorm. It stood next to a cellar with a couple of green tumbleweeds growing from its mounded dirt top. It appeared as though two or three decades had passed since anyone had occupied the house. The only other indications of purpose within view were the occasional feeding stations with salt licks and hayracks for the cattle.

Although never over a quarter mile from the highway, they had driven the winding path half a mile or more. Finally, Michaela steered around a thick stand of scrub oaks. Two gas wells and three rocking horse oil pump jacks came into view, clustered over about an acre. But, that was not all. Two pickup trucks sat parked side by side.

"Oh crap," Patrick hissed through clenched teeth. Michaela snapped a concerned look at him. "What are you *oh crappin* about?"

"That old cowboy on the left up there with the big belly and the broad-brimmed gray Stetson is Ned Barrett. The other guy is from Landers Energy. See that black and gold LEC oil drop logo on the truck door?"

Michaela slammed on the brakes and stopped. "Let's get out of here." She cranked the steering wheel to the right as fast as arms allowed to make a U-turn.

Patrick grabbed the wheel. "No, wait." He looked toward the two men, contemplating a move.

The two, talking across Barrett's truck hood, suddenly stopped and stared at them. It was clear enough now, word had already come down to prevent access. "We've already been spotted and it's kind of hard not to notice the giant KBTA painted on the van next to the network logo. Let's make the best of it. Get out and get the camera. We might still make this work."

"We're on that man's private property without invitation. Are you out of your mind?"

As he was getting out of the van, he replied, "Maybe, but let's do it anyhow."

"Okay," she said with a nervous warble in her voice. "Although, it's going to be difficult graduating from college while sitting behind bars for a couple of years."

Patrick grinned. "Nah, people graduate from college in prison all the time."

"That's about as funny as a bullet wound." She grabbed the door handle, but then turned around, hesitating momentarily. "What the hell am I doing?" she asked. She grunted as if diving into cold water, threw open the door and dropped to the ground.

While she stood at the back of the van between the open ambulance-style doors getting camera and paraphernalia from the metal case, Patrick got out and figured the best way to control the situation was to begin with friendly banter. Still some distance from the two men, he shouted, "Good morning. It looks like we might get some rain pretty soon. I bet you're happy about that."

"Sure am. We need more grazing. What can I do for you?" Barrett asked.

Michaela trotted to within a couple of feet behind Patrick, camera saddled on her shoulder.

Patrick glanced back and whispered, "Start recording and keep it rolling, no matter what." He looked back to Barrett. "I was wondering if I might get a comment from you about the class action suit that the residents of the Webber community filed against Landers Energy. You *are* named in the suit, too, right?"

"That's far enough. Stop right there," Barrett said. "I won't be makin' any comments or answerin' any questions."

Patrick continued walking toward him. "Can I take that refusal to comment as an admission of complicity?"

Barrett advanced aggressively. "This is private property and you were not invited to be here. Get back in that truck o' yours, turn around, and go back to wherever it was you came from!"

Patrick stopped. He looked to the Landers Energy employee standing beside the pickup truck behind Barrett. "How about you? Do you think these wells are responsible for the fouled water supply in Webber and the earth tremors?"

The man straightened and snatched a large adjustable wrench from the bed of the truck. "Oh, no. I'm not getting involved. I'm just a grunt roustabout trying to make a living. Worrying about stuff like that is far above my pay grade." He turned and walked toward a gas pipe terminal a few yards away. "Leave me out of this. I have work to do."

"That's as close to an answer as you're going to get," Barrett snapped. "Now, get in that truck and get off my damn property!" He kept closing the gap between them.

"There's no need to become angry, Mister Barrett."

"Oh, I'm not, but I have no problem taking that expensive lookin' camera off your girlfriend's shoulder and smashing it against a tree. I wouldn't even classify that as an action born of anger, just a way to make a point. If you choose to continue standing there after I've nicely asked you to leave, that's exactly what I plan on doin'."

"I just thought you might want to give your side of the story, that's all. We've heard plenty from the plaintiffs in the suit."

"I bet you have." Barrett walked past Patrick, heading for Michaela.

She clicked the camera off and backed away. Eyes locked on the old rancher, she dropped it from her shoulder and held it dangling in her hand, still back-stepping. "No need to damage valuable equipment, sir," she said and turned to leave. She hurriedly strode to the rear of the news van.

Barrett spun around.

Patrick had not moved.

"Last warnin'," Barrett said.

Patrick threw his hands up. "Okay, we're leaving. Sorry to have bothered you."

Michaela had already climbed into the van and had it idling, waiting.

Patrick opened the passenger side door and slid onto the seat. "Whew! That's was exciting."

"Yeah, but we didn't get an answer or a comment of any kind."

"Oh, but we did. His refusal to speak on the subject, and in such a forceful way, was perfect. Think about it. We edit together Landers' refusal to speak back-to-back with Barrett's little temper tantrum and voila! Two negatives make a positive. Refusals to speak by the principal defendants in a class action lawsuit is tantamount to an admission of guilt in the court of public opinion."

Michaela raised an eyebrow. "Sweet Jesus, man, you're ruthless." She dropped the van into gear and made a U-turn.

"Ruthlessness was not my intent. Forcing their hand is. When they see for themselves how secretive they appear on camera, it might make them come forward so I can engage one, or both, in honest dialogue instead of having to ambush them like this. I guarantee you that a time will come, and I bet very soon, when Landers and Barrett will be forced to publicize their side of the story or risk negatively tainting every jury pool in the state of Texas, maybe the whole country."

The van bounced over a rock in the road. "I get it. This is *a* story not *the* story, simply a way to force them into granting an interview."

"There ya go. Now you're catching on. I bet I won't have to call them again. Someone will be contacting me, probably an attorney for the company to set something up." Patrick looked up the road as the dilapidated old house was coming into view. "Hey, I have an idea. Take that little road that peels off to the right up there."

Michaela snapped a startled look at him. "Are you serious? Don't you think we need to hurry and get off his property?"

"The largest sinkhole is about a hundred yards behind that house. Can you imagine how much more powerful this story would be if I wrapped up with that gaping hole behind me after the audience hears both those guys vehemently refuse to talk?

"I don't think—"

"Then don't. Turn."

Michaela reacted and made the right turn. "Well, I've ceased worrying about Harry firing me now that the jail thing is becoming less a joke and more a reality. What are you getting me into?"

Patrick grinned. "I'm graciously allowing you to make an integral contribution to one of the biggest news stories Comanche Falls has ever seen... .and it's your first story ever. How great is that?"

She frowned. "You're so kind."

"I don't think the van will be visible from that rutted cattle trail they call a road we just turned off of back there."

Once Michaela stopped the van at the side of the old house, the hint of a driveway they were on disappeared entirely. "What if a wheel goes off in a hole that I can't see below those weeds and we get stuck?"

"Randy and I came this way when we did the sinkhole story. Just take it slow and go where I say."

She allowed the van to begin rolling and for the hundred yards or so down to the sinkhole, her right foot spent more time on the brake than the accelerator. Once there, she looked back in the direction of the better-traveled road they turned off of. "You're right. It's low enough here that even the top of the van should not be visible." She opened the door and got out.

"Grab the camera," he said.

This time there was no hesitation; she leaped from the driver's seat to the ground and then around to the rear.

Patrick joined her. I'll do a fifteen or twenty second stand-up as a wrap on the story from over there." He pointed to the hole.

She looked around the open rear van door to where he pointed. "That's much larger than I expected. One that size is big enough to swallow two, maybe three whole houses if one similar should open up in Webber."

"Exactly. That's one huge reason that this story is so important and worth the risk. If that should happen, this story would go national and guess who would stand to benefit?"

"You?"

"Not just me. You too."

"Me? Why me?"

"Cuz... you're my camera girl," he replied in his best little-boy voice."

"Oh hush. Let's get this done so we can get out of here before Barrett grabs a Colt .45, or some other cowboy kind of gun, and starts shooting at us."

While Michaela finished preparing the equipment, Patrick trotted to the edge of the sinkhole and studied it. It looked as if supernatural forces neatly lowered the earth in this spot about fifteen feet. The walls of the depression were almost vertical, the floor of it intact, appearing the way it had been before it sank. Two mesquite trees remained upright at the bottom of the hole. They seemed to have been virtually undisturbed and continued to thrive. Still, an area he judged to cover about half an acre had dropped straight down, rendered worthless. *Humans are a selfish and greedy lot. We can't seem to help ourselves. We screw with nature for personal gain and stuff like this happens. It's an endless cycle of upsetting the natural order. Will we ever learn? Or will we just keep squeezing this planet until it's uninhabitable?*

"Have you figured out what you're going to say yet?" Michaela asked.

Startled from his thoughts, he said, "I think so. I'm going to blame the entire human race for this hole, the earthquakes and the ignitable water."

"What?"

"Never mind," he said, stepping toward her. "Hand me that microphone and start recording."

Microphone in hand, he began backing up.

"Stop!" she shouted and quickly put the camera on the ground.

"What's the prob—?"

Suddenly the earth crumbled beneath his feet. As he staggered backwards, Michaela lunged at him, helping hand extended.

As Patrick grabbed her hand, the fracturing ground split beneath her feet as well.

She screamed as they both fell.

Patrick landed on his back. Air rushed from his lungs upon impact. "Oh, God," he moaned and then looked over.

"Ow," Michaela groaned, having landed on her back next to him.

"Are you okay?" he asked.

She rubbed a spot on her butt, spit dirt and then rolled her head to face him. "What an idiotic question. Do I look okay?"

He sat up. "Cynicism intact. Good. You're well enough."

She pulled a cell phone from the hip pocket of her jeans. "Crap, I landed on my cell phone and broke it."

Patrick remembered that he left his cell phone on the dashboard in the van. "Oh, man, we have no way to call for help."

Michaela exploded in cutting laughter.

"What's so funny?" he asked as he came to his feet and dusted his pants.

"You do realize, don't you, that if we called for help, word would spread fast what happened and KFAL would jump all over this. *We* would be the lead news story on *their* newscast this evening. They might even be out here before we could get out of this hole, recording video of our stupid faces while we're stranded in a sinkhole. What would you say then?"

Patrick dropped hands onto his hips. "Oh... yeah. You're right... don't want that."

Michaela turned a slow circle, examining the dirt walls. "Maybe before we attempt getting outside help we can try getting out of here on our own, since we don't have a choice at the moment anyhow." She added, "It may turn out for the better that we could not make a snap decision to call for help, just sayin'."

He sighed. "Maybe."

"Hey, how about that root sticking out over there?" she said. "If you can lift me up on your shoulders, I think I can reach it and I might be able to pull myself up high enough to get a hand on the base of the little tree growing above it."

"Worth a try." He walked the few feet to where the gnarled little

root protruded from the dirt wall about a foot down from the top.

He squatted. "Climb aboard."

Michaela planted a foot on one shoulder.

Patrick held up his hands, and she held them both.

He pulled her forward as she put the other foot on his opposite shoulder and began to rise. He grunted.

"Is that gnashing of teeth I hear? Don't even think of complaining about my weight. I'm not that heavy," she said, releasing his hands and leaning into the wall.

"It's not your weight. It's your boot heels. Besides, my back hurts from that hard landing over there."

"Whatever. Stop complaining and push me higher."

He placed hands on each side of her butt.

"You better not be enjoying that."

"Would it be so horrible if I were?"

"What would be horrible is if I knew you were enjoying it and could do nothing about it. Now, push, don't squeeze."

As he shoved her upward, her feet wobbled and she dropped from his shoulders to the ground.

"Are you okay? Did you lose your balance?"

She stared at him with a disturbed look on her face.

"What?"

She pointed up.

His eyes followed her finger, and he saw Ned Barrett peering over the edge, grinning.

Barrett shoved the brim of his gray felt western hat up with the tip of a finger. "Well, well, well. What have we here?"

"How did you know we were here?"

"Didn't. Heard a scream. Sounded like a newsman's scream... you know, sorta like a little girl." He laughed. "Figured out pretty darn quick this is where you'd be if you hadn't left the property yet."

"I can explain. We—"

"Doesn't matter." He removed his hat and scratched his bald head as he scanned the darkening skies. "Here's the way I see it. You two are about to get what you deserve, a good soakin'. Might even get a little sense knocked into you with a hailstone or two. It'd be country justice for sure."

"You mean you're not going to help us get out of here?" Michaela blurted.

"Oh, I'll help ya, darlin'," he said, drawling the words, "just not the way you might think." He backed out of sight.

"Hey, don't leave us down here," Patrick shouted.

Barrett reappeared with a coil of rope in his hand, the man from Landers Energy Company now at his side snickering. Barrett continued grinning. "I can see at least three ways you can get out of this hole using this rope, but I'll let you figure it out." He tossed down the rope. "I can't kill ya. That would be murder. I can't confine you because that would be kidnapping. Shoot fire, I can't even beat hell out of you. That would be assault. Sure would please me greatly, though, if I could." Barrett pushed out his lower lip, stroked the stubbly gray whiskers beneath his chin with the backs of his fingers and seemed to give that final idea thought.

Patrick cocked his head to the side. "Surely, you wouldn't seriously—"

"Consider it? Sure I would, but... oh well..." Barrett set his hat back on his head and pulled it down tight against increasingly gusty wind. The brim fluttered. "Tell ya what, here's what I *can* do. Ol' Rusty here will grab your camera, put it in your truck, and then drive it up to my house because we, of course, found these things abandoned on my property." He pointed west. "My house is about a mile that way. You two are welcome to walk on over and get it anytime ya like. That should give you plenty of time to think on the error of your ways." Barrett straightened abruptly and looked up. The brim of his Stetson fluttered from a hard, sudden wind gust. He put a hand on it to prevent it from flying off his head. "A big ol' raindrop splattered on my arm. Come on, Rusty. Let's get 'er done. It's about to storm. I want these yahoos drenched, not us."

"Hey," Patrick said, "don't leave us down here. What if a tornado drops out of the cloud?"

"Aw heck, if that happens you'll be safer down there than we will up here. Just remember to keep your mouth shut when it passes over so it doesn't collapse your lungs. But, since you're a TV man, keepin' that big ol' mouth of yours shut might present a problem." The old man guffawed, clearly for show.

Lightning lit the sky, followed by ground-shaking thunder. Barrett and the LEC guy disappeared from view.

"Aw, come on, guys..."

Patrick heard shared laughter, vehicle doors slamming and then the van starting. He gave up trying to get them back. "Okay, Michaela, the old man said there were at least three ways to get out of here with this rope. So, what are they?"

She picked up the coil of rope. "Well, this rope is a lasso." She handed it to him. "Conjure your inner cowboy and get a loop over that little mesquite tree I was reaching for."

"Humph, 'inner cowboy'... right." He uncoiled the rope and opened up the loop at the end. "Here goes nothin'..." He twirled the rope overhead one time and pitched it up toward the stubby little tree. It missed. He tried again and that missed as well. "Three's a charm," he said and tossed it again. This time the loop landed on top of the tree but was suspended on a small upper branch. He gently yanked on the rope.

"Easy," she said.

"Shh. My 'inner cowboy' needs to concentrate." He jostled the rope one more time and the loop fell to the ground encircling the small but adequate trunk."

"There ya go," she said. "Well, aren't you the stud?"

Patrick frowned at her, but otherwise did not reply. He tightened the rope on the three-inch base of the tree. "Okay, let's repeat what we were attempting the first time; except, now, it's with the help of a rope." He squatted down.

She climbed up onto his shoulders while holding the rope. He put his hands on her butt.

"I've barely known you a week and already you've grabbed my ass twice."

"Up you go." He pushed and then repositioned his hands on the bottoms of her feet and kept pushing. "Grab the tree."

"I've got it."

"Pull yourself out." He gave her feet one last shove and she was up and over the edge.

Rain began increasing. Lightning flashed.

"Your turn," she said, almost shouting over earthshaking thunder.

Patrick clutched the rope, planted a foot on the dirt wall and began walking his way up. As he neared the top, Michaela grabbed his nearest arm with both hands and pulled. After a final kick-off with a foot against the dirt wall, he was safely out of the hole.

"You're a pretty good rope climber."

He lay on his back breathing heavily. "Yeah, it was my preferred sport in middle school."

Michaela's head reared back as rain dripped from the tip of her nose. "Rope climbing is a sport...a real sport?"

He looked up at her. Raindrops rolled off his face. "Of course not. You sure are gullible." He flinched as a drop of rain splattered dead center in an eye.

"You better be careful. If you cry wolf too often I may not be listening when I should be. Get up. Let's get to that abandoned house. I'm getting soaked."

He rolled over and got to his feet. "You're right. We'd better take this storm seriously. I see rotation in that cloud. Take off," he said. "I'm right behind you."

Michaela began to run. Patrick noticed that her gait appeared as though running was not a new thing to her. Her movements were fluid and polished, not at all what he expected to see. He wondered if track, or some other sport, was in her past. Even as he struggled a bit to stay up with her, he became curious, wanting to know more about this girl. It wasn't far, a hundred yards or so up the hill, and they covered the distance in short order.

Patrick caught up to her and grabbed her arm, pulling her to a stop next to the cellar. "If a funnel drops out of that cloud, we might be safer in here." He yanked open the slanted door against the mounded dirt roof and then froze.

A large diamond-back rattlesnake sounded off. The three-inch rattle, twice as wide as his thumb, sounded more like water under pressure from the end of a garden hose than a rattle. Coiled and head reared, it lay on the top step inches below his feet. It clearly did not like being disturbed, or rained on.

"What's that noise?" Michaela asked, stepping in, trying to see around him.

"Stop!"

"Why?"

In a calmer voice, he quietly said, "Back away... slowly."

"I don't understand." She looked over his shoulder. "Sweet Jesus..." She disappeared from his peripheral vision. In extreme slow motion, he began backing away as well.

Once the snake was out of sight, the sound of its rattle changed. It slithered down into the darkness of the cellar, so far refusing to cease the alarmed rattling. Patrick had no intention of following and sharing a cellar with it. "Come on." He grabbed Michaela's hand and pulled her in tow behind him as he began to trot. "It would appear that the old house might be the safer choice after all. But I suppose that would depend on which possibility is most likely—damaging wind or a snake bite."

"I vote to chance one of the whirly things," she said as she shoved him to run faster toward the old house.

Suddenly a hailstone the size of a ping-pong ball thudded at his feet. He jumped onto the back porch, ignoring the two steps up to its surface.

Hail began pounding the ground and crashing against surfaces all around. Within a scant couple of seconds, a new life-threatening danger had just presented itself.

He tried the door. It was unlocked but jammed shut. "Ow!" he blurted as a hailstone struck him in the center of the back.

Michaela joined the chorus. "Ow!" she shrieked. Then again, "Ow! Ow!" She pressed her body into Patrick's back. "Put a shoulder into it, man, before we're beaten to—"

Suddenly Patrick felt her body, which had been tight against his, go limp and slide down. He glanced back.

Her hands fell away from his shoulders. She crumpled into a heap on the porch. One of those chunks of ice had apparently struck her on the head.

"Crap!" The sight of her lying helpless in a hailstorm was the adrenaline spike he needed. He slammed a shoulder into the door. The force of it splintered the jamb, ripping the metal latch-set from its mortise and sent it clinking across the floor. The door swung and banged into the wall, sending out a jarring rattle from metal venetian blinds that hung askew over a window in the door.

With a decided lack of finesse, Patrick grabbed Michaela's arms and dragged her limp body bouncing over the raised aluminum threshold to the inside and away from the door. Hail hit them both with brutal frequency. They were definitely going to have bruises.

He raced back to close the door.

As he reached to slam it shut, a hailstone smashed into his knuckles. "Damn!" he growled through clenched teeth but followed through, shutting the door.

Hail pounding the roof increased in number and intensity to become almost deafening.

He went back into the kitchen where Michaela lay on the floor. Kneeling, he swept away from her face the sodden strands of hair that had escaped the elastic band holding her ponytail in place. It struck him that this was the first time since meeting her that he had time to inspect her face without fear of being thought the lecherous old fool. So far, she had had no qualms telling him that, in roundabout ways.

She was beautiful—tall with the body of an athlete. She had long, thick, straight auburn hair about the same color as his, at least the part that had not turned gray yet on his own head, hanging down to the middle of her back. Starry eyes roved all over her face. Aside from the impact point on her temple where a red welt grew with a dribble of blood, her skin was smooth and blemish free. Gorgeous.

His eyes drifted down to the drenched, semi-transparent blue blouse clinging to her chill-enhanced breasts. His gaze lingered, and then reality abruptly set in, sending him crashing back to earth and shattering the moment. It was as if one of those lightning bolts popping down outside had struck him, when it occurred to him that he might, indeed, be a lecherous old fool. He grunted annoyance with himself and shook his head. *You are an idiot, Patrick Daniels, a real idiot. Don't you have enough woman problems?*

This time, slower and much more gently than when he dragged her into the house, Patrick lifted Michaela into his arms. She had begun to regain consciousness. In a whispery way, she moaned, and clearly with no conscious motivation, she wrapped her arms around his neck and nuzzled her head against him. Through the doorway into the next room, he noticed a mattress leaning against the wall. He went to it and pulled it over to fall flat onto the floor. An explosion of dust clouded around it as a mouse exited the mattress from a gnawed-out hole in its side. It squeaked displeasure at having been disturbed, racing across the floor and disappearing under buckled linoleum in the corner of the room that probably had not lain flat since the fifties.

Patrick placed Michaela on the mattress on her back. He released her but she did not relinquish the hold on his neck. He wanted to allow it to continue, to lie beside her until she fully regained consciousness. But he realized that once lucidity returned, it would somehow be his fault that they were lying together with her arms around his neck.

Caressing a bloodied knuckle, Patrick took a moment to inspect his surroundings. The old house may have suffered from lack of occupancy for an extended period, but it seemed solid enough and appeared that, with a little repair work, it could again be habitable. He wondered what life might be like, living isolated in the middle of a huge pasture in an old house. He would have to analyze it later when he had more time to think on it. There was something appealing about the isolation out here, or the perception of it. Why?

Michaela frowned and moaned again, unwilling to release him.

He began attempting to peel her hands off his neck. It was clear that only a thin veil remained over this beautiful young girl's consciousness. She tried pulling him closer.

He wondered who she thought he was. "Michaela," he whispered, "you need to let me go."

A lazy sort of smile came up on her face, seconds before eyelids parted. Swimming eyes looked up at him. And then, in a flash, those eyes popped large as full consciousness came crashing in. Her arms flew away from his neck as if spring-loaded to fly apart. "What the hell..."

"One of those chunks of ice coming down out there smacked you on the head. It happened to hit you hard enough and just right to put you down. You've been unconscious for a couple of minutes."

She looked one way, then the other. She then squeezed her eyes shut. "Oh, my head." She massaged the back of her neck and then danced fingertips over her temple, feeling the damage. "My head is pounding."

"I'm sure you'll have a headache for a while."

She opened one eye and looked up at him. "Ya think?" she asked, annoyed.

He shrugged his shoulders. "It could've been worse, a lot worse." Her face softened.

"I guess you're right." She again looked around. "We're inside that old house, aren't we? How did I get in here?"

"I dragged you in. I bet you and I will have bruises tomorrow. It was pounding us both pretty hard before I could get you inside."

"That explains the red welts. But why does my rump feel sore?"

"Oh. Sorry about that." He smiled. "You were limp and sort of bounced over the threshold when I pulled you across it... didn't have time to be gentle."

She sat up and scooted back, rubbing a sore spot on her hip as she slid toward the wall and then leaned back.

He mimicked the move and sat next to her.

She grimaced, squeezed her eyes shut and touched the spot on her head. "Crap, that hurts," she hissed through clenched teeth, and then opened her eyes for a moment to check for blood on her fingertips.

"Must've been a jagged chunk of ice."

"No doubt." She shuddered. "It's cold in here." She rubbed her arms.

"If I had a coat I'd give it to you."

"Yeah... well..." She shivered.

"Come here." He opened an arm, inviting her to lean in to him. She eyed him suspiciously.

"Oh come on, now. All I want is to share my body heat until you stop shivering."

Hesitatingly, she scooted sideways and put her head on his chest.

He draped the arm around her and pulled her tight into his upper torso. "Better?"

"I guess so." She drew her knees up, trying to make her body smaller.

The rain, the hail and the thunder created a noisy show of nature's fury, but it all moved into the background of his thoughts. Patrick stared down at the back of Michaela's head on his chest. Holding her felt good. It felt right. He hoped she did not warm up too fast. He enjoyed this. And, that scared hell out of him.

CHAPTER 7

It was almost the weekend. Margaret Daniels sat on a stool at the bar separating the kitchen and dining area of her home. Although mid-morning, she had not seen the need to change out of her pajamas. Why should she? She had nothing to do and nowhere to go. So, disheveled was the look of choice. The thought of having a job appealed to her. She had not worked since she married Patrick, except for a few part-time jobs along the way over their twelve-year marriage. He continued supporting her financially even though they had been separated for several months and were planning divorce. The time was coming, and fast, that he would no longer be doing that. So, to have an opportunity to be in the mainstream, working full-time, and making her own way in the world again sounded liberating. This was one important consideration. If she could develop her own income stream, she could then force the divorce issue and possibly make it happen faster. But there was still one other huge consideration. Was a divorce really what she wanted?

The Baker Mortgage Company business card that Randall Forrester had given her lay next to a cooling cup of coffee. She contemplated doing something against her nature—call him. She tried convincing herself that it was about the job, but it was more than that—much more. To consider such a thing was an odd mix of exhilaration and fear. She toyed with the card as if it were a hockey puck on the slick marble surface of the bar, flicking it with the finger of one hand to the other hand and then back, over and over.

It excited her that Randall might be a way to break a miserable cycle of despair and end a string of weekends alone at home. But what about potential pitfalls? Real possibilities or simply imagined? Or did any of it matter at all? Either way, scary caveats traipsed through her head. She had begun traveling a disconcerting path of overthinking it. *What if he's just a nice guy and laughs off the idea of a date with me? Or what if we should go out together, I do the rebound thing and dive in too deep too quick, to later discover that a relationship had only been a fantasy of my own making?* The notion of calling him teetered on the verge of derailing.

She rose from the stool and picked up the card, stroking its edges between her fingers. She stepped over to a cordless phone and lifted it from its charging port. She wandered through the house— card in one hand, phone in the other.

Margaret stopped to stare at the front yard through the window and glanced skyward. It had darkened further since the last time she looked out a few minutes ago. She figured it would be raining soon. Her jumbled thoughts went from Randall Forrester, to the prospect of a weather change, and then to Patrick—all in the span of two seconds. When her soon-to-be ex-husband dropped into the mix, indecision billowed like that thunderhead in the distance. It frustrated her. It should not have warranted consideration. None. Patrick should no longer matter. But he did.

As much as she hated his infidelity, she admired Patrick's ability to make quick decisions and then act on them. Sometimes his ideas worked, sometimes not, but he never quailed over failure. He modified solutions to something workable and moved on—a strength she envied. *Why is this scaring me so? Randall is just a man and this would be just a phone call. What's the worst that could happen? He turns me down. That's not such a big deal.*

A miniscule burst of courage sparked. Margaret held up the card to check the phone number. She lifted the receiver to dial but before she hit a single digit, it rang.

Startled, she dropped the phone onto the sofa. Embarrassed, she snatched it up, punched the talk button, and said sheepishly, "H—Hello?"

"Margaret... Margaret Daniels?"

"This is she."

"Randall Forrester. Remember me?"

Tension left her in a rush. She sighed. "Of course I do." And then she looked down at her appearance and became embarrassed. He may not have been able to see her, but she imagined that he could and began fussing with her hair. She then pulled her robe together in the front in a display of needless modesty.

"Have you given thought to dropping by and talking to me about an office manager position here at Baker Mortgage?"

"Uh... in a way." The notion of the job may have begun the thought process, but she hadn't really given that part much consideration—yet. It was all about Randall. "Are you seriously interviewing? I sort of thought you were just being polite and making conversation over coffee."

"I really need office help. This may be a one-agent office but I can't handle it all alone. Yes, I was quite serious. I started interviewing yesterday."

"Any prospects?"

"Not really. I may be overly critical, but of the three women and one man I've interviewed thus far, none have sparkled. So, I decided to call you."

"I'm flattered."

There was a pause, and then hesitatingly, he began, "I was wondering if you would consider dropping by my office about thirty minutes before six. That's closing time. I sure would like to talk to you about it." He hurriedly added, "I know this is short notice, but—"

"No, it's okay... really. I have time. I can do that. I would be honored to just be in the running for the job."

"Great." He fell silent for a moment. "I have an ulterior motive for wanting it to be the last thing I do at work today."

"Oh?"

"I thought that we might mix business with pleasure. I'd like to take you to dinner afterward."

She was about to blurt out "yes," but something indefinable stole her voice away. An awkward stretch of silence followed.

"Look," he said, "I know conventional wisdom dictates that to remain objective and unbiased, a potential employer should never do this sort of thing. That's why I need to tell you right now, I *have* been biased since our coffee break the other day. That lack of sparkle I mentioned has more to do with my predisposition toward those interviewees. So, if you have a problem with this then—"

"I'll do it. I'll come in," she interrupted. "Just minutes ago, I considered doing something unconventional. I think I'll go nuts if I have to stay home again. I'd love to go out with you." She heard a relieved sigh, and then added, "I can't think of anyone I'd rather be out with, and the idea of being in consideration for the job makes for two very good reasons. So, yes, it would be wonderful."

"In that case, pardon my language, but convention be damned, let's be avant-garde... if only for this one time."

CHAPTER 8

It was Friday, a few minutes before eleven, and Danica Crane had returned to the editing bay in the newsroom of KBTA. She clutched a fourth cup of coffee since that reluctant exit from bed earlier. "I guess I should stop drinking so much of this stuff," she told Randy, standing behind him and looking over his shoulder as he worked.

He did not seem obligated to respond. He sat at the editing console watching video on two different screens, searching for the perfect place to splice in silent B-roll over an interview with the local Rotary Club president about the award of a generous scholarship.

"This is your last day, isn't it?" she asked.

"Yep," he replied, still watching the monitor screens. "I'm packed and ready to hit the highway for Houston in the morning."

"That new girl, Mikki, is she good... I mean... capable of replacing you?"

"Her name is Michaela. She's persnickety about who she lets call her Mikki. And, yeah, she's very capable... smart too. She's a good girl. You'll like her."

Danica wanted to think the best of her, but Stan's goading earlier in the week left a bad taste in her mouth. "Does *Michaela* not come in until news time today?"

"That was the way it was supposed to be, but Patrick decided to take her as his photog when he found out you and I had this editing session planned. Stan and Harry got together and agreed to have someone else operate studio cameras for the six o'clock sequence. Patrick thought it was as good a time as any to let her test her wings in the field."

"He did? Are you saying it was Patrick's idea and not Harry's?"

His eyes remained fixed on the monitors. "Uh-huh. He called me at home last night and asked if I thought she was ready for field work. I told him that she would do him proud." He glanced sideways and grinned. "Of course, I could tell by the way he was talking that he had already committed to it, regardless what I told him. Not sure, but I had the impression he already promised her."

"What do you mean by 'do him proud'?"

Randy's nimble fingers suddenly went still upon the console. He snickered. "Out of everything I just said, *that's* the part you picked up on? Clearly, not what *you* think it means."

"Keep your dirty thoughts to yourself."

"Me? A dirty thought wasn't in my head until you put it there."

"Forget it. Finish the editing. I'm tired of this cramped, dark space. I'm ready to go to my apartment and shower."

"Is that jealousy I detect?"

She backhanded him on the arm. "Just wrap the editing and mind your own business."

He laughed. "Hey, we work in news. Minding our own business is *not* what we do; minding other people's business is."

"Yeah, well..." She turned up the last swallow of coffee and then whirled around, crumpling the paper cup and tossing it across the room at a wastebasket. It missed and rolled beyond it, but she didn't care and let it lay. "These are not exactly hard-hitting news stories that I need to be overseeing. I hope you don't need me for anything else. I'm outa here."

Suddenly, Randy became more businesslike. "Nah, go ahead. I'll finish up and get these stories in the video queue for the six o'clock sequence."

Danica softened. She stepped next to him until her hip contacted his shoulder and gave him a gentle shove sideways.

He looked up at her. "What?"

She lifted the thick, unruly wad of hair away from his forehead and kissed it. "I wish you well. I really do. You've been a good friend and a great co-worker. I hope your career skyrockets in Houston. KBTA will miss you."

"Gosh... thanks." He seemed genuinely touched.

She hurried from the room into the hall and headed for the front door. Stepping outside into the late morning brilliance, she squinted. *Not even noon and hot already, muggy hot. Geez!* Lack of a breeze put conditions firmly in the sweltering category. As her eyes adjusted, it was an ominously dark sky west of town that captured her attention. Since a line of clouds seemed to cover the entire western sky, it occurred to her that this was the cold front predicted to arrive. One particular cloud stopped her scanning eyes. It towered over all others, appearing twenty, maybe thirty miles out and she still had to tip her head far back to see its top. It had to be billowing up over forty-five thousand feet. *God, I hope it's not raining or hailing when I come back in a couple of hours.*

She got in her car and lifted the bill of her cap to check her face in the rearview mirror, disgusted by what she saw. *Oh, God. How could I have let people see me like this all morning?* She put on a pair of sunglasses and pulled the cap down to rest on top of the shades.

As she started the car the radio blared one of her favorite songs, an '80s hit by Bonnie Tyler. She only heard a few seconds of it before it abruptly stopped, and a series of electronic beeps sounded. A hollow, unprofessional and monotone male voice identified himself as a meteorologist from the National Weather Service and said, "A tornado watch has been issued for the city of Comanche Falls and surrounding area until two o'clock this afternoon. A 'watch' means that conditions are right for the formation of tornadoes. A severe thunderstorm with large hail and potentially damaging winds was reported over a rural area ten miles west of Comanche Falls moving east. Stay tuned to a local radio or television station for further watches and warnings."

"Great... just great." Danica dropped the car into reverse and backed out of the parking space. She took off for home with more acceleration than necessary, tires squealing. *Patrick, I hope you and your...protégé have enough sense to come in out of the rain.*

CHAPTER 9

Michaela lay against Patrick, head against his chest. His arm encircled her, holding her snugly. The chill had begun to subside but the shivers had not, and the warmth of his body felt nice. It was kind of him to do this. Was it simple kindness? She harbored cynicism and had not known him long enough to let it go. Although, it was beginning to seem that she may have inflated a preconceived negative opinion of him to an unfair degree. At the moment, a feeling of safety and security enveloped her. It came packaged in the arms of a brash, middle-aged television newsman by the name of Patrick Daniels. She did not want to believe she was attracted to him, but there was something there. Feeling anything for any guy was not part of her plan, especially this guy. She did not want to feel anything for him, other than respect for a good working relationship. He was too old, too established, too far down the road of life compared to her. As she lay perfectly still, head on his chest, listening to his heartbeat and thinking about it, other questions surfaced—the most important one: Did any of these conjured negatives really matter?

Unmoving, face turned away from his view, her eyes darted about but she saw nothing except confusing feelings and flashing pictures that seemed to be racing at light speed through her mind's eye. Even the dangerous storm raging outside did not rate an image in this menagerie of snapshots she attempted to sort.

Could it be that she had spent so much time with school and career that such close proximity to a man—any man—excited her? Is it possible that this tingle was creating the shiver, not cold, wet clothes? Had she missed the closeness of a man that much? For heaven's sake, this guy annoyed and aggravated her, aside from all those other reasons. How could she lie against a man she scarcely knew and have an overwhelming desire to remain as long as he allowed it? It did not make sense.

Involuntary shivers continued but she was becoming convinced temperature had only a small part to play. Desire deepened, and she swallowed hard and struggled against an illicit inclination that stalked her.

"Warming up?" he asked.

"A little, but I'm sure if I pulled away now that the breeze blowing through this old house would chill me all over again."

"Then stay right where you are. There's nothing we can do and certainly no better place for us to be until the storm passes. We *can't* walk out into a hail storm, and I *don't want* to walk in the rain."

She pressed her legs tighter yet against his. "Me neither." She paused. "Okay then, here's where I'll stay," she said, but quickly added, "Don't read anything into my willingness beyond a desire to remain warm. Got it?"

She did not have to look to know that he was grinning when he replied, "Got it. Not a problem."

Even though it was the answer demanded of him, she felt it came too fast and too easy. *'Not a problem.' What did he mean by that? Maybe I want it to be a problem. It's a problem for me.*

Michaela thought back to a time not so long ago when she and girlfriends from school who shared journalism classes would gather Friday nights at her apartment. It had become a regular thing to have news-watching parties and compare coverage, videography and each station's approach to stories and slants on them. That's how the parties began, but after copious amounts of wine or beer the gatherings often went from serious to funny as they metamorphosed into demeaning personal shots at the anchors—clothing, hair, voice and, of course, building on and fictionalizing stories picked up around Comanche Falls about each on-air personality. To college girls with no money, it was a cheap, entertaining way to spend Friday nights, and good for a few laughs. She was right in there with them, especially when it came to Walter Peck, the chief anchor at KFAL, making insulting remarks and laughing loudest about them. Good old Walter was near the bottom of a list of people to be nice to, or about. She knew him better than she cared to.

There was something else she remembered, becoming uncomfortable and quiet when they attacked Patrick Daniels. Even back then, there was something about him. His looks, style and mannerisms fascinated her. That was long before having been introduced to him. She knew him only in passing at the Lazy S Bar, the shared watering hole for local news media—television, radio and the lone newspaper. It was clear that first evening on duty with KBTA that he did not remember her. Still, it was those Friday night parties that cemented an opinion of Patrick that she now believed was not even her opinion, merely borrowed, and not at all flattering.

Several minutes passed and she still had no appetite for separating her body from his. *What am I doing? The man is literally old enough to be my father. He's twice my age for Christ's sake!*

The moment of self-incrimination may have been noble, but went nowhere. More than a sexual desire had been sparked. She wanted to learn everything she could about this man, from him, not from stories that may or may not have been true and were nearly always alcohol induced. "Patrick..."

"Yeah."

"I know it's none of my business, but what's the deal with you and Danica?"

"You're right. It is none of your business." He sighed deep and long. "But... I suppose if we're going to work together... and sometimes quite closely it would seem," he said, snickering, "we should be honest with one another."

After the snicker, the arm draped over her shoulders squeezed a little tighter, and then he patted her arm. It seemed affectionate. There was that tingle again. "Uh... well, you don't have to if talking about it makes you uncomfortable."

"I'll make a deal with you; if you don't mind answering my questions about you then I don't mind answering your questions about me. Deal?"

She had to think about that. She had nothing to hide but had not thought about opening up her life for him to question after knowing the man for only a few days. It must be the stigma of becoming an on-air personality because she had no qualms about asking him personal things. It was worth a second thought. She had no more right to ask than he did to ask it of her.

"I don't hear an agreement," he said.

"I suppose it's only fair."

"Look," he said, "with your more than pleasing appearance, education and obvious talents, you will one day be sitting behind an anchor desk somewhere and your private life will be wide open to speculation. .by everyone. Lord knows mine is."

"Interesting. I was just thinking about that."

"I've hit the age where it doesn't matter much anymore. It all seems a bit funny now. I can't help but be flippant about it all. I suppose my attitude toward it makes me seem arrogant, but rumors and innuendos fly like bullets around Comanche Falls."

That explained a lot, but that last comment shocked her. Mere seconds ago she was remembering how her opinions of him had formed. Those parties where they did exactly that, speculate ad nauseam.

"The way I see it," he continued, "is that people *you* care about know the truth, the real truth of who *you* are, not a patchwork of half-truths and, sometimes, pure fabrication. That said, there will be hundreds, even thousands, who will believe you to be something that you are not. Don't worry about them, ever. They don't matter."

"You do have a way with words."

"It's what I do. Since we have time and nowhere to go and no way to get there, let's trade questions and answers. Okay, what's on your mind?"

"Danica?"

"Oh, yeah. Danica Crane. Beautiful woman, isn't she?"

"Yep, she is. Do you consider her your girlfriend?"

"That's a matter of interpretation."

"I want yours."

"She thinks of herself as my girlfriend. I think of her as a beautiful co-worker that I got too close to."

"So it's a charade."

"Humph. Well, that seems like an overly neat way to button an explanation. It's a bit more complicated than that."

"Regardless what you want to call it, why continue it?"

"Now, that's a question I ask myself all the time. The answers vary but there is a central truth... a selfish one I suppose; nonetheless, true. Danica's career and mine are linked, meaning our number one news rating in this market is because we make a good on-air team. We work well together. If I, or she, do anything to upset that balance, it might irreparably damage both our careers. You've heard about the proverbial rock and a hard place? That's where I am, smack-dab between them. And I stupidly put myself there. I like Danica and don't want to hurt her. Unfortunately, bursting that romantic bubble she nurtures would likely do just that."

"If what you say is true, I hope you realize hurting her is going to happen. It's inevitable. It's not a matter of *if* but *when*."

"I know. It gnaws at me. I don't at all look forward to that day." Patrick's voice shifted from glib too solemn.

It was now clear that he was not a player, just a man who succumbed to temptation and now grappled with what to do about it after allowing it to continue for so long. To take this situation so seriously showed heart. "Is Danica the reason your wife filed for divorce?"

"Mostly, but not entirely. We had a few issues, none big. The simple fact is, I blew it. Margaret's a good woman. She deserves to be happy and, most certainly, with a better man than me. Although, I am having a little trouble letting her go."

"Any kids?"

"No, we kept putting it off and then one day we found out she could not conceive anyhow. We had a few conversations about adoption but never followed through. As it turned out, it was for the best."

Sharing his personal life, as he did, tugged at her heart. And here she was, a virtual stranger. It drew her closer to him. Her ideas and opinions about this man crumbled. "Understandable," she said, "but what about—"

"Hang on a second. It's my turn."

"Okay, shoot."

"Is there a significant other in your life, other than Mama and Daddy, I mean?"

"Not since high school."

"Seriously?"

"Seriously."

"Do you date?"

"Sure, but not often."

"Are you gay?"

For the first time, Michaela lifted her head off his chest and looked up at him. "What is there about me that made you ask that question?"

"It's just that you're strong willed and opinionated with an in-your-face style of conversation. It makes you... come off as... well—"

"Butch. Is that the stereotypical label you're searching for?"

"Whew! Sure glad you said it. I didn't want to." He laughed.

She slapped him on the stomach and thought about that impression. "It's a practiced thing the way I am. My education and career have been the center of my life. I can see where I want to be a few years from now and don't want obstacles getting in my way. I know things out of my control will happen, but I can sure prevent self-induced problems. I discovered long ago that to be nice to people, guys in particular, caused them to misinterpret intentions."

"I can see that happening, and frequently. You have the look and grace of a model and the intellect to pull the whole package together nicely."

The flattery surprised her. "Uh... thanks. Anyhow, I didn't want the distraction of people buzzing around me like green flies on a dung heap."

"That's a colorful image."

"Yeah... well, I developed the habit of not engaging in conversations with strangers and certainly not starting them. I'm not even into direct eye contact with people I don't know. If I find myself in a situation I can't walk away from, I discovered that a little abrasiveness goes a long way."

"I must say, all that practice paid off," Patrick said, chuckling. "It apparently didn't work on you."

"No, but I'm pretty good at poker and reading faces. You have *a tell*."

"And what might that be?"

"Whenever you say something for effect, that you may or may not believe, your eyebrows lift, not much, just a little. It's subtle... and very cute."

"I'll have to work on that."

"Hey, you hear that?"

"What?"

"The hail stopped and the rain is letting up. I don't think the wind is blowing quite as hard any longer."

She sat up, as if cued to do so. "Oh.... okay..." It should have been great news but she did not feel like smiling about it. This all-too-brief interlude created by the oddest of circumstances may never happen again. She liked it and she discovered that, much to her surprise, she liked him. It saddened her that they could not while away the hours on a musty rodent-infested mattress in an abandoned house and get to know one another.

Patrick checked his watch. "It's almost one o'clock. It'll take about fifteen minutes to walk up to Barrett's place and get our van."

He rose and went to a westerly facing window that had been broken out. He looked to the sky. "It looks as though I won't have to miss the six o'clock sequence after all." He looked back down at her sitting on the mattress. "I really was worried about that for a while."

Michaela wondered if she had created a conundrum that might become difficult to cope with—an attraction to a man who happened to be out of bounds for a lot of reasons. "All right then, let's beat a trail west. I want to see where Ned Barrett lives."

"Do you have to operate a studio camera for the six o'clock?"

"Not today, thanks to you and this story," she said with considerable relief in her voice. "And, with this headache, I'm thankful." But there was more to it than a throbbing head. She needed time to process things, alone in a quiet place, away from everyone for a while. She could not allow herself the luxury of letting sentimentality show. Slowly, not really wanting to, she rose to her feet, dusted her hands and began the process of pushing it all out of her mind, for now.

She removed the elastic band holding her ponytail in place and re-gathered her hair. Stringy wet clumps had escaped. She re-banded it. *Okay, that's it. I need shorter hair...much shorter.*

CHAPTER 10

Patrick walked through the kitchen of the dilapidated house and stepped out the back door onto the porch. The air had been washed and then hammered clean by hail. Under different circumstances, the smell of the air would have been welcomed. Water continued running in rivulets off the roof, splattering into an old galvanized washtub at the corner of the house, creating a rhythm that faintly resembled a song he could not quite identify. Otherwise, the rain had stopped falling. The sky looked no less ominous though. "Come on, Michaela. Let's see if we can walk to Barrett's place before we get another round of weather. It doesn't look like it's through with us yet. That sky still looks angry."

"Should we walk back to the highway first, and then over?"

"I don't think so. Heading straight across the pasture might be a little hilly, but I don't see obstructions that would slow us much. I think we can walk due west across his land without many problems." He scanned the sky. "Besides, going back to the highway first would add a few minutes to the trip. I'm not so sure we can afford the time, judging by the looks of that other cloud northwest of here."

"Are you sure? It might mess up those expensive-looking loafers."

"I'm okay with it... as long as damage is confined to the shoes."

"You're the boss." She took off walking at a fast clip, right around where he stood."

"That's the first time a woman has ever agreed with me so fast."

"Get a move on. I don't care to have another hailstone drive me to the ground. I don't want two concussions in one day. I already have one knot and a headache. Sure don't need more."

Patrick watched her long, determined stride in those tight blue jeans as she marched up the gentle slope. He smiled, envisioning a dancer gliding across a stage. *She has the grace to be one if motivation should push her that way.* But it was more than a graceful stride. It was the whole package—beauty, quick acerbic wit, and intelligence. It was worth a moment for an admiring look. *Michaela Ross, I want to know more about you.* He then hurried to catch up. As he came alongside her, "Michaela?"

"Yeah?"

"You're a goal setter..."

"Sure am."

"You mentioned that you knew where you wanted to be in a few years. Where do you see yourself in five years?"

"I had thought about an anchor position, but this taste of investigative reporting is intriguing. I think I might like to do this at the network level someday."

"Great aspiration. I like your style."

She looked sideways at him. "Thanks."

He met her glance. "Are we friends yet? Can I call you Mikki now? Two syllable names are okay, but three's a stretch." He began to fall back and snickered.

"You think you're funny, don't you?" She slowed and allowed him to again walk alongside. A slow smile creased her cheeks. "Okay," she said, "here's the deal: My dad wanted a boy. I was supposed to be Michael, but when he saw a baby girl come out in the delivery room, it was at that moment I became Michaela." She lengthened her stride and was again several steps ahead, but glanced back and abruptly added, "Or so I've been told. My memory of that day is a bit foggy."

He laughed. "I suppose that wonderful story—that, by the way, was no answer at all—means no, I can't call you Mikki. Too bad. To be granted the privilege would make my day."

"Let's wait a while on that. Whaddaya say?"

"Hey, it's your name. I'm just passing through."

She smirked and shook her head.

He wondered if he might be overreaching, searching for some indication of generalized acceptance of his friendship. Clearly, she found it amusing. She did grin. He wanted to know if she softened toward him. It seemed as though she might be leaning that direction. Maybe she needed more time. He would have to be satisfied with small advances for now—more smiles, frequency of eye contact and that sort of thing. He saw improvement and wanted to build on it.

Michaela clearly took pleasure in playing the name game. She continued on up the hill, never breaking that military-like march across mostly open grassland. "How about you," she asked, "got a nickname?"

"Not really. Daddy used to call me Trouble. Fortunately, it didn't stick."

She laughed. "You should *not* have told me that."

"Why?"

"It fits. I like it."

"Oh, Lord, what have I done?"

"The name Patrick Daniels and Trouble are now, and forever will be, inseparable in my head."

He abruptly stopped walking. "You're not seriously going to start calling me Trouble, are you?"

She stopped a few paces ahead of him and turned. "You're right. It really doesn't sound respectful of an elder. Now does it?" She spun back and continued on.

His step faltered. He stopped. "Elder! You see me as an elder?" He walked on, but at a slower pace.

"How else would I see you? You're old enough to be my father... literally. To be perfectly blunt, you're only a year younger than Dad. Although, he does happen to look older and acts *much* older. But, that's a conversation for another day."

He quickened his step, caught up to her, and stared sideways at her. "Hmm."

"Now what's on your mind?"

"I've come to a decision."

"Oh?"

"I think I'd rather be called Trouble than elder."

She laughed. "I wasn't offering a choice. They are both perfect identifiers for who you are."

"In that case, I'd like to request that you not call me Trouble...ever. And, for heaven's sake, never use that label, 'elder' again, not in reference to me anyhow."

"Doggone it! I was really looking forward to calling you Trouble. That would have been such a cool nickname." She walked on quietly for a moment, and then added, "Seriously, I think a person is only as old as they think or feel. I don't see you as anything but an experienced newsman. I was kidding about the elder thing." She looked to the sky.

As she turned her back to him, his annoyed expression transformed into a smile. He had witnessed his own brand of sarcasm coming back at him. It was endearing. He liked it.

"That cloud is looking meaner by the minute," she said. "Come on, we're wasting too much time." She picked up the pace.

After a couple more minutes of hard marching they came to the top of the long, gentle slope they had been ascending for some distance. Ned Barrett's home and headquarters lay before them, about three hundred yards beyond a dry creek bed at the bottom of the hill they had just crested. If it had been a sunny day, it would have been a view worthy of a Texas postcard; a sprawling one-story ranch house set in the center of numerous pecan and oak trees of substantial girth. Beyond the yard lay a broad expanse of treeless land covered in irrigated grass tickling the bellies of fat cows that gathered against the fence, bunching close together.

"Why are those cows doing that... crowding together against the fence?" Michaela asked.

"Do I look like a country boy to you?" He looked to the sky and began an honest examination of the conditions. "But, if you think about it, it would appear they might be smarter than us about what's probably coming." Although early afternoon, the sky had darkened to a dusk-like state, dim enough that two mercury vapor yard lights operating on photo cells mounted on tall poles near Barrett's house came on. The stiff breeze that had been blowing stopped abruptly. Chirping birds, rattling wings of locusts, even gnats buzzing in Patrick's ears went silent. Sounds of nature ceased, now disturbingly calm and quiet. The air felt heavy. "Judging by the cows and the eerie quiet, I get the feeling something is about to happen."

"Patrick, look!"

His eyes followed her pointing arm skyward. "Oh crap!" The cloud rotated and tightened. It seemed in slow motion. "Run for that dry creek down there!"

As they sprinted the hundred yards, a funnel formed from the center of that rotating cloud. Patrick sped up and passed Michaela. "Hurry!" he shouted. As he ran by, he grabbed her hand and pulled her in tow.

The hill was not steep but enough so that Michaela began moving faster than her legs could carry her. She stumbled, and her hand ripped from Patrick's grasp.

A sudden, hard blast of wind hit Patrick in the face, forcing a stuttered step that broke his stride. He did not stop moving and was again running all out.

"Patrick!"

He glanced back to see that Michaela had fallen.

She attempted getting back on her feet just as a second harder gust knocked her back down.

Patrick tried stopping. He skated over loose gravel for a couple of feet until forward momentum ceased. He reversed and ran back to Michaela, now up on hands and knees trying to stand. Her slender frame proved problematic against the force of high velocity gusts.

The funnel touched the ground, doing a slow motion, rope-like death dance toward Barrett's house.

Working fast, Patrick grabbed the back of Michaela's shirt and unceremoniously yanked her up. "Come on! Fight!"

The wind could no longer be called gusty. It was more like sustained shotgun blasts, each one abrupt and in excess of seventy miles per hour, he guessed. Running unconstrained became impossible.

By the time they reached the dry creek bed, the wind reached such velocity that his shirt collar slapped his face repeatedly at machine-gun speed, feeling like scorpion stings. He leaped down the four-foot embankment to the rocky bottom and pulled Michaela down after him.

He dragged her, stumbling across the uneven, rock-strewn, dry creek bed to the other side beneath a jutting stone overhang. He squatted beneath it and jerked her down next to him.

She sat and then rolled onto her side, curling into a fetal ball, hands over her head.

He fell onto his side and lay facing her in equivalent shape. He had to yell over the roar of the wind. "Are you okay?"

Profound fear translated as wide, staring eyes and a fast, affirmative nod from Michaela.

Then, as suddenly as the wind began, it stopped—not a breeze, not a sound.

Patrick's ears rang, and the hair on his arms rose. He could not discern if it was from static electricity or fear.

Michaela lay still, staring wide-eyed.

Patrick put a hand on her shoulder and, without a word, indicated she should stay down. He uncurled, reached up, and clutched the rock shelf over his head. He cautiously pulled himself up, fearing a blast of wind that could blister his face, blind him, or worse yet, send a pebble through his head like a bullet. There was no such thing as overly cautious when it came to the power of a tornado.

The weight of the air seemed to add gravitational force against him. No horror movie could be scarier.

As he rose, the world to the west came into view, and he saw it. A very narrow undulating funnel swept the ground as it moved within several hundred feet behind Ned Barrett's house. Shingles left the roof in large patches and took flight; fifty-five gallon drums lifted and swirled as if they were weightless child toys. Debris of all manner became dangerous projectiles slamming into the house, the barn and other outbuildings.

Although some distance away, the roar of the tornado was like a highballing freight train. Yet it remained deathly calm where Patrick and Michaela took shelter in the creek bed.

Like a large invisible hand pushed it, Barrett's pickup truck tipped over onto its side. Patrick looked but did not see the news van anywhere within the yard. A storage building was pulled apart so fast, it appeared to explode. Two large pecan trees and an oak tree uprooted, lifted and then tumbled over onto their sides in the yard.

Finally, the funnel began to lift, and a blast of wind caused Patrick to duck back down below the jutting rock above his head. Michaela lost control. She cried, grabbing for his shirt.

He wrapped his arms around her.

The wind abruptly stopped, but only for a scant second. Another harder explosion of wind came across overhead, carrying tree branches at deadly velocity. And then, as abruptly as it started, the wind stopped again.

Patrick did not move. He lay uncertain and wondering. After a few more seconds he looked up to the sky. The funnel had receded into the cloud. It moved northeastward, directly overhead. The danger seemed to be passing.

Patrick drew a long, slow breath. He felt as though he had been holding it, and may have been.

Michaela remained on her side, making her body as small as possible. She whimpered and refused to unfurl from that tight fetal position.

He pulled her away from him. "It's okay. It's over... for us anyhow." He watched the funnel cloud move on.

She spit dirt and then pushed hair away from her eyes. Patrick read utter disbelief on her face, unwilling to let it go. Fear retained control.

He rolled onto hands and knees and stood. He looked east, the direction the storm traveled. The cloud, boiling and rotating, looked as though it might tighten into a funnel all over again and attack somewhere else along its path. He turned his attention to Michaela. "Come on." He offered her a hand up.

"I—I'm not sure I can stand. I'm numb." Tears created two muddy streaks on her cheeks.

"I know what you mean. I can't seem to control my breathing. I was just as scared." He grabbed her hand and tugged.

She sprang up fast enough but, as feared, her knees buckled. She threw her arms around his neck and held tight. "I'm sorry."

"Don't be sorry. Just hold on and take as much time as you need."

"If it weren't for you, this paralyzing fear would have gotten me killed by a flying tree limb or...something."

Her face, inches from his, caused his already uneven breathing to become even more ragged.

Her eyes locked on to his.

Without thought to consequences, he kissed her.

She did not pull away.

Suddenly, he realized the foolishness of it. "I'm sorry. I should not have done that."

"No big deal. We're just very happy to be alive right now."

He felt heat of embarrassment rise in his cheeks.

"It's okay," she continued. "It just happened, that's all."

"That it did, but that's not the problem."

"Oh?"

"I suddenly have no desire to let you go. I don't care if you can stand on your own or not."

She pecked him on the cheek. "You must." She removed her arms from around his neck and pushed him away. "This private moment, of which we will never speak...to anyone...*ever* has been brought to you by a damaging tornado. We now return to our regularly scheduled programming."

"Funny." Before more impulses came over him, he climbed the short embankment to level ground higher up to get a better look.

Aside from that one small storage building, Barrett's house and barns were battered but appeared intact from this view. He offered a hand down to her as she attempted to follow. "Take my hand. Let's go make sure everyone is okay." She slapped her palm into his and he pulled her up.

They began to jog, but with less urgency than when heading for the shelter of the creek bank. Patrick stopped at a barbed wire fence and held two of the strands apart. "Come on through."

Michaela bent at the waist and began the ultra-careful passage between them. Despite her best effort, a sharp barb snagged her shirt below the collar. The top button popped off and unfastened the second. In that awkward bent position, she attempted pulling the fabric from the twisted piece of wire to prevent further damage. She could not get it done without ripping fabric. "Damn it," she muttered.

Bent over as she was, Patrick knew what the problem was but could not see where she was caught. The taut upper strand of wire tested the limit of his strength. If he was going to help he needed to get it done before the top strand slipped and drove a couple of barbs into her back. "Let me help," he said hurriedly. Keeping a foot on the bottom strand while holding the upper with a shaky hand, he reached beneath her and patted across her chest searching for the snag. "Whoa, Bucko! Careful what you're grabbing. The snag is a little higher."

"Oops." He found the entanglement and worked the fabric from it. She went on through and then turned and held the fence strands apart for him.

He came through.

Michaela let the wire go, backed away and was re-attaching the button of her shirt that had not torn off. "I swear. This is starting to feel creepy."

"What?"

"We've been alone on a ranch for less than an hour and you've grabbed my ass twice and now copped a feel of my boobs."

"Yeah, tough job. But someone has to do it." He turned and continued on toward Barrett's house.

She followed.

He glanced back. "I don't think I like your characterization of our time together today as 'creepy'?"

"Okay, I'll back off that one. It might have been a little too harsh. But even you would likely see it as odd if it happened to someone else, wouldn't you? I bet you'd have a hard time believing it a coincidence of circumstances."

"I guess you're right."

The nearer they came to Barrett's house; the more concerned Patrick became. The damage appeared worse than first imagined. They walked through the gate into the front yard. The decorative wrought iron gate hung by one lag screw on the bottom hinge. It lay askew off to the side. Patrick kicked a patch of roofing shingles off the sidewalk. He pounded on the front door. "Hello? Anyone here?" he asked in raised voice.

No answer.

"Hey," he shouted louder yet, "is everyone okay?"

Still no answer.

Michaela turned away from the door and ran a smoothing hand over strands of hair that had escaped the ponytail band. She surveyed damage elsewhere around the yard. "I guess ol' Ned just—"

"Shh!" Patrick cocked an ear.

She spun back around and moved closer to him, standing close enough behind him that their bodies touched. "What is it?"

"Hear that?"

"Uh-uh. I don't hear anything."

"Someone's calling for help, but it's muffled. It sounds like it's coming from the backyard."

"Hey, I do hear it." She backed away.

"This way." Patrick jogged toward the end of the house.

As they rounded the house into the backyard, a massive live oak tree came into view. It had been uprooted and fallen over onto a closed cellar door. Large limbs on the opposite side of its broad canopy had crashed through the roof at the back corner of the house. Patrick ran for the cellar and pounded on the metal door with a clenched fist. "Anyone in there?"

He heard a moan from somewhere behind them toward the house. It came from the vicinity of a foot-thick limb that had collapsed the wall and part of the roof. "Oh crap." He raced over to see Ned Barrett pinned beneath that oak limb. Piled debris from the collapsed wall prevented the limb from crushing him, but it was tenuous. His head lolled side to side. He was semi-conscious but injured. "It's Barrett! He's trapped!"

"Oh no, oh no, oh no," Michaela chanted as she ran to catch up.

"It appears he was looking out the bedroom window when the tree came down. We've got to get that limb off him before that pile of splintered wall studs beneath it shifts. That's all that's keeping it from crushing him, and it sure doesn't appear stable." He looked around the yard, searching for something that might be used to pry the limb up. Nothing.

Barrett lifted a limp finger and pointed. "Barn... chainsaw..."

Barrett's hand dropped to the floor. He fainted. The older man had numerous lacerations over his face and arms, and although blood streaked, it did not appear that anything had impaled him.

Patrick ran the few feet to the back door. It was unlocked. "While I find that chainsaw, you go inside, get some towels, sheets or something like that and try to slow that bleeding."

"Okay." She whirled around and began to follow through with the plan.

He grabbed her arm before she could take a step. "Hey, you be careful around that debris...okay? It's wobbly and dangerous."

"Don't worry about me." She ran on into the house.

Patrick wanted to linger and admire her burst of courage but had no time. He sprinted to the open door of the large red building sheathed in sheet metal about seventy-five feet from the house. The door was open, the news van parked inside. He ran to the passenger side and saw his cell phone on the dash. He dialed 911. It rang once.

"What's your emergency?" the female voice asked.

"A small tornado uprooted a tree and has a man trapped beneath it. He's partially conscious but losing blood from numerous cuts over his upper torso."

"Location?"

"It's the home of Ned Barrett on the Cattle Trails Ranch, ten miles west of Comanche Falls."

"An ambulance is being dispatched. Please don't hang up. Leave the phone line open."

"Got it." He placed the phone on the dash.

Frantically, he looked this way then that, searching for the chainsaw. He finally saw it lying on a workbench. After reading the sticker on its top as a refresher on how to start it, he flipped it on its side, removed the gasoline tank cap, and peered into the darkened well. Fortunately, it had plenty of fuel. He snatched it up and ran for the house.

When he got there, Michaela was tearing strips from a bed sheet. She had already wrapped Barrett's arms in a couple of places and had bound a wadded rag onto his forehead. "Good work," he said as he prepared to pull-start the saw."

"Wait," she said. "Think about this for a second. The limb is perched on this pile of debris, and not solidly. If you cut the limb on your side of it, this side may hold this end up but the tree will roll and crush him. We need to find something stout to put beneath it on that side to keep it off him in case it does shift."

"You're right. I hadn't thought of that." He put down the saw and picked his way over tree limbs and debris to stand over her. "I'm no lumberjack. That's for sure."

Michaela continued bandaging the sources of every blood streak she could find on Barrett.

Patrick saw a short, octagonal bedside table that looked stoutly built. With a sweep of his arm he shoved a pile of books and a lamp from its top. "This looks sturdy enough." He slid it beneath the limb next to where Barrett lay. The limb was suspended a couple of inches above the table. He snatched up a couple of the books from the floor and wedged them between the table's surface and the underside of the limb. "This should hold it up."

Michaela grimaced. "I'm not as confident. If either side of the cut rolls, we wouldn't be able to stop it. But we have to do something before that limb decides for us."

Patrick made his way to the chainsaw. He had to pull it a few times, but it finally cranked. He stepped over to the log—one foot inside the house, one foot out. He then yelled above the scream of the saw held to full acceleration, "Back out of the way."

Michaela rose and went to the opposite side of the bedroom.

Patrick didn't let up, holding the trigger to the full-on position. He touched the top of the limb and engaged the spinning chain on the trunk side of the limb next to the bedside table beneath it. The blade was dull. He was forced to apply more pressure on it than he felt comfortable with. Progress was slow. Wood chips flew back onto his pants and shoes as the chain blade made a slow descent through the stout limb. The heavy branch bounced and tried to roll beneath the jumping chain bar.

As the saw ate its way through, it became clear that the limb was the only thing keeping the remainder of the tree from rolling. When the cut could be completed, Patrick would become the target of branches above his head.

As the cut neared completion, he began flinching.

The saw cleared the kerf. The tree began to roll.

Patrick dropped the saw, and it died.

"Run!" Michaela shouted.

Patrick only managed a single step backward before an upper branch came at him, hitting him hard in the chest, throwing him onto his butt in the grass. Smaller branches came to rest over him.

"Patrick!" Michaela screamed and then appeared, running from the back door around to where he lay. "Are you okay?" She was frantic.

"I think so." He began backing out from under the small branches as they snagged and tugged at his clothing.

She grabbed his shoulders and pulled, lending an assist.

"How's Barrett? Did that end of the limb stay up?"

"So far," she said.

He rolled over onto hands and knees and groaned. "This is twice today that I've landed hard on my backside. My butt is sure going to be sore in the morning."

"Can you stand?"

"Yeah. I'm just complaining."

"I hope so, because I still don't trust the other end of that limb. We have to get the old guy out from under it, pronto."

Patrick followed her back through the house into the bedroom. As soon as he came in, he heard an ominous popping sound. The bedside table used to prop up the tree emitted cracking noises. It seemed to be on the verge of collapse.

"Can you lift that limb a few inches?" she asked.

He hurried to the sawn end extending beyond the small table and grabbed hold. Using all his strength, he tried lifting. No good. Sirens became audible.

He looked and saw an ambulance followed by a county sheriff's vehicle and a black and white state trooper's car turning onto the long driveway off the main highway.

"I'll keep doing what I can here. Run around front and meet them. Get help back here as quickly as you can. We need more muscle power."

She turned and sprinted toward the front yard.

No use trying to lift the log until help arrived. There would be no one to pull Barrett from beneath it even if he did budge it, but he needed to find additional support. Only a few steps from where he stood he saw a broken limb about the right size. He hurried to it and swiped it from the ground, jamming it beneath the precariously perched log next to the little table. He felt a measure of comfort that it might hold a bit longer, albeit small. The little table stopped creaking and cracking—the menacing sounds of an imminent collapse.

The sirens ceased. Seconds later, Michaela reappeared around the back corner of the house followed by two emergency medical technicians, a deputy sheriff and a state trooper. "Hurry, guys! I need muscle over here before this log comes off a makeshift perch and crushes this man."

The deputy, state trooper and one of the EMTs positioned themselves and grabbed the heavy green limb. Patrick and the other EMT were already prepared, each holding one of Barrett's legs ready to pull.

The deputy asked, "Ready?"

"Yes," came the reply in unison.

"Lift!"

The three burly men groaned, and the log came up.

Through clenched teeth, the deputy yelled, "Pull him clear!" Patrick and the EMT pulled Ned Barrett's limp body from beneath the limb and clear of it. "I'll get his shoulders," the EMT barked.

Patrick now had control of both Barrett's legs.

They lifted and carried him over the collapsed wall into an open area in the backyard and placed him on the grass. "Damn," Patrick complained, breathing hard. "Ol' Ned needs to go on a diet. He's heavy!" He bent and dropped his hands on his knees, allowing time for air intake to do its job.

Barrett moaned. He began regaining consciousness.

"What's his name?" the EMT asked.

"This is Ned Barrett. He owns this ranch."

The EMT dropped to his knees next to the old man. "Mister Barrett, besides the cuts, where else do you hurt?"

Barrett had not opened his eyes yet but was lucid enough to understand the question. He lightly rubbed a spot on his chest where the log struck him.

"That's what I thought," the EMT said. "I think he has a few broken ribs. He'll be lucky if that's the only bones broken." He quickly checked Michaela's makeshift bandages. "It looks as though the wrap job on the cuts will suffice for now."

Barrett reached for and grabbed a handful of the EMT's pants bottom. "Thank you...for getting here...so fast," he said, laced with groans and grimaces.

"You need to be thanking this man," he replied, pointing to Patrick. "If it had not been for him and his friend over there, you'd still be trapped and wondering how to get help, much less when it would arrive."

Barrett lolled his head toward Patrick. He squinted, smiled weakly and said, "I bet you'd like your news van back."

Sweat-streaked and breathing heavily, Patrick grinned. "That would be nice."

"The keys are in it."

Two men rolled a gurney next to Barrett and collapsed the rolling legs to their lowest point. Others came and gathered around to lift him onto it. After getting the portly man onto it, they lifted the rolling bed to transport height and locked the legs into place.

Barrett labored for a good breath. "Mister Daniels..."

"Yeah."

"That interview... still want it?"

"Sure."

"You got it. And it will be exclusive. Promise."

Patrick snapped a glance at Michaela. A giddy expression sprouted on her face. She offered a bouncing upturned thumb.

CHAPTER 11

"Although I really wanted the job, I didn't think I'd get it," Margaret said.

Randall Forrester, sitting across a table for two in the crowded restaurant, smiled. "You know that sparkle I said the other applicants lacked?"

"Yeah."

"You've got it, plus some. What you lack in clerical skills you'll more than make up for with potential customers walking through the door, and all you have to do is be yourself. I can teach you everything else. You're a charmer. You need to hear it, understand it and believe it."

"But—"

"No 'buts'." He reached across the table and gave her hand a reassuring squeeze. "If you typed a hundred words a minute and operated a calculator at lightning speed, what good would it do if nervous people coming in to talk about insurance don't feel welcome and comfortable in our office?"

"Our office," she thought. *That has such a sweet ring to it.* Margaret listened, her head tilting humbly. She lifted a wine glass to her lips and sipped.

"You already have the skills," he continued. "You need a chance and time to become re-acquainted with them, that's all."

"Thank you. You don't know how much I treasure your confidence in me."

"There is another side of the equation."

"Oh?"

"It's a small office. You and I will be the only two working it. Why would I not want to hire someone pleasant to be around eight hours a day, five days a week? Believe me, you own those qualifications."

She blushed and became fidgety—not because he made her uncomfortable—quite the opposite. It was because she liked him and was becoming too comfortable with that notion alarmingly fast. Affection for this man bloomed at lightning speed as she attempted hanging on to a smidgen of modesty. "I. uh, thank you for the lovely dinner." She circled the rim of her wine glass with a finger as she looked into his eyes and began falling into them. She abruptly retracted her hand from the wine glass and broke eye contact, realizing the gesture had suggestive overtones. Her feelings and actions toward Randall, still a virtual stranger, scared her.

He must have noticed and sensed nervousness. "Look, it's still early. Care to go to O'Reilly's, that little pub downtown? I haven't been there yet, but I've heard that a really good jazz trio plays there nightly."

"Can I take a rain check? I think I'd better go home." She paused but then added, "Please, don't read too much into that decision though. This evening and your kindness have been wonderful."

He smiled. "Sure." He removed the napkin from his lap and dropped a fifty on the table. "I'll take you back to your car."

From the restaurant to the car, she wondered if she might have blown her one and only chance with this man. But then she thought about that. *Do I really want a chance? Sure, he's great looking and wonderful company, but he could also be a serial killer.* As they walked, she stole analytical glances at him for at least the suggestion of reassurance that he wasn't a psychotic masquerading as a gentleman, while trying to get a handle on her ratcheting feelings toward him.

The glances did not go unnoticed. That was obvious. He smiled, clearly feeling each glimpse, but he kept staring straight ahead toward his car.

Randall drove at a leisurely speed back to his office and pulled into the small parking lot next to her car. He got out, walked around and opened her door.

As she took his courteous hand and got out of the car, she said, "I have to say again how much I enjoyed dinner and your company." She bounced a shrug and grinned. "I think I might have lost my mind, spending another Friday night alone with a pot pie and a rented movie." She took a moment to admire this handsome man's face in the glow of the streetlight in front of his office.

He met her stare and stepped closer, placing his hands upon her shoulders.

Moths swarmed the light and June bugs fell at her feet. It did not matter. Her eyes were fixed on him and she had no desire to stop it. At that moment, the world could have been crumbling beneath her feet and she would not have cared, as long as his attention and his hands were on her.

His eyes roamed over her face. He leaned in to kiss her.

She reacted unintentionally, turning her face and pulling away from the advance. "Okay then, I'll see you bright and early Monday morning."

The dreamy look on his face turned to surprise but then metamorphosed into a smile. "Sure. Monday morning. Looking forward to it." He turned and took a couple of steps.

"Randall?"

He stopped and turned. "Yeah?"

"I... uh..."

"What's on your mind?"

"Nothing important. Thanks... thanks for a wonderful evening and for the employment, but not just those things. Thanks for being you."

Margaret hurriedly got into her car and drove home. She pulled into the garage and hit the remote to close the big door behind her. Contradictory thoughts piled one upon the other as she sat, fingers hooked over the top of the steering wheel, hands hanging limp. Tears filled her eyes as she let her head fall onto the backs of her hands.

After a few moments of competing thoughts, she sprang upright and shouted through the windshield to the garage wall, "Damn you, Patrick! I can't stop loving you!"

She began to cry.

CHAPTER 12

"I like your new hairstyle," Danica told Michaela as she sorted through scripts under the glare of studio lights on the news set.

"Thanks. After the day we had Friday, I felt it was a needed change if I plan on continuing on as a field videographer. Long hair gets in the way."

Danica smiled, but did not look up from proofreading scripts. "You certainly have the face and body structure to pull off the look. It must feel strange, though, going from extra-long too extra-short in one sitting."

Michaela leaned from behind the camera. "It does. My ears feel naked. But I left the sweeping bang as sort of a style statement," she said and then pulled the long bang aside to reveal an injury on the side of her forehead.

Danica glanced up. "That's a nasty looking scratch and bruise you have there." She looked back down and continued reading scripts.

Getting no immediate response, the ensuing silence became obvious. Danica looked up to see the young camera operator step out from behind the camera and move to a position between the two cameras trained on the news set. Michaela grinned at Patrick. "It's a little sore, but it's not as big of a bruise as the one Patrick put on my butt."

Danica's hands, busy with splayed news scripts, abruptly stopped and her casual demeanor hardened. "Did you say your butt?" She looked to Patrick sitting next to her on the set. "Care to explain?"

"Come on, Michaela, don't toss out a comment like that with no explanation. You're gonna get me in trouble," Patrick said.

Danica looked to Patrick, then to the young girl, and then back to him, seeing them both grinning, enjoying some kind of private joke. "It would seem you two bonded over a news story. That must have been quite the adventure for you two Friday."

"Oh, Miss Crane," Michaela said, "I had no idea that field reporting could be that exciting. It turned out to be so much more than a news story."

"*So* much more," Patrick said, topping and reinforcing the young girl's comment.

The tone of the conversation irked Danica.

"Thirty seconds to intro. Get ready, guys," Michaela announced. An idiotic smile remained steadfast on the young girl's face. It appeared as though they shared an inside story that amused them, but refused to share.

Danica looked sideways at Patrick—his expression no less foolish. What the hell went on out there Friday? Had something happened between them that had nothing to do with television news? Jealous anger bubbled in the pit of Danica's stomach. Did he have so little respect for her that he would flaunt this college kid young enough to be his daughter in front of her, as if... well hell, as if he wanted to end things between them? Many thoughts whirled through her head in a single second, topping with: *That must be the reason he hasn't signed those divorce papers yet. He never did see us as a couple.* There was no time to flesh out the facts. The intro video came up on the big studio monitor followed by News Channel 12's signature music.

"Stand-by," Michaela said. She raised a stiff arm. "Coming to you, Patrick, in five... four... three... two... and..." She brought her arm down to point at Patrick.

Danica forced a pleasant expression as she and Patrick alternated story teasers, but inside, a stew of suspicion simmered. As the six o'clock sequence progressed, that distrust threatened to become a rolling boil several times, as Patrick and Michaela shared looks and banter that did not seem at all professional and, more importantly, did not include her. During commercial breaks, Danica fought the urge to yell out, "What the hell is it between you two?" She did not, managing to keep it bottled up. Still, she felt heat rising in her face and did a poor job of concealing anger simmering just below the surface.

Finally, the sequence was in its final few seconds, with Danica finishing the last story, "...and that nine-year-old academic prodigy not only made the high school varsity basketball team, last night she was high scorer as well." She paused. "And that's all the time we have for News Channel 12's *News at Six*."

Michaela zoomed the camera out for the concluding two-shot. "Have a pleasant evening, everyone," Patrick added, ending the show.

Studio lights went out as backlights came up to leave the pair silhouetted and the outro music abruptly blared in the studio, signaling all microphones had been clipped and were no longer live.

Michaela hung her headset on the pedestal ring of the camera base. "Another great show, guys."

"Thanks," Patrick said, "but not as great as the one yet to come. Am I right?" He stripped the small microphone from his lapel, rose and came around the desk.

Michaela approached him. "If all goes well, you're absolutely right."

Danica watched Patrick study Michaela's face. He finally justified the protracted gaze at the young girl, saying, "I agree with Danica. That new hairstyle is stunning. You could be a runway model with that look."

Michaela blushed and took an aw-shucks swipe at the floor with the point of her toe, and then clasped hands together at her back and bounced on her toes like a little girl on Christmas morning.

Their behavior annoyed Danica—too jovial, too friendly, overly familiar and it once again left her on the outside of whatever it was they had going on. She sprang from her chair and came around to cut Patrick off before he and the girl could close the gap any more. She grabbed his arm and pulled him to a stop. "How about we—you and I—go down to the Lazy S for a drink?"

Patrick shrugged, "I don't see why not. Sounds good."

Stan Brister stepped out of the director's booth.

"Hey, Stan, we're going to the Lazy S. Care to join us?" Patrick asked. The invitation stunned Danica. "That's not what I—"

"Stan, if you go, I'll go," Michaela said, chiming in.

"I can't think of a better way to start a work week," he replied.

A group party was not what Danica intended. She leaned into Patrick and whispered, "I changed my mind. How about you and I head back to my place and have a quiet evening there?"

He chuckled. "Sorry. The plan is set. You're out-voted."

"Okay then, how about you and I sit off to ourselves? We haven't had one-on-one time in almost a week."

His smile wilted. "Ah, come on, it'll be more fun as a group." Dismissively, without waiting for a response, he stepped around her to join Stan and Michaela, smile springing right back. "I'll buy the first round."

Everything about the way Patrick was acting annoyed Danica. She hoped it was simply fatigue after a long day that adversely affected her opinion and mood. She wanted to believe that. Still, the idea of a lighthearted gathering at a bar had totally lost its appeal. Thoughts of blowing the whole thing off and going home welled up. She broke away from the huddled cluster of three co-workers chattering about the events of the day and took steps toward the door. Then it occurred to her that the obvious bonding between Patrick and the girl might blossom into something more serious if she did. That could not be allowed. Patrick was hers. She had to be at that bar to find out exactly what that news story was all about, why it deserved so much of Patrick's time, and why that time had to be spent with that girl. For God's sake, he barely knew her. On top of that, that kid was half his age—a fact that circled her mind nonstop. She feared the hydraulic fracturing piece was fast becoming a side issue, or worse yet, an excuse to be together away from the station. Could the real story here be a budding romance? She had to find out.

Sighing deep and long, Danica returned to join her three coworkers. "Don't just stand there, people," she barked. "If we're going drinking, let's get on with it."

CHAPTER 13

"Okay," Danica said, looking first to Patrick then to Michaela. "Would one of you like to explain what bruises on her butt have to do with *you*, Patrick?"

Stan gagged on a swallow of beer. He coughed, grinned, and then laughed. He looked around at the faces of nearby patrons of the Lazy S. Those near enough to hear laughed along with him. Random snickers went up as the odd question was shared throughout the bar. Setting the beer bottle on the table, Stan rested his chin on an open palm. "I think I'd like to hear this story too." Stan neared inebriation— movements sluggish and erratic.

Michaela shot Patrick a frown. She wanted to say, "Just tell the truth and everything will be fine." But she was afraid that Danica might interpret that as code for "Tell the story at your own peril." So, she said nothing, hoping Patrick had the common sense to craft an answer that did not put her between them. His expression was bothersome and more than a little unnerving. The idiot enjoyed Danica's discomfort. He must have had a good gin and tonic buzz on because that smirky grin on his face was holding steady. After a lengthy awkward silence, Michaela determined that Patrick taking the high road on this was not to be and felt obligated to break the silence, since she was the object of the question. "Don't just sit there smiling like a drunken lump," she demanded. "Explain it to Danica before you get me into trouble."

"Yeah, Patrick, explain it," Danica added.

Patrick, still with a silly grin, casually took another sip of gin and tonic. As he pulled the glass from his lips, he said, "Why don't you tell her, Michaela? You were there."

"Well... yeah... but I wasn't conscious."

Stan readjusted his chin resting upon his palm. "This keeps getting better and better."

"No, it doesn't!" Danica snapped at Stan. "Quit grinning, you big ape... you too, Patrick."

Stan lifted his heavy head off his hand for a single second. He offered an apologetic look, in a drunken way. "Sorry."

Patrick set his glass on the table. "Calm down. I see it all over your face. You're visualizing all kinds of things, and I'm pretty sure none of them flattering to me."

"Then quit stalling and start explaining."

"To make a long story short, Michaela and I were running for the shelter of an old house on the ranch to get out of a hailstorm. We were already being pelted. She happened to catch one about the size of a golf ball on the head; thus, the knot. She lost consciousness for a short time, a couple of minutes, I'd say. I felt speed of action ruled. When I dragged her through the back door into the old house, her butt hit a raised threshold pretty hard and, voila! It bruised."

Danica's eyes shifted to Michaela.

Michaela began nodding once she figured out that Patrick was still sober enough to tell it honestly and not go for the laugh. "That's the truth," she said. "He was trying to keep me from getting hit anymore." She pointed to a bruise on her bare upper arm. "See this? I have them all over my body and would've had more if he had not moved as quickly as he did."

"Ya see, nothin' to it," Patrick said as he lifted the drink and gulped the last swallow. He then put the glass down and quickly added, "By the way, just in case you're wondering, I'm taking Michaela's word for it that there is a bruise," and then with fake modesty added, "I have not had the privilege of seeing her butt." He snickered.

Stan laughed.

"Come on, guys, making me the butt of your jokes isn't—"

Stan had to fight to keep from spraying a mouthful of beer, and Patrick exploded in laughter.

Michaela could not prevent a smile from wrinkling her cheeks. She shook her head as it wilted forward. "Crap. I can't believe I said that." She raised her head and looked to Danica, who was clearly not amused or satisfied with Patrick's explanation. "Look," Michaela said, "let me buy you another glass of wine. I can't speak for these two idiots, who clearly don't need more alcohol, but I think you and I could use one more drink. I wasn't meaning to make light of your concern."

Danica's expression eased. "Well..."

"Go ahead, take that glass of wine," Stan said, chin still resting on his palm. His eyes had begun to swim, as he worked on his fifth bottle of beer. "You can't be without a drink while Patrick tells us the rest of the story."

Danica's head reared back. "There's more?"

"Oh, yeah... how two wet people share body warmth. It's a hoot. Ya gotta hear this."

A knot kinked Michaela's gut, instantly angry. "Patrick," she whined, "you told Stan?"

Patrick mimicked the whine. "Stan, I shared that in confidence." Danica sprang up so fast, her chair tipped over backward and slammed the floor.

The crowded bar went silent. All eyes turned to their table.

"I don't want another glass of wine! And I certainly don't want to hear about you two sharing body warmth in a deserted ranch house!"

Michaela stood and came around the table. "Danica, wait." She touched Danica's arm. "It's not what you—"

"Don't touch me!" She slapped Michaela's hand off and stormed out.

Patrick stood and placed a hand on Michaela's shoulder. "You stay with Stan. He'll need you to drive him home. I've put off the talk long enough. It's time." He turned to follow Danica out of the bar.

"Wait," Michaela said. "Are you sure you're sober enough to do it gently?"

Patrick looked back and gave the question a moment of silent thought. "Let's put it this way, I'm drunk enough to get it done this time. As for that 'gently' part... well, we'll have to wait and see."

Michaela watched Patrick leave, wrestling with competing thoughts. She did not want to see Danica hurt, especially if blame of 'the talk' came back on her. Danica was a woman in love, about to have her heart handed to her. She was a lovely person and did not deserve such pain. She now believed that Friday's ranch adventure emboldened Patrick to do what he should have done long ago, and this assumption alone indicated volumes. Patrick had feelings for her. She suddenly felt giddy. By tomorrow, Patrick would be available. Her eyes lit up, but she then squeezed her eyes shut, trying to push silly schoolgirl optimism out of her head. It wasn't fair to Danica, or to her own aspirations, to think such things. *You dumbass! What are*

*you thinking? You don't need romantic entanglements...
with Patrick Daniels or anyone else.* She shook her head,
frowned and sat down.

"What's the matter?" Stan asked. "You seem to have
a serious concern of some sort."

"Oh, just thinking about graduating from college and
getting on with a career."

A slow, calculating smile came up on Stan's face, his
bleary eyes swimming in their sockets. "Sure you are.
And I'm perfectly sober."

"Oh shut up."

CHAPTER 14

When Patrick exited the Lazy S, he saw Danica remotely unlock her car door across the parking lot. He shouted, "Danica, wait!"

Ignoring the plea, she yanked open the car door and slid in.

He began to jog.

She started the car, dropped it into gear, and backed from the parking space, tires screeching. With equal verve, she accelerated toward the exit onto the street.

Patrick stopped the futile attempt to catch up to her. He watched the car squeal out onto the blacktop. *I'm not giving up this easily.* He hurried to his car and followed.

After traversing the breadth of Comanche Falls, Danica wheeled into the lot of her apartment complex and pulled into a parking spot so fast that her car bounced back from the curb.

Patrick pulled in behind her, blocking any possible attempt to continue running from him.

She got out and shouted, "Go home and leave me alone!"

He got out and walked toward her. "I can't do that. We need to talk."

"Talk to yourself." She spun and headed for her apartment, fumbling with the key ring, searching for the door key.

He followed. "Come on, Danica..."

She unlocked and opened the door. "Go away and leave me alone!" She stepped inside and attempted slamming it in his face.

He grabbed the edge of the door, disallowing her anger to win. "Please, Danica, calm down. This is not accomplishing anything."

She tossed her hands into the air and stopped trying to close the door. "Whatever." She marched to the sofa and dropped onto it. "I don't know what you need to say. Your actions spoke louder than any explanation could."

Patrick sat down, leaving space between them. He studied her face, searching, watching tense body language, waiting for an opening. He figured nothing needed to be said right away, hoping reason might encroach on that anger if extended silence became uncomfortable enough. As he watched her squirm in silence at the other end of the sofa, it occurred to him that he had never taken the time to look beyond her beauty to the person inside. Why? How could he have taken this gorgeous creature to bed without ever taking the time to get to know her? He thought he already did, working next to her for so many years, and never thought about it. But it was at this exact moment that it struck him, he knew nothing about her—nothing. He shuddered at his own callousness.

"You wanted to talk. So, talk," she said.

He reached for her hand.

She snatched it away.

He forced the issue, grabbing her hand and holding it tight. "Danica, you and I make a great team, and—"

"If we make such a great team, why are you getting cozy with Michaela Ross?"

"You don't understand."

"Then help me understand."

"When I say we, you and I, make a great team, that's sincere and from the heart but Danica, I don't mean it in a romantic way."

Her tight, angry face sagged.

"You and I are a winning combination for KBTA and for the two of us."

Tears welled in her eyes.

"Our careers are inescapably entwined, and I'm not so sure either could survive in the business without the other."

Tears spilled, streaking her cheeks. She did not interrupt, or respond.

"I like you... I always have. But I messed up by allowing the illusion of a relationship where one never existed. I was scared to set it straight, plain and simple. Fear you would refuse to work with me, fear that you would hate me, fear that your career would be ruined, and selfishly, fear that *my* career would be ruined."

Hand shaking, she swiped away tears dribbling down both cheeks.

"I am so sorry I allowed these uncertainties to leave an impression that my intentions were more than they were. They weren't. Because of things going on in my life at that time, it just... happened, and then it quickly became self-serving to perpetuate it. God help me, it was at your expense. I'm so very sorry about that. It was wrong then and wrong now because of what it has done to you. I didn't want to hurt you, but the longer I let this thing go, the more likely it became that I would. I want... no that's not right... I *need* your forgiveness. I can't imagine the rest of my life without you in it... but as a friend."

Danica openly wept, refusing eye contact. After a few seconds, she straightened. He saw building resolve. Her face now turned to tear-stained stoicism. "You've said what you came to say. Now leave." The response was monotone. She rose and meandered toward the bedroom, appearing despondent.

It worried him. He could not be sure of the depths to which he drove her. "I hope you can forgive me. You are my best friend. I don't want that to change."

Danica's movements were as lifeless as her words. She went into the bedroom and closed the door behind her.

Patrick felt as though something else needed to be said or done but instead, he simply stared at the closed bedroom door feeling neither satisfaction, nor closure. *Just how broken am I leaving her? I'm such a doofus. What the hell is wrong with me?*

He walked to the front door of her apartment and began to step outside. He paused and looked back one more time at the closed bedroom door. It was a symbol, possibly an omen, and not a good one.

* * *

Patrick walked through the door of KBTA much later than usual Tuesday afternoon. Jeanie, the receptionist, was her usual cheerful self. "Good afternoon, Patrick. Aren't you running a little late today?"

"Afraid so."

She held out a pink message slip for him. "Mister Alexander wants to talk to you."

"What about?"

She batted her eyelashes. "You flatter me... thinking I would know. How sweet is that?" She giggled but then dropped the grin. She shielded a whisper with the back of her hand. "He wasn't smiling though. That's something I think you should know."

He snatched the message from between her fingers. "Thanks." *I hope this isn't what I think it's about. I knew coming to work today was a bad idea.* He marched down the hall, through the door into the studio.

Stan Brister met him at the door. "Hey, man, Harry is waiting for you in his office. He's pissed. The old man actually lost an easy win in our chess game this morning."

"Crap." Patrick kept walking. "That's what I was afraid of."

He marched through the studio and pushed open the full glass door into the newsroom. Fingers of several reporters pecking out stories suddenly stopped. Patrick felt the stares. The aisle between rows of cubicles ending at the news director's office came into sharp focus. *Dead man walking. That's all I am, a dead man walking.* Even if he wanted to put off this meeting, it was now impossible. Harry's office wall and door were all glass. Patrick saw that he was noticed as soon as he came into the newsroom.

He drew a breath and walked the distance. Without having a chance to knock, Harry waved him in. Like a child sent to the principal's office, he pushed open the door slightly and poked his head in. "Jeanie said you need to see me."

"Come in."

Patrick stepped inside and let the door close behind him.

"We have a problem, and apparently you're the only one that can fix it."

"Me?"

"Danica came in early to see me this morning."

"Oh." A knot tightened in Patrick's gut. "What about?"

"She quit."

"Oh shit," he mumbled.

"That's as good a way to describe my feeling as any. And it would seem we're deep in it. I almost begged her to at least stay through sweeps. She refused. Hell, she wouldn't even give me a two-week notice, for Christ's sake. When I asked for an explanation, she said, 'Ask Patrick.' Her eyes were swollen and red. It looked like she had been crying all night." Harry contorted his face and whined, "Daniels, what the hell did you do?"

Patrick's head drooped. "I screwed up."

"Let me guess, the operative word in that sentence is 'screwed.' Right?"

He sighed. "Afraid so. I don't think it's fixable."

Harry calmed somewhat. "You two had such great chemistry on set." He sighed. "I suppose it was impossible for that chemistry to be turned off like studio lights after a broadcast. I've seen it happen time and time again. You sure it's not fixable?"

"I don't think it is. I tried breaking off a romantic entanglement without jeopardizing our work relationship. I was a fool to think it was possible."

"Yeah, you were. Behemoth ratings you two built together will plummet." He squeezed his eyes shut and massaged his forehead. "And to make matters worse, May Nielsen sweeps begin Thursday... this week, for God's sake! Forgive me for thinking of me and this station over your love life, but hell's bells, man, couldn't you have at least waited until after the ratings period?"

"Crap! I wasn't thinking about sweeps month when I decided to have that talk with her."

"Your timing stinks. You'll be without Danica, or a co-anchor of any kind. It'll be all you, Patrick."

Patrick drew a deep breath, and then on the exhale, said, "Well, it seems it has suddenly become of paramount importance that the interview with Ned

Barrett not wait. We need something big, something promotable... and it has to be exclusive. I have a feeling that if we have a shot at maintaining our ratings, it will hinge on that hydraulic fracturing story on the Cattle Trails Ranch. In fact, it should be a series of stories that build to a strong finish over the course of the sweeps. I'll get with Michaela and we'll get on it."

"Oh yeah, Michaela... I had a chance to scrutinize her work. She's a videography natural, very talented. The girl is showing signs of being a real artist with that camera."

"That she is. I'm sure glad she came over from FAL and is on our side."

Harry pressed and rubbed a tiny circle on his temple with his finger. "Now that Danica appears to be irretrievable, I hope you're not putting that girl in your crosshairs."

Patrick reared his head back. "You seriously think that I—"

"Yes. I do," Harry interrupted, his voice ratcheting into a higher octave.

"Aw, Harry..."

"I've known you for a lot of years, Daniels." He pressed his lips into a thin line and waggled an accusing finger at Patrick but said no more about it, and then waved dismissively. "You can leave now. I'm going to pop a handful of ibuprofen. I need to think, and I can't do it with this damn headache."

Looking at his friend and news director, Patrick watched him age ten years in a few minutes. Thinning gray hair looked even thinner, stomach paunchier and wrinkles deeper on a sallow face. Suddenly, Patrick felt the same ache in his gut that came over him last night in Danica's apartment. He wanted to say something to ease Harry's mind, to tell him that everything would be okay.

But he had just said the most encouraging thing he could think of by trying to expedite the series of stories backed by Ned Barrett's interview, and even that went to a negative place. What else could he say? He came to his feet, but hesitatingly so. *It looks like I'm screwing up lives comin' and goin' now.* He then thought of Michaela.

CHAPTER 15

Margaret Daniels stood before the bathroom mirror, outlining beneath her eye with an eyeliner pencil, her hand a bit shaky. She was putting the final touches on her makeup before leaving the house to go to her new job. She took extra time to achieve perfection, or as close as she could come to it. The red dress she wore was low-cut, but tastefully so, a bit snug but clinging to her slender figure in all the right places. She fingered and fidgeted with shoulder-length dark auburn hair, puckered her lips and then pulled them in to assure even coverage of lip gloss.

This was more than a job. Randall Forrester was more than an employer. That man and that job held promise for something better, lighter, happier—a giant step forward in her life. She had glimpsed a future free of emotional shackles, the strongest of which was reluctance to relinquish the spirit-robbing hold that Patrick seemed to have over her. She yearned for contentment and reasons to smile. An infant vision of happiness flickered on the distant horizon of her mind.

The first day under his supervisory tutelage went well—the second even better. As of yet, her nervousness had not abated, though. She did not want to be simply adequate. She wanted to be perfect at her new job—for him, for her. Now it was Wednesday. She had been narrowly focused on getting the job right; therefore, she had not thought much about the flipside of this work arrangement, an escalating romantic fascination with her new boss. It was clear Randall felt the same. As a result, she did not see a need to be overly cautious about the clothes she chose to wear. She wanted to please him as an employee, but also as something else—something not quite ready for a label. This made even the act of dressing in the morning a balancing act between businesslike and sexy. She wanted both.

Randall never missed a chance to put a hand on her arm, touch her hand or simply invade her aura over a shoulder while pointing out something on a document lying on the desk in front of where she sat, near enough that his intoxicating smell filled her nose and senses. That alone sent fantasies into overdrive. Each time he came close, there was no way to remain focused on job guidance. And, although his feelings toward her were obvious, he was a gentleman and always knew where the line was that he should not cross while in the office. Romantic inventions of the mind took control and her head, hands and body always drifted his direction when he came near.

Now that the job had developed a modicum of routine, her mind had begun drifting from learning duties of the job to the handsome man instructing her. She stopped trying to prevent it, but in thought only, not deeds. She had not been able to shake the tendency to automatically resist Randall's subtle advances, a subconscious thing she struggled to override with little success so far. She remained torn. *I should confront Patrick and force him to sign those divorce papers. If I don't, I'll blow it with Randall before it ever starts.* Margaret growled frustration at her self-induced paralysis as she hurried through the house on her way out to go to work.

She pulled into the small parking lot fronting the insurance office and shut off the engine. She sat for a moment thinking about that first date with Randall. She had denied him a good-night kiss. *Why did I do that? It didn't have to mean anything more.*

The simple act of pulling into this parking spot had turned into a reminder of that episode, that romantic failing. Just like Monday morning when she parked here, she was again assaulted by regret. She wanted to kiss the man. Her fantasies that kissing would lead to sweeter things had begun taking deep roots in her thoughts. She liked the visions created by those thoughts and savored this moment to let her mind go there and flesh out a scene that would end in bed. After all, it was just a fantasy. Right? Time passed. She suddenly snapped back to the moment and checked her watch. She was now two minutes late, after having shown up five minutes early.

The insurance office was a converted vintage home built in the twenties, with a multi-level steep, pitched roof and three tall, narrow chimneys. It was tan stucco with the appearance of exposed timber framing in the style of old English wattle and daub construction. It looked like a cottage in the woods from a Currier and Ives print. Margaret saw Randall through a picture window with a diamond-shaped pattern separating the panes to imitate leaded glass. The view she had of him was dappled with shade from the massive old live oak tree in the front yard. He sat at his desk, staring in her direction. He smiled and waved. This view was comforting, as if coming home.

I'm not sure how I could have been so lucky. I hope I don't disappoint him. She smiled and returned the wave as she hurried to the front door and then went on inside. "Good morning, Mister Forrester. Sorry I'm late," she said in a melodic way to his closed office door.

He came out. "Did you seriously just call me 'Mister Forrester'?"

She grinned. "I did, but not seriously."

"That's better." He had a number of folders under his arm. "Although I can think of many better ways to spend this day, I suppose we should get some work done."

"Gee whiz, boss, I'd rather play," she joked as she hung the strap of her purse over the back of her chair and sat, pulling the wheeled chair up under her desk. "What have you got for me?"

Hearing no response, she glanced up. He had opened his mouth to speak but stood motionless, sporting a surprised look. The wheels of his mind were clearly spinning. *Uh-oh, bad joke.* "But you're right, work first," she quickly added, and then took the folders from him. "We are all about insurance and keeping the customer happy."

He nodded, but remained quiet a few seconds longer. He then sighed. "Yeah."

In that single word, she heard dejection.

He bounced a quick smile and pointed a finger at the folders. "Fill those forms out like I showed you yesterday and prepare them for signatures." He went back into his office and closed the door behind him.

Margaret busied herself with the task before her, but did so in a perfunctory way. An hour passed, and she still was not finished, but she didn't care. Fantasies occupied her, flitting from one romantic scenario to the next, all focused on Randall in various ways. But every fleeting thought became tainted with a picture of Patrick materializing somewhere nearby. It finally became frustrating and over-the-top annoying.

She slammed a folder onto the desk with a force that reflected her attitude. *Please, Patrick, get out of my head!* She then hissed, "Damn it!"

Seconds later, Randall opened his door. "Everything okay in here? Need help?"

She felt her cheeks flush. "You heard that?"

"Clearly."

"Sorry, didn't mean to say that aloud, and certainly not to be overheard. Thanks, but I don't need help. I just had an aggravating thought about a chore left undone. That's all. I suppose I've become accustomed to being by myself too much." She thought about that. "Say, how about tomorrow evening we celebrate Hump Day. I'll buy your dinner after work. Now that I'm gainfully employed, I can do that. Besides, it's my turn to buy."

"Sounds wonderful."

"And that trip to O'Reilly's downtown I begged off of Friday? How about I cash in that rain check tonight. Let's do that, too, this time."

"Good food and good jazz music shared with a beautiful woman. Sounds like a date to me. I accept."

"Great!"

Randall stepped back into his office and closed the door.

Margaret looked out the window to the busy street beyond. Her eyes followed a blue jay diving at and aggravating a neighborhood cat. She grinned at the comparative symbolism, disruptive thoughts of Patrick at the worst times. *Yes, Randall, it is a date... a real date... one that will end the way a date should when two people like each other.*

CHAPTER 16

"Why so glum?" Michaela asked. She reached past Patrick into the rear of the news van and snapped large camera batteries into a charging port sitting on a side shelf. "That dour thing you appear to have going on is not a good look." She unlatched and flipped open the camera case next to him before beginning a perfunctory inventory of equipment. She retrieved the spare battery from the case and was about to charge it as well.

Patrick leaned out of her way against the other van door—arms crossed, staring at the ground. A weight seemed to pull his shoulders down. "I can't stop thinking about Danica."

Before she reached the charging port, extended hand holding the battery, she froze—suddenly very interested in what he had to say. "Why?"

"She quit yesterday."

Michaela fumbled and then dropped the battery onto the floor of the van. "She what?"

He lifted his gaze to meet her wide-eyed stare. He then looked to the newsroom door next to where the van was parked. He seemed to be wondering if he wanted to talk about it. "I guess that on days you don't have to work you don't watch our news, or you would've noticed I was alone on the set for the six o'clock news yesterday and made no public comment on her whereabouts."

"Normally, I do watch, but I had too much studying to do and a paper to write. Graduation may be a year away, but it'll fly by if I don't stay on top of my studies. I don't want to blow it at the finish line. Enough about that. What happened?"

He nodded. "Well, she's gone."

"Just like that?"

"Just like that. I was told that Danica poked her head into Harry's office, announced it and left... no letter of resignation, no two-week notice... nothin'. I hurt her bad, really bad."

Patrick was no longer that brash newsman she first met—just a man regretting his actions. She now believed her initial perceptions of Patrick as cocky and arrogant were undeserved labels, byproducts of gossip with no basis in fact. Right along with her Friday night news viewing college friends, she had fallen into the trap of believing it all to be true. What she now witnessed was an open display of heartfelt feelings toward another person. It appeared genuine, as if a razor blade opened him up and his soul was spilling out. It had nothing to do with cameras, lights or anything dressed up for public consumption. She closed the lid on the metal camera case and shoved it deeper into the van, then sat on the bumper between the open rear doors. She patted the surface next to her. "Sit."

He sat next to her, and then glanced sideways at her. "I always figured her feelings would be hurt and that she would be angry. That's why I put it off for so long. Even so, I underestimated how such a talk would crush her. Sure, I didn't love her, but I liked her...a lot, still do. I've taken a wonderful friendship and pissed it away." He slumped forward until his elbows rested on his knees.

His emotion and sincerity touched her. In a low, conciliatory tone, she said, "I have something to say that might help... if you're willing to listen."

Patrick slowly came up to sit straight, shifting his stare from the ground to straight ahead.

"I know I'm much younger with less life experience, but I think I can offer a gender specific take on your situation as an outsider looking in."

He drew a deep breath and shrugged his shoulders, and then within a sigh he replied, "Go ahead. I'm listening."

"First of all," she touched his hand that rested upon his knee, "just my opinion, mind you; you had no choice, you had to tell her. I wasn't there, so I don't know the words you chose, but the door had to be closed on the issue definitively, no wiggle room for hope. *If*, of course, you truly did not love her and did not wish there to be hope for a future relationship. Did you?"

He offered an almost imperceptible, negative headshake.

"Okay then, I see where it came at her like a bullet between the eyes and broke her heart. The way I see it, the affair that set you guys on the path was a shared responsibility. That wasn't all your fault. She was a willing participant and should shoulder an equal amount of that blame. Early on, if you would have broken it off, it might not have even brought tears and she would've gotten over it quickly. Time wasted, I'm afraid, is all on you though. I believe this to be a sound assessment."

"You're right. I should never have succumbed to lust in the beginning." He slapped a knee, clenched his teeth and railed to the sky, "It was so damn juvenile and thoughtless! Consequences be damned! I did it anyway!" He drew a breath and lowered his eyes to meet hers. "If I hadn't thought only of what pleased me, none of this would have happened, but no... not me."

She smiled and looked down at her feet.

His face screwed down, perturbed. "What? Why are you grinning?"

"If candy and sugary nuts were ifs and buts, we'd all be fat and wondering why. I'm smiling because it happened. There's no turning back. You did what you thought was the right thing to do the other night...albeit a little late." With a tilt of the head, she gathered her thoughts. "Look, as a woman, I can tell you that no matter how tough we like to think we are, when it comes to affairs of the heart, all that toughness goes right out the window." She quietly studied his profile, waiting to see if what she told him helped. Interpreting his bland expression was not an easy task.

"Don't stop there," he said. "Now that you have a firm grasp of the story, what advice would you offer... from a woman's perspective?"

"Glad you asked. I do have advice. The quick answer is to give it time. I know that's a cliché, but it's quite true. Let Danica get reestablished somewhere else. And then, maybe, you can reconnect as friends someday. But I believe there is nothing you can do right now, or anytime soon, that will change the situation whatsoever. In fact, you might make things worse if you tried something now. She has to heal, find new friends and, maybe the distraction of a new man in her life. As for you, keep your eyes forward. I think you have good things waiting for you in the near future."

"You sure talk like someone much older than twenty."

"I am older."

"You are?"

"Where the heck did you get the idea I was twenty?"

"Not sure. Just threw it out there. How old are you?"

"Twenty-two... twenty-three in November."

"Regardless, how did you get so wise at such a young age?"

"My daddy likes to say I was born with an old soul. I've always been smart... not braggin' either... just am. Unfortunately, sometimes too smart for my own good. I tend to over-analyze a wee bit, heavy emphasis on anal." She grinned. "The big surprise here is that you listened to me, a mere youngster."

"Would you drop all the talk about age difference? Every time you mention it, I age a few years."

"Hey, you started it." A smile wilted away. "You do realize that I'm only kidding about the age difference, don't you?"

"Yeah, but even if I'm having no trouble with a mid-life crisis, I will be with a regular diet of that kind of talk." He paused. "Although, I have to admit, it would feel worse coming from someone else."

She patted his knee and then sprang to her feet. "Come on, time's tickin' away. We don't want to keep Ned Barrett waiting. After the pain of his injuries go away, his thankfulness for you and I saving his life might go with it. Thanks to sweeps month starting soon and the absence of Danica Crane, that interview has gone from simply a wonderful opportunity to vitally necessary for ratings health and career security."

"I don't think I've ever known any other part-timer that would give two toots in hell about ratings, as long as they got their paychecks. You really are smart enough to see beyond the end of your nose and beyond Saturday night parties, aren't you?"

"Told ya." She stepped away from the rear doors, and Patrick closed them. She stared at him as he walked around to get into the passenger side of the van. There was a tingly rumble deep in the pit of her stomach, threatening her own professed toughness. A continued softening of her opinion of this man was definitely moving to a different higher level. *I wonder if he will sign those divorce papers.*

* * *

Idling at a red light near the edge of town, both hands on the steering wheel of the news van, Michaela glanced over at Patrick. "When did Barrett get out of the hospital?"

"Yesterday afternoon. He was lucky, only a couple of broken ribs. He told me on the phone that although someone drove him home, he could've done it himself if he'd had his pickup truck at the hospital."

"That tree could have killed him." The light turned green and she accelerated heavily.

"Yeah. Even if it had stayed put until other help came, he would've suffocated from the pressure on his chest." He smiled at her. "Ol' Ned again voiced appreciation for us showing up when we did. But, ya know what?"

"What?"

"When I asked for an appointment to get this interview, I could hear it in his voice. He's having second thoughts about going public with an honest opinion of a drilling process that Landers Energy has a large investment in." He turned to her for emphasis. "If he answers truthfully, it will most certainly be a negative affirmation on the safety of hydraulic fracturing. I understand his hesitance. He may only be one landowner out of thousands that do business with Landers, but if one breaks rank and speaks up, it will have national, possibly even global, repercussions. Barrett is a very credible spokesperson because he has a financial stake in perpetuating the hydraulic fracturing process."

As she drove past the Comanche Falls city limit sign, Michaela accelerated to highway speed. "Let's say the truth gets out and it is proven beyond reasonable doubt that fracking is indeed responsible for quakes, sink holes and gassy water wells; do you think they'll stop the technique."

"Nah. What it will do is create a chain of accountability for property damage that companies like Landers are so vehemently denying. The world is still far too addicted to crude. Long answer short: we still need it. So, Landers and all the others are going to continue fighting against culpability in the matter. They don't want a slice of profits going to repair or replace property damage. In the meantime, the process will go on and on into the future." He grinned and leaned toward her. "But, it only takes one to speak up and then the balance of power shifts. That behemoth energy conglomerate has far-reaching tentacles and, in this case, they wouldn't have to reach far at all, just a few miles west to the Cattle Trails ranch. I think Barrett is becoming afraid for his safety. Still, I have skin in this game and I'm going to follow through and hold ol' Ned's feet to the fire to keep his promise. I don't care how nervous he is."

"Don't you think Barrett might just be agonizing over possibly losing the income from those wells?"

"I don't think he cares that much about the money."

"Really?"

"That man was wealthy from the cattle business before those wells were drilled. He lives alone. His wife is dead and his children are successful business people. I don't think preserving royalties is a strong consideration in his case."

"Then what?"

"The old guy is scared, but now feels obligated to keep his promise. Think about it. He may confine his answers to what's happening on his ranch, but Landers has control of, or an interest in, hundreds of such projects around the world, many of them right here in the United States. If only one person with a vested interest in even a single project involving hydraulic fracturing speaks out honestly, it might force costly regulatory legislation. If that should happen, Landers Energy would lose not billions of dollars, but tens of billions, complying with mandated government regulations. Plus, private and class action lawsuits would be flying at Landers from all directions. I think Ned is afraid for his life."

"Seriously?"

"Yep. There are people out there that would kill to prevent companies from bleeding that kind of cash. No doubt, Ned realizes that. He's a man with a vested interest in *not* sharing the whole truth. That makes whatever he should say honestly more credible, to the point of toppling energy empires."

"How about you? Are you sure you're not having second thoughts?" She checked her watch, staying on schedule as she held the news van at a steady seventy miles per hour heading west, the morning sun at her back.

"I can't afford the luxury of backpedaling. I need this as much as he doesn't want to do it. Maybe I can advise him on things to say publicly that may add a layer of security. As much as I want this interview, I don't wish the old guy harm. He seems pretty nice, even has a good sense of humor..." He chuckled. "...leaving us in a sinkhole to fend for ourselves with a storm coming like he did."

Now familiar with the route to ranch headquarters, Michaela steered into the main entrance and stopped before a solar-powered automatic gate. When the van interrupted the sensor beam, both sides of the double gate opened inward. The entrance was as big and bold as the ranch itself. The double gate was tall, detailed ironwork with intricate bends, swirls and cut metal to create a single scene across both sides—cowboys chasing cattle on horseback. Judging by the intricate detail and quality of the craftsmanship, it appeared as though it may have been designed by a true western artist. It stood between two square, enormous, mortared stone columns at least fifteen feet high, anchored across the top by a massive debarked cedar log that looked as though it might have been the entire trunk of a rather large tree. It was certainly big enough and quite impressive, worthy of a Texas ranch.

"What time is it?" Patrick asked.

"A couple of minutes before nine."

"Right on time."

Before it had completed its slow-moving cycle, Michaela accelerated through the opening gate and stopped in front of the house. Men with chainsaws worked to remove the monstrous tree, preparing the way for carpenters and craftsmen to begin repairing the collapsed back corner of the sprawling one-story ranch house.

"I'll go ahead and have a chat with Ned and try to ease his mind and make him comfortable. When you get the camera equipment together, come on in."

"Got it." As Patrick headed for the front door, Michaela went to the rear of the van to get the camera.

Even as her hands engaged in the work of collecting equipment, she watched Patrick standing on the porch pressing the doorbell button. The earlier conversation about Danica lingered. Respect and admiration for Patrick was on an exponential rise, as was deepening affection for the handsome middle-aged man. These thoughts were unavoidable, and more than a little bothersome. As feelings moved toward a higher plane, so did obstacles in the path to her goals. It shouldn't be this way. Her ten-year plan had not allowed for these burgeoning feelings toward Patrick, or any man. She had vowed not to become romantically entangled for years yet. She wanted to finish her education, establish a career, succeed at it and then advance in it before becoming involved to the extent she drifted toward right now. Her head told her not to make room for such encumbrances, but her heart spoke a different language. This fantasy, ill-conceived fascination, crush or whatever the hell it should be called had to stop. She had a future to build before allowing herself freedom enough to use her head for a sexually charged playground. Some little girls dreamed of having babies and being mothers. Even as a prepubescent child, dolls and playhouses never entered her mind. Michaela's vision had always been toward making a mark and leaving a solid thumbprint on the world—something memorable, like breaking the news story of the century. Now, at the age of twenty-two she found herself involved in what might turn out to be a way to get there faster than she dared dream, possibly even before finishing her education. How great would that be? Unfortunately, it happened to tie her closely to a man she could not help but eye for other reasons.

Ned Barrett opened the door and stood with an elbow close to his side, protecting sensitive ribs. He and Patrick exchanged words for a couple of minutes, and then Patrick waved her over to join him.

She shook off the musings, shouldered the camera and hurried toward the two. "Coming." She appreciated her new short hairstyle and how it prevented her hair from becoming tangled in the shoulder saddle of the camera. It was a small thing, but liberating. As she passed into the house, Patrick closed the door behind her.

"Michaela, would you give Mister Barrett and me a few minutes alone?"

"Sure." She removed the camera from her shoulder and set it on the richly-aged Saltillo tile floor in the front foyer. Patrick and Barrett disappeared through a door to the left down the hall.

Following the tornado, when the race to save Barrett was underway, she never entered the front part of the house at all. Now, she had a chance to take in the style of the place. Like the front gate, it was an over-the-top representation of all things southwestern, cattle and cowboys. Chairs made from the horns of Texas Longhorns, upholstered with cowhides that still had hair on them, set on each end of a Mexican-inspired rustic side table—tall, narrow and left purposely rugged and natural with a debarked cedar wood frame, topped with rough-sawn cedar planks and varnished to a high-gloss. A massive chandelier made of deer antlers hung from the tall ceiling above her, and the walls were covered with artwork depicting ranch life, several appearing to be Frederick Remington originals. Other works by lesser known western artists were interspersed with Texas stars of varying sizes. Mounted heads of deer, pronghorn antelope, bobcats and other indigenous animals lined the hallway toward the room that Patrick followed Ned into. It was definitely a display of wealth, Texas style. Patrick may have been right about Ned not being all that concerned about the oil and gas royalties.

After a short time, Patrick poked his head out of the room down the hall. "I think we're ready to do this thing,

Michaela..." he said and then quickly added, "...if you are."

His tone of voice infatuated her. It was the first time to hear concern for her and what she might think about the situation. It may have meant nothing to Patrick, but it deserved her smile. "Be right there." *His attitude toward me is changing. He's feeling this... something... too. He's softer, less abrupt and definitely less sarcastic.*

She snatched the camera from the floor and shouldered it. She took a hurried step, but then stopped. *Or, is fascination for the guy clouding my judgment?* She wanted to analyze it more but had no time. She had to get her head into game mode. This interview that was about to get underway could have broad-reaching and dangerous implications. She, Patrick and Ned Barrett were, quite literally, at ground zero.

CHAPTER 17

In Barrett's home, Patrick held the door to the small library/study open for Michaela. As she stepped inside, hesitating long enough to scope out the setting, she smiled at him. He glimpsed at the surroundings and then looked at her again, this time long enough to wonder about the source of the odd smile. There seemed to be a thought behind her expression. He became curious. Was it something humorous, perhaps? *Yeah, that's probably all it is. She saw something in here that amused her.* He stepped around her and glanced back at her once again. He returned the smile and then dismissed it as unimportant.

Barrett's bookshelves were lined with Louis L'Amour and Elmore Leonard novels. Even the man's pleasure reading was all cowboy. *Maybe that's what amused Michaela*, Patrick thought, but he had no time to delve into it. "Tell ya what, Michaela, this time let's do it right and set up the tripod and a couple of filtered lights. I want this as studio-like and professional as we can get it."

"Sure." She set the camera on a nearby chair and headed back to the van to retrieve the tripod and lights.

"You really think that if I say those things during the interview it will provide a level of protection?" Barrett asked, sitting behind a cluttered desk, nervously picking at a thumb cuticle with his index finger.

"Yes, Mister Barrett, I do; in fact, a rather solid measure of it."

Barrett sighed. "Okay." It was not difficult to hear lack of faith in that one-word reply. "Let's get this done before I lose my nerve," he added and then fidgeted, looking for a more comfortable position.

Sore ribs elicited a grimace as he twisted his upper torso and he abandoned the effort to get more comfortable.

"You okay?"

"Well, thanks to you and your gal pal, I'm better than I would have been. So, yeah, I'm fine. It'll heal."

"Gal pal?" Michaela asked as she clumsily came through the door with equipment under each arm.

Old Ned grinned, but it was mirthless.

"Has a nice ring to it, don't you think, Michaela?" Patrick asked, attempting to lighten the mood.

She shrugged her shoulders. "In a way, I suppose." Again, she drew that odd smile.

There's that funny grin again. He pointed to where she stood. "Just set up right there and throw indirect light on him from each side of the desk. That should lessen shadows, yet still appear intimate."

"Got it." In less than a minute she was set, had the camera locked onto the tripod and ready. She framed a shot over Patrick's shoulder as he sat across the desk from Barrett. "Recording," she said, followed by a couple of seconds of quiet. She then whispered, "Anytime, Patrick."

There's no turning back now. He drew a deep breath. "Mister Barrett, I am honored that you chose to speak frankly and honestly on the subject of hydraulic fracturing. It may be a necessary process to supply this country's energy needs into the future, but it's also a controversial process that critics say needs substantial regulation. Potential dangers to nearby homes and lives have been repeatedly dismissed as unrelated by major energy companies and a few high-ranking politicians as well. Yet there is strong anecdotal evidence and growing support for the notion that it's destructive and potentially dangerous. Tell the audience, if you would, events that took place after those wells on the eastern edge of your property were drilled."

Barrett answered in striking detail about the sinkhole, gas leaking into the adjacent Webber community's water wells, and earth tremors. That paved the way for Patrick to explore each issue individually with question after question. It was more than an interview. It was a fifty-two-minute conversation covering every downside of the process and what appeared to be a massive cover-up. There was no mention of names or companies. It was one of those things Patrick said might help protect the old man.

Barrett finished answering the final question and took a sip of water. "Mister Barrett, one final question: "Aren't you concerned for your personal safety after admitting to all this?"

The old guy looked into the camera lens for a couple of seconds. "Before I answer that, I want to say that I'm no geologist or expert of any kind. I'm just an old rancher that knows a whole lot more about raisin' cattle than gettin' oil out of the ground. So, I can't say one way or the other if the drilling process is responsible for those problems, but it's hard to overlook the coincidental timing. The Cattle Trails Ranch has been in the Barrett family for three generations, and nothing like these problems have ever occurred before those wells were drilled and the hydraulic fracturing process used...not once in a hundred-twenty-two years." He paused, looked down, pursed his lips and then back up, this time staring firmly into the camera. "And... yes. I am very concerned for my personal safety after talking to you about this."

"You do have a vested interest in the wells on your property, right?"

"Yes. Those wells represent tens of thousands of dollars to me personally each year."

"Why do it?"

"I felt compelled for personal reasons that are not relevant to this discussion."

"Any final comments?"

"Just one. If anything should happen to me after this interview airs, it certainly will not have been an accident. That would be another one of those coincidences with miraculous timing, and certainly not to my benefit. The public needs to know my feelings on this."

Patrick allowed several quiet seconds to pass, as Michaela held steady the tightly-framed shot of Barrett's face and then nodded approval. "That's it, Michaela. We're done."

"Wow..." Michaela clicked off the camera.

"We'll break this into a series of stories, probably five," Patrick said. He turned his attention back to Barrett. "That final comment will end the last story in the series and that's what should serve as a vital protective element for you, sir."

"I hope you're right. I may be an old, fat and ugly cowboy, but I'm not ready for that pine box yet. Still, I owed it to you. It's done. We're even."

"Thank you. You're not only a man of your word, but courageous as well."

"Yeah, well, please leave. I'm gonna pop a hydrocodone and take a nap. The ribs are killing me."

* * *

"Do you really think what he said will protect him, or was that just something to appease him?" Michaela asked as she sped eastward down the highway, back toward town and the television station.

"I was sincere. It'll be difficult for anyone to do something when the whole television viewing audience has been warned to watch for it. There will be no way to create an accident. It would have to be a straight-up assassination, and that would be a suicide mission that no amount of money would cover. Granted, it may not be foolproof, but it does offer that extra layer of protection I spoke of."

Michaela smiled—that odd smile.

"Why the funny grin? That's the third time I've seen it on you this morning. What's on your mind?"

"Oh, I was just thinking about and admiring your work."

"Is that all? Gosh, thanks."

"I might even be on the verge of admiring you personally."

"Do I detect a hint of sarcasm?"

"Nah. I only give back what I get when it comes to that. Although, I think I am moving in that direction though." Her response was uncharacteristically gentle. There was a shyness to her smile this time.

"Which direction are you referring to, sarcasm or admiration?"

"I'll let you wonder about that. Regardless, I probably do need to apologize for my negative opinion of you when we first met. You're certainly no Walter

Peck. I'm sorry for thinking you were just another player like him."

"So, I'm now moving away from being a dick to... something else."

"Hey, that's *exactly* what I thought you were. How'd you know?"

"I didn't... not specifically anyhow, just a guess but understandable.

Are we friends yet?"

She glanced and smiled sideways at him.

"I'll take that as a resounding yes," he said.

"Talk about sarcasm. That sure sounded like it to me."

"Hard habit to break. It's just too much fun."

"I'll give you that *one*."

"If all goes well, we'll have the networks clamoring for this story. I bet it goes national before the series ends."

"What if it does... and, oh, what if they offer you a job?"

"My answer to them will be simple but in two parts. It'll go something like this... 'Yes, but only if Michaela Ross can remain my partner and videographer.'"

Michaela bounced a quick smile, and then stared down the highway. Her eyes moistened.

Daniel Lance Wright

CHAPTER 18

"This was a wonderful idea," Randall said. He slid a hand across the small cocktail table to cover Margaret's and squeezed it.

As had become the pattern, Margaret fidgeted at the personal public display of affection. She had to consciously make her body comply to leave her hand where it lay and allow the gesture. "I'm glad you think so," she replied, eye contact fleeting. She could not rid her nagging fear that if she stared into those handsome eyes, she would get lost and fall into them. But was that not the whole point of the evening...to do that, specifically that?

The jazz singer on stage mere feet from where they sat fondled the microphone stand as her soft, mellow voice filled the room of mesmerized aficionados. The pretty blonde sang in the style of Diana Krall, or maybe Nora Jones. She was wonderful and talented enough to make Margaret wonder why she wasn't performing in Dallas or Houston. Comanche Falls and this little downtown bar were lucky to have her. "This is the first time I've been to O'Reilly's," she said. "Now that I'm here and listening to the music, I don't understand why I've never been here before. I will be back often. I'm glad you had the idea to come."

"I'm glad you invited me."

Although she watched the singer, she flicked glances at Randall. He stared at her with an alluring expression. He was clearly more interested in who sat across the table than who performed on stage. She wanted the attention. Yet she could not stop fidgeting. She needed it. She needed him, but remaining relaxed and simply enjoying the evening was not coming easily for her. It had been so long. This was not something she was accustomed to, but wanted to be. She struggled against what was fast becoming an antiquated sense of right and wrong. After a minute of that examining gaze she became compelled to meet it. "What?" She smiled and blushed. "Do I have spinach on my lip or something?" She snickered.

"Well..." He extended a finger and began reaching across the table toward her mouth.

Her amusement vanished. "Oh my God. Do I really?" She reached for a paper napkin next to her wine glass.

"The napkin isn't necessary. I've got it." Randall placed the finger gently on her lower lip and ran it entirely around her lips. Margaret drew a ragged breath at the touch.

"Just as I suspected. Nothing here but a beautiful mouth."

"Oh, Randall..." She wanted to respond with something clever, but nothing came to her. The rising heat between them addled her. She could produce nothing aside from a sexually charged tingle followed by a shudder strong enough that he may have noticed.

"I realize I shouldn't ask, but I can't help myself. Margaret Daniels, would you care to make this evening last a while longer... in my apartment?"

Numerous mental snapshots flashed through her mind over the next two seconds, the final one a wedding picture of her and Patrick she packed away just this morning before going to work. The answer that came out surprised even her. "I'd love to, Randall Forrester."

CHAPTER 19

"You two have been editing that footage for over three hours," Stan said, having just completed editing a thirty-second commercial in the adjacent partitioned bay of the editing room at KBTA. "I'm surprised to see there isn't smoke curling up from the monitors." He laughed.

Michaela dropped her hands into her lap, straightened and stretched her neck side to side. She looked up at Stan. He rested his chin upon folded arms atop the dividing partition between booths. "Yeah, but we have no choice. Nielsen sweeps began today. If Patrick's news ratings are to stay in a number one position in this market without Danica next to him, this series has to be promoted heavily this afternoon for the debut in today's six o'clock sequence, and then continuously promoted for the duration of this series, spread judiciously over the sweeps period."

Patrick stepped sideways and tapped Stan's arm with the back of his hand. "Sounds like she's been doing this for years, doesn't it?" he asked with pride.

Michaela glanced up and smiled appreciation at the compliment. Stan nodded. "That she does."

"It's a new world in this, the post-Danica Crane era. We have to do more and do it all better than Peck and his crew at FAL," Michaela said as she again scrolled through raw interview footage with Ned Barrett. She cut in a few shots of Patrick asking questions to give the interview the appearance of having been shot with two cameras. She also searched for places within Barrett's answers that would look better with B-roll footage of the wells or sinkhole and to get off the talking head for a few seconds to break it up and keep it interesting.

Stan abandoned the relaxed pose and faced Patrick. "About that..."

"About what?"

"Danica. Harry and I were in a chess game back in the newsroom yesterday while you two were out at the ranch. He got a call from her."

Patrick straightened and stepped away from looking over Michaela's shoulder. "What about?"

"It was a quick conversation. She told Harry she had a new job, and then she gave him a mailing address to send her final check."

Michaela listened. She did not like where the conversation was sure to go. A twinge of jealousy kept her ears tuned to their conversation while her eyes remained trained on two video monitors, raw footage on the left to be dubbed across and edited onto the other. That's what her hands were doing, but the focus of her attention was the conversation behind her.

"Maybe I shouldn't be telling you this..."

"You got that right," Michaela breathed, not meaning to be heard.

"...But the address Danica gave Harry was that station Randy went to work for in Houston. Apparently, she doesn't even have an apartment yet but landed a reporter's job covering city hall in Houston shortly after getting down there."

"Damn, that was fast." Patrick drew a deep breath and blew a big sigh. "It sure is great news, and a relief. I was afraid she might get hungry, having bailed out of here so fast." He put a finger to his lips, hatching a thought. "Maybe I should—"

"No you should not," Michaela blurted, "if *call her* was how you planned on ending that sentence."

Stan and Patrick stared down at her.

Her eyes darted between them. "What?"

Stan grinned. "Wow! You sure seem passionate about it. And you should care because...?"

"Hey, I'm just looking out for both their interests. Danica doesn't need the burden as she goes through an orientation period down there. And, you, Patrick," she held a stern, stiff finger toward his nose, "have important things to do right here, right now that require *all* your attention."

Patrick inflated his cheeks with air, raised his eyebrows and then blew it out. He shrugged his shoulders. "You're right."

"I agree," Stan said. "But I have to say, Patrick, I'm amazed you took her advice so quickly. You're not the type to accept advice so readily from...from anyone, actually."

Harry Alexander breezed into the editing room. "How's it going, guys? Have you given birth to a ratings boost yet?"

"Not yet. But I've been watching the labor pains," Stan said in that gravelly voice and then grinned.

"I wasn't asking you, Brister."

Stan snickered. "Shut up, old man."

Alexander ignored him. "You have the first one ready for this evening though, right?"

"Yeah," Patrick said. "We've already loaded it into the producer's video file. Also, every half-minute slot without a commercial in it has been logged to carry the promotion this afternoon. It's set to saturate for the remainder of the day up until the start of the six o'clock sequence. Michaela sent two versions to master control a few minutes ago. They're meant to rotate all afternoon."

"Great! What's the length on the first story?"

"Three-minutes-thirty-seven seconds," Michaela said.

"Good. Keep 'em all about the same." He turned to leave but then hesitated and turned back. "Regardless how this affects our ratings, I want both of you to know that the work you've done is excellent, network quality for sure."

Michaela swiveled around. "Thanks. You don't know how much it means to hear that."

The old man smiled and pointed at Patrick. "I *expect* that kind of quality from this yahoo but you, Michaela, have all the makings of a news professional with star potential that can make it in any facet of this business you choose."

Michaela blushed. "If it weren't for Patrick guiding me, I assure you the work would not be up to this level. We make a good team."

Alexander did not answer right away, but slowly began to nod and then held a gaze on Patrick. His expression appeared accusing. "Good team... yeah." He left and closed the door behind him.

Michaela did not know how to take that final comment. It was a compliment, of sorts, but sure didn't sound like one.

"Well, that's my cue to get out of here and let you two finish up," Stan said. "Besides, it's about time to get graphics together for that all-important newscast coming up in a few hours to get us launched successfully into the ratings period." He headed for the door.

"Stan, how about we get together afterwards for drinks at the Lazy S?" Patrick asked. "It's partially to unwind from a hectic day, but I also want to talk over with both of you how best to air this series over the ratings period. We have four weeks but only five stories."

"You know I'll be there. You didn't have to ask," Stan said.

"You sure you want my opinion?" Michaela asked.

"I haven't turned away any of your advice yet, have I?"

"In that case, sure, I'll be there."

"Besides, it's your turn to buy," Patrick said.

Michaela blew a melodramatic sigh through rounded lips. "Oh great. I stepped right into that one."

* * *

"What do you think was on Harry's mind with his reply about you and me as a team?" Michaela asked. She pushed condensation from her beer mug down to the soaked cocktail napkin beneath it.

"Not sure, but I have a good guess," Patrick said. "I think it was a backhanded reference to my poor handling of the situation with Danica, because she and I were a good anchor team."

"So, which is it; are we a good team or not in his eyes?"

"Why do you care what the old fart thinks?" Stan asked, chin cupped in his palm next to a nearly empty beer mug.

Michaela sat straight. "Seriously? Hello! Earth to Stan! My future in this business is pretty much in Harry's hands at the moment. So, yes, I care what he thinks... very much."

Stan snickered. "Just kidding."

"No you weren't," she fired back. "You and Harry have been going at one another for so long that you've forgotten how many good strings that man could pull for me or anyone else in the television news business." She growled frustration with Stan's drunken sense of humor.

Still, that grin born of inebriation on his face didn't waver. Patrick snaked his hand across the small, round table and patted the back of hers. "Don't get upset. Stan's just yankin' your chain." She looked to Stan. He was bleary-eyed and sported a toothy grin. Patrick offered a disbelieving shake of the head. "It's a great source of entertainment for him. Keep responding to his inane comments like you did and he'll keep right on poking at you."

"I see that now." She rolled her hand over beneath his and held it, a move without forethought. Propelled by anxiety, she shook it. "It's just that this series of stories may be a good opportunity for you, but a *great* one for me."

"I understand. I really do." Patrick's eyes dropped from hers to their interlocked hands."

Michaela's eyes followed his. It finally occurred to her they were holding hands across the table, neither letting go. His touch and expression were enough to make her not want this affectionate moment to end, not yet. She had consumed enough beer to dampen the more practical, goal-oriented side of herself. Sober, she would never have allowed a moment as this to take wings. But it was certainly off the ground and now beginning to soar. Thoughts shifted to lustful things. She wondered if the tingle she felt channeled through to him.

"Yep, you two make a great team all right," Stan said, and motioned for the waitress to bring another beer. "And I figure that scares hell outta my old friend, Harry. It's no secret that the story will garner national attention and network interest, maybe even job offers coming y'all's way. If so, that would mean KBTA will lose not *just* a news anchor/reporter or *just* a videographer, but a crack news *team*...oh, and I would be utterly remiss in forgetting to mention the recent departure of Danica Crane."

That sobering comment broke Michaela's spell. She snatched her hand away and returned it to duty around the half-empty beer mug. "That makes too much sense," she mumbled.

"Yeah, it does," Patrick said. "It's probably that prophetic sense the old toot has for anticipating the future. He's good at it, always has been."

The conversation veered back to a nuts and bolts discussion about the series of stories and strategy to wring the most ratings from them in the sweeps month just beginning. They exchanged ideas and a plan came together to present to Harry on the best way to promote and air them. During the half-hour strategy session, Michaela had a problem keeping her head on topic, snapping back frequently to that wonderfully warm sensation that washed over her when she and Patrick held hands.

"Well, guys, if there is no more to discuss, I have to get out of here," Stan announced. "If I hang around any longer, I'll order another beer, and I certainly don't need it. I have no desire for a hangover at work tomorrow." He stood, listing sideways, clearly unaware that he did. He began to stumble.

The waitress who had been waiting on them rushed to his side. "Stan, do you need a ride home?"

He swung his head around as if it floated on liquid. "You're a good woman, Darlene... the best." He craned his head toward the waitress with puckered lips, but she pushed him away, looking embarrassed by the advance.

Patrick sprang up and caught him before he teetered from the waitress's loose grasp to inevitably fall, crashing to the floor like a tall, grizzled tree. "Whoa, buddy, you can barely stand. You're crazy if you think I'm going to let you drive home."

"You got him?" Darlene asked.

"Yeah," Patrick said. "Thanks."

Stan's inebriation seemed to ratchet up fast now that he was on his feet. "Crazy? Yep. How can I debate such an informed assessment? The wisdom of it is... is... very wise."

Michaela snickered. "You *are* drunk."

Patrick struggled to keep Stan's rubbery arm around his neck so he could help him out of the Lazy S Bar.

"Hang on," Michaela said. "She pulled a wad of cash from her jeans pocket, counted it out and dropped it on the table. "I'll help you."

Stan forced them to stop pulling him along and turned to the waitress, Darlene, as she walked away. "I'll be back to see you soon, my sweet," he announced, kissing his finger and then stabbing the air in her direction.

As she and Patrick guided Stan toward the door, they walked past the crew from KFAL. Walter Peck, apparently no more sober than Stan, blurted, "Hey, Brister. What's the matter, can't handle your beer anymore? You must be gettin' old."

Stan's head bobbed around. He stuck his tongue out at Peck and blew rattling slobber toward the competition's chief anchorman." Stan looked at Michaela. "That one was for you, Sweetie."

Michaela recoiled from the cigar and beer stench of Stan's breath but smiled anyhow. "You're a good friend, Stan."

They managed to get Stan outside where the night air revived him slightly. Patrick opened the passenger-side car door.

Michaela helped Stan in. "Give me your keys, Stan. I'll drive your pickup truck and follow." She rode to the Lazy S with him, so no vehicle would be left behind at the bar, although her car would be left in the television station parking lot.

Driving Stan's dinged and battered old red truck, Michaela followed Patrick out of the parking lot. On the way, her mind freewheeled, exploring the dizzying array of possible futures waiting for her. One possible path included Patrick. She envisioned the two of them heading off together, as a team, to New York or Los Angeles, becoming journalistic forces to be reckoned with. And then, maybe, somewhere in time, becoming more than a news team. She drifted toward that notion, an idea shifting from the possible column into the probable. It was on the verge of billowing into more than a fantasy; in fact, a worthwhile goal to work toward.

She and Patrick helped Stan up the outdoor stairs to the second level of the complex where he lived, and then over three doors to his apartment. She unlocked the door and from behind, gently pushed him inside. She dangled the keys in front of his bleary eyes. "I'll put your keys right here." She pecked the surface of a small bookcase next to the door with her other hand. "Got it?"

Stifling a belch, Stan merely offered the okay sign with circled fingers at the end of a drifting hand, and then turned and meandered toward the sofa. He collapsed onto it, facedown, one arm and one leg hanging off the side.

Patrick followed and leaned over him. "Gonna be okay, buddy?"

"Uh-huh," was Stan's only response, followed seconds later by a soft snore and a rivulet of drool stringing onto the sofa cushion beneath his open mouth.

Michaela hurried to a box of tissues, yanked one and wedged it beneath Stan's open mouth and the couch cushion. "Our work here is done," she said.

As she stood to walk away, Stan mumbled, "I'm comin' for ya, Darlene."

Michaela looked back at him and snickered. "Okay," she drawled in a distinctly southern way. She looked to Patrick. "Does he have a thing for that waitress?"

"Not sure, but if so, it's about time. Stan is the oldest teenager I've ever known. Come on, I'll take you home."

Michaela followed him down the outside stairs to the parking lot. She watched Patrick walk, charmed by the package that, when looked at as a whole, made the man. She engaged in a fast, halfhearted attempt at finding flaws, but could not—not without further, deeper analysis. And in the brief span of only two weeks, she had moved from cynical about this man to an attitude of not wanting to know too much, for fear of bursting a swelling romantic bubble. Under this moon, on such a comfortable night with the added internal glow from three mugs of beer, why tip all these feelings in an undesirable direction?

The ride back across Comanche Falls was made with minimal conversation. Michaela assumed Patrick had his own thoughts where this night might lead. They drove past the college campus and into an upscale but older residential area a couple of blocks away. "At the next house, don't pull into the driveway on this side, but the one at the other end of that two-story red brick."

Once on the driveway, the car's headlights illuminated a two-car garage with living quarters above it straight ahead. "So, you live in a garage apartment."

"Yeah. My roommate and I found this place our first year of school and have been here since."

"Roommate?"

"Belinda." Michaela smiled. "She's the reason I was soured on you before I met you. It wasn't all her fault though. Walter Peck played a hand in molding that opinion. After that fiasco of a date I had with Peck, Belinda naturally assumed all anchormen were the same, arrogant players. And... well, I sort of fell into that line of reasoning with her. At the time, I couldn't argue if I had wanted to. And the situation being what it was, I didn't want to. Her personal assessment of what you were like seemed reasonable enough. So, her opinion became my opinion."

"How about now?"

Michaela's grin eased, less amused. "Improved. Greatly, I'd say." She wanted to ask him inside, but apprehension over opening a possible Pandora's Box suddenly bound her. An awkward silence followed.

"I suppose I should be getting back to my own place. Tomorrow, we've got to—"

"Would you like to come in for a while?" she blurted.

"What about your roommate? Won't we disturb her? It's kind of late."

"She's in San Antonio...some kind of family thing, but she told me it was no real emergency. She just wanted to be there when her mother had surgery."

"I don't know if I should. I kind of like being a good guy in your eyes now."

"No need to worry about that." She held up a hand. "Promise." He stared for a moment, searching her face.

"I have one beer in the fridge... if Belinda didn't drink it before she left. I'll split it with you."

"I guess I can stay for half a beer," he finally said.

As she led the way, ascending the outdoor wooden stairs to the small apartment over the garage, she glanced back a couple of times, knowing how hesitant Patrick seemed in accepting the invitation. She felt as though she needed to justify the over-the-shoulder looks. "Watch your step. These stairs are old and rickety."

"They seem pretty solid," he said, just as she stepped onto the small landing in front of the door.

She unlocked it, stepped inside and held it open. "Come on in."

He bounced a fast smile, appearing nervous. He had to turn sideways to breach the threshold with her standing in the doorway. His arm brushed across her breasts.

Her breath hitched. She swallowed.

"Sorry. That was clumsy of me."

"You're... uh... it's okay," she stammered.

Patrick stood inside and looked around the room as she closed the door behind them. "Nice apartment," he said.

She breezed through, picking up clothing strewn about on the backs of chairs and from the floor. "Thanks. But, as you can see, neither I nor Belinda are into good housekeeping."

"Hey, no need to apologize. I don't know about your roommate, but I've known you long enough to realize you couldn't have much time to devote to it."

She gathered papers and books together off one of the sofa cushions. "Thanks for the vote of confidence, but when this day began, if I would've known I'd have company tonight, I certainly would have made time to straighten up this place." She dropped the armload of college materials on the floor at the end of the sofa, which was small, more the size of a loveseat. "Please, sit. Make yourself comfortable."

"Honestly, Michaela, I'm a little scared about that."

"What... being comfortable?"

"Not just comfortable, but *too* comfortable... in *your* apartment... with just the two of us here."

She smiled. "Good answer." She stepped into his aura and kissed him lightly on the corner of the mouth. "Your hesitance is sweet, endearing really. But, from my vantage point, it's unnecessary."

"Oh, Michaela..." He put his arm around her waist and pulled her back in. He kissed her, long and deep. As their lips parted, he said, "I have a feeling I'll be going straight to hell for this, and when I get there, the devil will look a lot like Harry Alexander."

Michaela took his hand. "Still want half a beer?"

"I really don't."

"Neither do I." She led him toward the bedroom. "You may fear hell, but I'm expecting to hear angels sing." She glanced over her shoulder and wrinkled her nose.

Michaela opened her eyes reluctantly, lids drooping and heavy, coming out of a deep, dreamless sleep. The morning sun streamed through in broken rays between white metal slats of blinds covering an eastward facing window of her second-floor garage apartment. She lolled her head to the side. Patrick continued sleeping soundly on his stomach. A single sheet covered them both. She reached and gently pulled it down to reveal his back and buttocks. Urges of last night again swelled within her, and her breathing quickened. Then her eyes drifted up to see the big, red numerals on the digital clock next to him on a small table, and her lust-enhanced breathing abruptly stopped. It was ten minutes after nine. "Crap!" She rolled over and off the bed, dragging the sheet with her. "Wake up, Patrick. We've overslept."

He moaned and then licked his lips. "I don't want to get up." He lifted his head and looked at the clock. "I don't have to be at work for another couple of hours, and I might be able to get away with being even later than that."

"I have class. It started ten minutes ago. I've already missed one in the past couple of weeks. I can't afford to miss another." She did not take time to put on panties, snatching up her jeans from the floor, and then falling back onto the bed, jerking them on, both legs at the same time. She was back on her feet before Patrick stopped bouncing on the other side of the bed. "Please get up. Come on," she pleaded. "Did you forget that Stan drove me to the Lazy S last night? I left my car at the television station. You *have* to drive me. Get up, get up."

"Oh... yeah." He scratched his head. "I did forget." He sat up and yawned. He looked to her and frowned quizzically. "How come you didn't remind me last night, so I could take you to your car?"

"Are you complaining it turned out this way?"

"Bad question, huh? Sorry. Let's blame it on being addled, coming out of a sound sleep."

"Put some snap in it, would ya?"

"Okay, okay." He slipped his boxers on. "Do I have time to pee?"

"No, but go ahead."

He grinned and dragged his pants and shirt to the bathroom. When he came out, he was dressed except for shoes and socks.

"Good enough," she said. "Let's go."

She flung open the door and ran down the stairs, flip-flops slapping on each tread of the creaking and wobbly wooden stairs outside her second-floor garage apartment.

Patrick followed, but not enthusiastically, carrying shoes and socks. "Ouch, ouch, ouch," he barked with each footfall on worn and splintered stairs with peeling paint. He then ran, tiptoeing across the graveled walkway from the bottom of the stairs to the smoother driveway. Once on the concrete surface, he lazily leaned far enough forward that he had to break into a jog to keep from stumbling. He wasn't fooling Michaela in the slightest. She saw that his rush to get to the car was a pretense for her benefit. Still, she appreciated the effort, contrived or not.

The car had not even had time to warm up before they reached the campus. "Turn here!" Michaela ordered abruptly.

Tires squealed as Patrick suddenly spun the steering wheel, steering off the street onto a circular drive. He braked to a hard stop at the centered front door of a broad four-story building, just one of many campus structures, all covered in the same boring red brick.

Without thinking, Michaela leaned over and kissed Patrick on the cheek.

Apparently not good enough, Patrick cupped her cheeks between his hands and returned the kiss—the signature deeply romantic and mutual. "You're quite a girl, Michaela Ross."

Michaela's rush slowed as it occurred to her that Patrick's standoffish attitude of the night before had disappeared. With no time to consider the implications, the reflective moment evaporated. "In the light of day, I'm now wondering if I might have screwed up a good working relationship last night. Did I?" She threw the door open.

"Too early to tell," he said, and then smiled, "but there is no way I'm going to say I didn't enjoy it."

Michaela took a deep breath and huffed it out, then nodded. "Me too." She hurriedly bounded out of the car, but took time to lean down and look back through the open window. "I have a friend in this class who owes me a favor. I can get her to drive me to work afterwards. I'll see you at the station this afternoon."

As Michaela left Patrick behind and trotted toward the building, an odd feeling came over her. She had a growing internal conflict brought on by a convolution of desires. Her life's goals were now muddied almost beyond recognition. *What is it I want? Patrick?* The thought of him pleased her, but a smile it began to produce did not complete before fading away. She jerked open the door. Her forward momentum stuttered as she stepped through into the building. *Have I begun to manipulate him to get what I want? If that's the case, how come I find myself racing to class late after a night lying next to him? Aw, geez, I think I'm falling in love. Damn, damn, damn!*

She ran down the deserted hallway toward her nine o'clock class, flip-flops slapping her heels. It was nine twenty-five.

CHAPTER 20

After Patrick left Michaela on campus, he felt no urge to rush the morning. On the way back to his apartment, he stopped at a small diner and ate a leisurely breakfast. It gave him time to think. As he held a coffee mug to his lips, steam bathing his face, he sipped the hot coffee while he wondered how the public viewed his first hydraulic fracturing story that KBTA aired during the six o'clock news yesterday. Various scenarios circled his imagination. As imaginings swung from positive to negative and all degrees in between, optimism remained high. He could think of no reason that this series of news stories would not turn out successful, but he could think of many ways they would serve as a positive game-changer for his career. His star was finally rising. He sensed it deep down and it brought a feeling of satisfaction. Comanche Falls and the nation would recognize the importance of the story, and he was becoming more certain than ever that an honest national debate would be ignited on the issue of how to treat the hydraulic fracturing process so that it would be fair to all parties involved. And now it was possible thanks to old Ned Barrett's willingness to talk. Over the course of the next four stories still in the can waiting to air, he and Barrett would become known in network television circles and, possibly, even household names. Patrick figured his time at this level of the news business would soon be at a favorable end.

After breakfast, he went back to his apartment, showered, put on fresh clothes and went to the television station. He arrived at the station a few minutes before eleven o'clock. He bounded from the car, walked with a joyful strut to the front door and breezed on into the lobby.

"Oh, Patrick. Look," Jeanie Fromme blurted as he came through the door. The pretty, young, freckle-faced receptionist waved a bulging pile of pink message slips at him.

"My God," he said, "all for me?"

The redhead giggled. "Yeah. Can you believe it?"

"All good I hope."

Her head bobbled as a more serious look came over her. "Uh, not all." She thumbed through the pile and pulled out a particular slip. "Since you asked, maybe you need to read this one first. It was the first call I answered this morning after opening the switchboard."

Patrick snatched it from her hand as she continued clutching the remainder in the other. The hair stood up on the back of his neck as he read:

"There are more forces at play than you can even imagine. It was a mistake to slap that hornet's nest before considering the number of powerful people you angered and the size of their stingers."

"Well, I can't say it was unexpected," he mumbled, feeling a sense of dread.

Jeanie pouted. "The man was very rude, almost screaming in my ear to make sure I wrote it down correctly, to the point of insisting that I read it back to him. When I asked his name, he slammed the phone down in my ear. I didn't like him at all, Patrick. He scared me."

Although nervous about the threat, Patrick smiled. "Don't worry, sweet Squeaky. It wasn't about you. He's pissed at me." He took the remaining messages from her and then squeezed her hand. "Thank you." He gazed into her eyes for a moment. "Gonna be okay?" He shook her hand playfully.

That effervescent smile popped right back. "Sure."

Stan Brister exited the control room down the hall near the door into the studio. He leaned against the wall, holding a folded newspaper, tapping his thigh with it. "Been waitin' for you," Stan called out.

"Oh?"

Patrick glanced down at Jeanie. "Thanks again." He walked toward Stan. "I see you made it to work okay. Hangover?"

"Nah. I'm a drinking pro. It takes more than a fast six-pack to give me pain." Stan waved a hand over his head. "Can you feel the gathering clouds?"

"What are you talking about?"

"Buddy, I think you're in the process of seeding a shit-storm." Patrick frowned. "Your sense of humor sucks."

"Sorry, but I have been holding that one all morning, waiting for you to show up."

"Poor stab at humor aside," Patrick replied, holding up the offensive message, "I think you might be right after having read this."

"It's not just you. Apparently, you had help with the seeding process."

"What are you talking about?"

"Are you familiar with Amanda Pine... that young aggressive reporter for the *Falls Tribune*?"

"I've read some of her work, never met her. Why?"

Stan slapped the folded newspaper section into Patrick's stomach. "I think she's trying to make her bones with this fracking story, just like you, but in her own way. She covered a city council meeting in Sawyer, north of the metroplex. A few members of Sawyer's city council are attempting to get a proposed ban on fracking within the city limits on the ballot."

Patrick shoved the wad of pink message slips in his pocket and took the paper section from Stan. He perused the article.

Stan continued talking. "If a ban happens to be approved, it seems Landers Energy is the one that will be hurt most by it. No surprise, right? Some current and former Texas officials are backing Landers' right to drill within the city limits of Sawyer and actively speaking against Sawyer's attempt to get the ban approved. They even have a former Texas Supreme Court Chief Justice on the payroll who has found a loophole. According to him, the city of Sawyer *cannot* legally ban it, vote or no vote. He says state law supersedes the city's authority. As you read, you'll notice that Amanda Pine is going after that former judge, hammering him hard, actually accusing him of using his status to trample people's rights in favor of a fat paycheck. The girl has guts, I'll say that for her, but taking facts and then tacking on a personal editorial spin is dangerous. There's even a paragraph in that article about the governor talking about allowing state law to supersede *all* city ordinances, under the guise of stopping the 'patchwork of laws and ordinances' in Texas that are so different from one city to the next. Terribly coincidental, don't you think? This was never an issue until powerful people wanted to drill within city limits. It seems to me to be a way to legitimize the fracking thing in all Texas cities, leaving no local control."

Patrick let out a breathy whistle. "God Almighty, this thing seems set to explode. I think you're right."

"It's a good article, though. She might be doing a better job of pissing people off than you. She doesn't pull any punches; although, there are a few well-placed adjectives in that article that I don't think her editor should have allowed."

As Stan spoke, Patrick continued scanning through the article, nodding as he read. Finally, he said, "Wow, I'm impressed. But you know what? I'm afraid she may have not just poked the bear, but drawn blood as well. She's *too* critical, and you're right. She *did* salt the article with opinion. Stupid move... and dangerous. The girl is inviting hell to rain down on her. Landers has got to be feeling pressure this morning to do something fast. Even though Barrett's little operation and Sawyer's problem are simply drops in a bucket for Landers Energy, it could quickly reel out of control for Landers if the situation goes viral nationwide. I think it will. It could cost the company billions in legal problems and lost fracking opportunities."

"You know it," Stan said. "Two separate news organizations from the same Texas town, breaking similar stories on the same day, will get attention." Stan suddenly became serious. He grabbed Patrick's arm. "You and that Amanda Pine chick may not have collaborated, but you have successfully put two boots in that bear's balls at the same time. Be careful and very aware of your surroundings, now that you've put this thing into motion."

"That's the second time in five minutes I've been warned to watch my back."

"Who else?"

Patrick shoved the threatening phone message into Stan's shirt pocket, patted it down and walked away.

"Now that you've gotten Mikki involved in this mess, you really should have a talk with her...a serious talk."

Patrick continued walking away.

"Ya hear me, Patrick?"

"Yeah. I hear you." Patrick did not look back. "I will. I promise." *I've got to let her know there could be serious downsides to investigative reporting. The bigger the rewards, the bigger the risks.*

Patrick went to his desk in the newsroom, one of many cubicles lining two sides of the room ending at Harry Alexander's office door at the rear of the large room. He sat in the wheeled desk chair and pulled himself into position at the keyboard of his computer, intending to look over the producer's story list for the six o'clock broadcast coming up in a few hours. Fingers resting on the keys, he instead stared at the slowly spinning and rocking KBTA logo screensaver, as if mesmerized. His mind and heart went elsewhere.

It struck him that concern for Michaela's safety was only a single facet of a growing obsession with the young woman. It may have begun as physical attraction, a simple infatuation. After all, she was young and beautiful. What man in his right mind could think otherwise of Michaela Ross? Beauty may be only skin deep, but Patrick saw unimaginable depth to Michaela's true beauty. She was the total package. It only started with appearance, but those physical attributes plus her intelligence, passion, and wit were all extremely attractive. On top of it all, she had a personality Patrick melded with so easily, so perfectly.

He drew a sudden deep breath and shoved away from his computer terminal, realizing, for the first time, he was developing deeper feelings for this girl than intended and moving to the precipice of losing himself to them. This abrupt realization shocked and frightened him. He wondered what life would be like if she should suddenly disappear from it, a picture he saw as still developing. What if she got a job in a different part of the country? What if he did? What if, God forbid, something should happen to her as a result of the fracking story, and only because she did nothing more than stand too close to him?

That thought was too vivid. He shuddered and sprang to his feet.

The prospect of not having her around, whatever the reason, was more than he cared to consider right now. It was crazy. He missed her, although it would only be another two or three hours until she would be here at the station, and only about the same length of time since he last saw her. As he had done so many times with Danica, he attempted shaking off deeply personal thoughts to focus on work. With Danica, it was a rather simple process to compartmentalize thoughts and feelings about her. With Michaela, it did not work. His heart overrode an ability to think rationally about Michaela, taking his mind to events of the night before in her apartment, above that garage, in that squeaky bed and, of course, the smell of her natural scent. *God! What have I gotten myself into this time?*

The phone in his cubicle rang. It startled him from highballing thoughts that would have shortly hit a wall if left to reel like they were. He snatched up the receiver. "Daniels."

"This is the front desk. You have a visitor in the lobby."

"Thanks, Squeaky. On my way."

He left the newsroom and walked through the darkened studio. As he exited the other side of the studio into the long corridor with a clear view of Jeanie Fromme's desk in the lobby, he saw Margaret standing there talking with the young receptionist. She was not smiling.

He had an inkling what it might be about. But why today? He was in no mood, and had no time, for divorce talk. Some other day perhaps, but for God's sake not this one. He had other things on his mind, serious things, and far too many to give her the attention she deserved. As he approached, he called out, "Hi, Margaret. What brings you here?"

She did not offer a quick reply. Instead, she waited until he closed the gap, and then asked barely above a whisper, "Is there somewhere we can talk...privately?"

"I really don't have time—"

"Please, Patrick, it will only take a couple of minutes. I promise."

He pursed his lips, held it, and then sighed. "Okay. Let's go to the breakroom. There's usually no one in there this time of day."

Patrick led the way to a small room off the corridor. Vending machines lined one wall. On the opposite wall stood a buffet bar with a coffeemaker, and small round tables with chairs were randomly placed in the center of the room. As he suspected, there were no other employees in there at the moment. He went directly to the coffeemaker and lifted the carafe. He swirled it at eye level. "This looks fairly fresh. Want a cup?" he asked.

"If you'll drink one with me."

He wanted to say no, but the look on her face seemed faintly sad and her words pleading. "Okay...sure. I'm a bit frazzled this afternoon. I can use some coffee."

"Frazzled, huh?"

"Yeah. It's this fracking story." He grinned. "And I don't mean fracking as a euphemism for another dirty word. We started a five-part series yesterday."

"I saw the first one. It was excellent."

"Thanks." He handed her a steaming paper cup of coffee. "Please, sit." He pulled a chair out for her. She lowered onto it, appearing apprehensive. He sat on the opposite side of the small table.

Margaret lifted the cup to her lips, held it for a couple of seconds, sipped, and then continued holding it near her mouth a while longer. As she slowly lowered it, she asked, "Patrick, do you still have those divorce papers?"

"I believe they're in my desk. Is that what this is about?"

She nodded.

Her tone sounded conciliatory, making him wonder which way this was going.

"Although I had them hurriedly drawn up, you may have noticed I haven't pushed for your signature...aggressively anyhow. The reason is simple. After the heat of anger subsided, I wasn't sure it was what I truly wanted. I can only assume your hesitance to sign was for the same reason."

"It was."

"For heaven's sake, Patrick, we've invested twelve years in one another. It's not something that should be taken lightly or ended in a fit of anger."

"That... *thing*... with Danica was a huge mistake. I—"

"Please, let me finish. For your sake and mine, I don't want to take up any more time than I have to. I have to get this said quickly or risk not saying it at all, and I realize you have a lot of work to do."

Patrick studied Margaret's eyes. In them, he saw desire to reconcile. It seemed obvious. He began to formulate a response.

"I met someone," she said quietly, eyes downcast.

A surprised jolt at the unexpected comment widened his eyes and slackened his jaw. "You did?" A chilled shock washed over him. She nodded. "And I have a job now."

"You do?"

"My employer's name is Randall Forrester. He manages a small insurance office here in town, in that English Tudor style house at Tenth and Elm.

"I know the one."

"Randall has become much more than my employer. He has become a very good friend."

"Friend?" Patrick asked, eyebrows raised.

Margaret rolled her eyes, mildly frustrated. "You know what I mean. Here's the thing; you're always in my thoughts. It doesn't matter if I'm at work, on a date or any other kind of social situation. I can't function. I spend too much time and energy wondering what you would think about every move I make, every step I take. It's... it's maddening."

Margaret's tone sent mixed signals that Patrick could not yet differentiate, but it seemed that she headed in the direction of reconciliation. It sparked a twinge of panic in him. He was convinced she wanted to get back together and try to work things out. Just last week he would have welcomed it as a life-simplifying thing to do and felt he still had time and the interest in doing so. Then, only a few minutes ago he attempted coming to terms with skyrocketing feelings for Michaela. What the hell was he to do? What should he say? He began to squirm. The last thing he wanted was to hurt this woman who was still his wife.

"I realize this is an uncomfortable topic." She smiled weakly and glanced around. "It's not exactly an ideal setting for such a discussion either." Her smile faded. "But the time has come to decide a course for the rest of my life and see if you and I can agree and then move forward."

There could be no more procrastination. A gauntlet had been figuratively tossed down. He had to say something. "I love you more than you know... always have, always will. Having said that, my indiscretions will always be a cloud on our relationship if we should get back together."

"Back together? You don't understand. That's not why I'm here." He abruptly straightened. "It's not?"

"No," she continued. "I think the only way for me to get on with life is to sever this thread that binds us, the legal part of what once was a marriage. I thought you wanted it, too. Don't you?"

"I—uh..." He suddenly was unsure again, but then blurted, "Yes... of course. You deserve happiness."

Margaret continued, "Although those divorce papers may only be a thread, lately the lack of a legal decree might as well have been an anchor chain. Patrick, I'm here to not simply ask, but plead with you to sign those papers. You see, now that Randall has this branch office of Baker Insurance Company running smoothly, he's being recalled to the home office in Dallas and promoted. They'll bring in a lesser experienced person to maintain and manage what he has set up. He has asked me to go with him."

Patrick could not control his slumping body language. "He has?"

She nodded. "Yes. Please let me go. Let me wake up tomorrow with a fresh sense of myself and a brand new outlook. Please, don't keep me tethered to the past. I—I think I'm falling in love with Randall." Margaret's eyes drifted downward, as though embarrassed. "And I want to go with him," she whispered hesitantly.

"When?" Patrick asked.

"Within the month," she replied.

Silence between them followed, but oddly, it was not at all uncomfortable. It was a particular type of quiet that existed between two people who had known one another as long as he and Margaret had. He dropped his hands limply into his lap. Shock melted away and was replaced by a smile.

At the same time, a worried frown upon Margaret's face softened and then faded.

Patrick reached across the small table and gently touched her fingers that surrounded the paper coffee cup. "There's nothing I want more than to remain friends. And I don't mean that to simply soothe this situation. I mean real, honest friends that stay in touch," he said. "I'm so sorry that my indecision locked you in limbo. I'll not let you suffer another minute." He put a contemplative finger to his lips. "Tell you what; I'll not only sign the papers; I'll hand deliver them to your attorney this afternoon. How's that?"

Tears moistened Margaret's eyes. "Thank you."

"Can you ever forgive me for what I did?" he asked.

"Already have." She lifted his hand from the tabletop and kissed his knuckles, then rose.

Patrick suddenly wanted to ask her to stay longer, but even that small gesture would be counter to what he had just promised, that he would let her go and get on with her life.

Margaret turned to leave and took a couple of steps, stopping, turning, and silently blowing Patrick a kiss. "Have a good life, Patrick."

He said nothing, just smiled and nodded but felt tears stinging his eyes.

She turned and walked away.

As Margaret left the room, Patrick felt an unsettling sensation deep in his bones; this was likely the last time he would ever see the woman he had been married to for twelve years.

*   *   *

On the way back to the television station from the attorney's office, Patrick felt strangely off balance, as if that "tether" Margaret spoke of was not figurative but literal. Once cut, it left him aimless, waving like a flag in a randomly changing and twisting wind—not what he anticipated, nor did he like the helplessness of it. He knew this was what he needed to do, so why did he feel such a sense of loss? He clutched the steering wheel with a white-knuckle grip. His mind raced, searching for a lifeline that might ground him. As he steered into the parking lot of KBTA, he saw Michaela's black Volkswagen Passat, left there from the night before. He suddenly calmed and relaxed his grip on the steering wheel. *You've come into my life at just the right time,* he thought.

He pulled into the empty parking space next to Michaela's car and got out. He stroked the top of her car, needing reassurance of Michaela's presence, not only here at the television station, but in his life. He wondered if she felt as he did. After the morning episode with Margaret, he felt vulnerable and lonely. He was not a young man. Chances for building a new life and finding happiness with a woman would likely begin declining soon. Once begun, it would probably happen quickly. Hollowness in his gut must have been the genesis of desperation, wondering if Michaela's friend had brought her to work yet. His eyes went from her car to the main entrance of the station. He suddenly had a strong desire to see her, not just think about and daydream of her. He hurried for the door.

The instant Patrick pushed the door open, he encountered a group of KBTA employees excitedly discussing something, Stan Brister and Harry Alexander included. "What's going on? Why is everyone huddled in the lobby?"

Harry approached him. "I guess you haven't heard."

"Heard what?"

"An employee of Ned Barrett found him dead in his house this morning...apparent heart attack."

"Dead! Are they sure it was a heart attack?"

"No, but the emergency medical techs believe it to be the most likely cause. He was found in the bathroom with an open bottle of aspirin in his hand. Apparently, he didn't get to it in time."

Patrick was already shaking his head. "No...no, I can't believe that. The timing is too convenient, too coincidental to the airing of that first news story. For Christ's sake, Ned expected this!" He paced one quick tight circle. "Crap, I should have ended the first story with his statement of fear for his life. I screwed up. I screwed up bad."

"Now, calm down, Patrick," Harry said.

Stan came to stand at Harry's side. "Don't be jumpin' to conclusions and blowin' this thing out of proportion. Think about it, Patrick. Barrett was injured and severely traumatized by a tree after that tornado. Add to that his age, his weight, and the worry of revealing his deepest thoughts on the fracking issue. Sounds to me, if he had any problems at all with his heart, it was a perfect storm of reasons for an attack... natural reasons."

"Stan's not usually right about much," Harry said, "but on this issue, I agree with him."

"I don't know." Patrick let his head slump, hanging loosely from his shoulders, staring at the floor. He stuffed his hands in his pockets and chewed the inside of his cheek, thinking. "True or not, it's a strong reminder to keep our guard up and watch our backs."

"I think that's good advice all the time, not just in this case," Harry said.

Stan nodded. "Yeah, it is."

"Since Barrett died alone at home, an autopsy will be performed. It's the law in a case like this, regardless what the EMTs and doctors believe. If anything out of the ordinary is found, we'll know for sure then," Harry said.

Patrick reluctantly nodded. "You're right. No use letting my imagination run wild. Has Michaela come in yet?"

"Haven't seen her," Stan said.

"She should have been here by now. Maybe that friend of hers forgot to pick her up after class. She may need a ride." He retrieved his phone from the inside pocket of his sport coat and hit quick dial.

It rang twice and began a third, interrupted by an unfamiliar female voice. "Michaela Ross's phone."

"Uh...who am I speaking with?"

"A triage nurse in the emergency room of Comanche Falls Medical Center."

"What? Why are you answering her phone? Is she all right?"

"Please, calm down. She's fine, sitting right here. She asked me to answer for her while the doctor examines her."

"What happened?"

"Car accident. But she and her friend are fine. Miss Ross sustained a few scratches and had the wind knocked out of her upon impact by the seatbelt. Here, why don't you talk to her?"

"Michaela?"

"Yeah."

"An accident? Was it really?"

"Of course it was an accident. Beverly, a friend from school, picked me up and we were heading for the station when some joker decided he needed to get around us in a hurry. When he cut Bev off, his rear bumper clipped our front and sent us up over the curb into a light pole. Sure, the guy was a jerk and should be severely fined for carelessness, but it was an accident. It scared him worse than it did us." She chuckled. "Last time I saw him, he was still apologizing, which he had been doing from the second he jumped out of his car and ran back to check on us. I wouldn't want to pay the traffic fine that he's facing."

Patrick breathed deep and let it out in a huff. "Sit tight. I'll be there in a few minutes to pick you up."

He hurried out the side door of the newsroom to his waiting car. As he accelerated out of the station's parking lot onto the street, a thought struck him. He pulled his cell phone from the inside pocket of his jacket and dialed the Comanche Falls police department.

The final ring was interrupted. "Hello," came a reply.

"Yes, hello. This is Patrick Daniels with KBTA Television news. May I speak to the detective assigned to the Ned Barrett death?"

"Hold, please."

Patrick glanced quickly around at traffic as he came to a stop at a red light. He heard a click on the phone.

"Detective Solomon. May I help you?"

"Hey, Loyd, this is Patrick. You got the Barrett case, huh?"

"Yeah, I did. How are things in the TV biz?"

"Rocky, but that's a side issue at the moment. An autopsy is going to be performed on Barrett, right?"

"Sure, but it's a formality. The body is en route to a forensics lab in Dallas as we speak. The consensus is that it was just a heart attack."

"That's what I heard. Tell me, aren't there ways to induce a heart attack that are extremely difficult to detect?"

"True. Are you saying you don't think it was from natural causes?"

"I don't know, but I am suspicious. That said, I would suggest that the forensics folks look for specific markers to that end. Did you watch our six o'clock news yesterday?"

"Sure did. Good piece on the fracking issue, very thought provoking."

"That's why I'm saying what I am about Barrett's heart attack. The man put his safety at risk by broaching the subject publicly like he did. It's one thing for a scientist or politician to talk about it. Their opinions can be refuted by other scientists and politicians. But for a landowner who is actually profiting from producing oil and gas wells to go public and talk about the dangers to property and lives is quite another... and a helluva lot more credible."

"Excellent point. I'll pass the word along to forensics. Thanks. Tell me more."

Patrick explained in detail the hydraulic fracturing story, the tornado, and the interview. He then invited Detective Solomon out to the station to see Barrett's comment that if something should happen to him, even if it appeared to be an accident, that it would likely be a murder meant to appear natural or accidental. That comment was not scheduled to run until the end of the final story in the series and had not yet aired. As he wrapped up a more in-depth explanation, he approached the small parking lot next to the emergency room and began to decelerate. "Loyd, would you keep me in the loop on the Barrett case?"

"You got it. Talk to you soon."

By the time the conversation ended, Patrick eased by parking spaces at the rear of the Comanche Falls Medical Center. There were none available. He did not care and pulled in behind a car bearing a hospital logo and blocked it.

He walked faster than the automatic sliding doors could open, slipping sideways between them. A blast of cool air smelling of alcohol and cleansers assaulted him. He walked swiftly to the check-in counter.

A round-faced nurse with bright red hair looked up from behind the counter. He saw the instant she recognized him. She beamed a brilliant smile. "Mister Daniels... hi. I watch you every day. Your news is my favorite."

"Thanks. There's no way I could ever hear things like that too often." He bounced a quick smile but quickly went serious. "Where is Michaela Ross? She was brought in from a car accident. We work together."

The nurse slid a finger down a sheet of paper on a clipboard. "Michaela Ross... Michaela... here she is. Try triage room number three, down the hall to the left."

Patrick had already begun walking away. "Thanks," he said over his shoulder and then added, "Keep watching. I need all the fans I can get."

"You got it," she called out.

As he rounded into the room marked "Triage 3," Michaela sat alone on the end of a padded examination table, legs crossed at the ankles swinging them like a little girl sitting on a low-hanging tree limb, as if concerned about nothing. "Are you okay?" he asked.

"Sure. The doctor just wanted me to sit here for a while in case some post-trauma kind of thing kicked in and I passed out. I didn't want to, but he said it happens frequently after even minor accidents."

Patrick cupped her chin and examined a bruise under her eye and a red welt on her cheek.

She reared away from his hand. "It's nothing... really. The airbag popped into my face, that's all."

"I'll take you back to your apartment."

She hopped off the examination table to her feet. "No way. I want you to take me to work."

"You should rest."

"I can rest tonight. I'm a part-timer. Remember? I need my hours at work. Still have to pay rent and buy groceries, you know. Besides, it will soon be my turn to buy the beer again."

Her smile and tip of the head was cute. It also served to ease his anxious mind. He stared at her for a moment longer, but finally acquiesced. "Okay, but I'm going to keep a close eye on you."

She smiled. "I sort of hoped you would...even if I hadn't been involved in a car wreck."

He shook his head. "Come on, silly girl, let's get out of here." Michaela saw her friend sitting on an examination table in one of the other triage rooms and abruptly stopped. "You okay?"

"Yeah, just pissed about my car."

"Need a ride? I bet Patrick wouldn't mind giving you a lift."

"No, not at all," Patrick chimed in.

"Thanks, but my brother is already on his way."

"In that case, see you in class." Michaela continued on to the main desk, Patrick at her heels. She hurriedly signed out and they left.

On the way back to KBTA, Patrick told Michaela of Barrett's heart attack. Afterward, there was little conversation. It appeared he was not the only one wondering about the day's events, and especially the timing of them.

As the fifteen-minute drive was coming to an end, he steered into the parking lot of the television station and finally broke the silence. "I think I'll get Stan to set me up a stool in the studio and I'll record a disclaimer to begin each of the remaining four Ned Barrett interviews."

"The next one is Monday, right?" she asked.

"Yeah. Stan told me that the promotional spots were set to saturate over the weekend."

"Do you really think his death and my accident are linked?"

"I sure hope not." He glanced at Michaela, but even as he looked away, an image of her face remained, burned into his consciousness by worry. A deep, hollow feeling in his gut mirrored his billowing concern.

CHAPTER 21

Patrick walked with a committed sense of determination as he came through the door of the television station Monday afternoon. He knew how he wanted to re-edit the Barrett interview. Breezing through the building, focused on a singular purpose, speaking to no one, he headed for his cubicle in the newsroom to begin writing a script while still fresh in his mind. The overhaul would create an additional sixth story, replacing the one scheduled for this evening's broadcast, and would begin with an opening disclaimer announcing Barrett's death. Patrick planned to use Barrett's statement of how he feared for his life instead of waiting till the final story as originally planned. He should have led the entire series with Ned's statement of extreme apprehension about doing a broadcast interview. This lack of forethought sickened him and blackened his mood. Still, there was nothing he could do at this point except try and do right by Ned Barrett from this point forward. This evening's report deserved a measure of respectful solemnity. The disclaimer that he planned on airing to introduce the Barrett statement should open with him in a chair in a limbo set in the studio, announcing the old rancher's death and funeral services scheduled for Tuesday morning and then end with Barrett's statement of fear as a chilling close.

It occurred to him that he should rerun Barrett's statement again after the final report as sort of a dramatic punctuation on the entire series. It was dicey in this business to dramatize a news story that way, a presumptive editorial, and there was plenty of drama without forcing it, but damn it, he owed it to the man. He was compelled to make Barrett's words and face linger in the hearts and minds of everyone that happened to see the series of stories. He became committed to freezing the old rancher's face on screen immediately upon completion of his statement, hold it silently for five seconds, and then slowly pull in super-imposed text over it with his full name, birth date and death date to end the six-story series. Patrick wanted the world to know beyond doubt that the man feared the possibility of dangerous reprisal from forces within the monolithic oil industry, although never mentioning Robert Landers or Landers Energy by name.

After typing the opening disclaimer, which was mostly a perfunctory obituary announcing the man's passing and importance to the story, he had second thoughts on how to end the report after running the piece where Barrett spoke of his fears. Should he just end it there and go straight to commercial? Or maybe come back to the studio for a live wrap-up of some sort? As had been the case for many years, when indecisive on a way to go, he headed for Harry Alexander's office for input.

Patrick opened the news director's office door a crack. "Hey, Harry, got a minute?"

Harry looked up from the yellow tablet he took notes on. "Sure. Come on in." He tossed the pen onto the tablet, leaned back and rubbed his eyes. "I've been staring at that damn tablet too long anyhow. What's up?"

"I plan on opening with a brief update on the fracking story to remind the public of Barrett's involvement, followed by a death announcement and scheduled funeral service for the old guy. Then go directly to that part of Barrett's interview where he states flatly that he will be afraid for his life when these stories air."

"I see nothing wrong with that approach. That was his fear and words right from his own mouth."

"Here's the thing, Harry; I want to wrap the story instilling questions in the minds of viewers on the power of money over people's lives. Why should a man fear for his life, just because he told the truth? Does the rule of law become vague and easy to skirt when wealthy corporations or individuals are involved? Does a strange kind of blindness exist in the halls of government when laws are broken by people with vast amounts of money to donate for political causes and candidates?"

"Those are all valid thoughts and mostly true I'm sure, worth looking into, but they should be handled as a separate investigative report. Once you attempt to tie all that into the hydraulic fracturing issue, it gets muddied. You'll be walking a tightrope of opinion versus fact. At the very least of the problem, rabbit-trailing like that into generalized points of debate will detract from your topic... hydraulic fracturing and its cover-up. Stay on point. It sounds to me like you're allowing personal feelings to get involved and cloud your judgment." Harry raised an eyebrow and dipped his chin. He wore an all-too-familiar suspicious look. "Are you?"

Patrick chewed the inside of his cheek and nodded. "You're right. I probably am." He suddenly became frustrated and slammed a fist into his open palm. "But, damn it, Harry, I'm feeling like the world is reeling out of control and I have a shot at making a difference! The only way I know to get it done is to put the truth out there to as many as I can as quickly as I can."

Harry nodded. "Let's not call it 'truth.' Instead, let's refer to it as verifiable truth. I personally believe every bad thing said about Robert Landers and that behemoth energy conglomerate of his. But, Patrick, if you slip up by offering what you and I know to be true without sourced proof, Landers will own you, me, and this whole damn television station. And nothing will have changed for the better. Be smart and choose your words carefully. You do have the power to make a difference... a huge difference."

A slow smile began stretching Patrick's face. "I knew I would gain some perspective from you. Thanks."

Harry smiled warmly. "Are ya feelin' overwhelmed?"

"I guess so," he replied and then paused. "Yeah... overwhelmed. That's probably it and as good a word as any for it. I'll see if Stan and his crew can set me up in the studio to record the opening disclaimer. I'll close the story live on the set this evening and simply promote the next one in the series before I throw the commercial. I appreciate the input."

"No problem. Talking it out is always best."

Patrick went back to his cubicle and wrote a subdued version of the wrap-up, sticking to suspected problems created by the controversial process and where the truth might lie. As he worked his way toward the end of it, his fingers suddenly stopped, now idle upon the keyboard, wondering how best to close it out. He had a notion. *I have to say it. I just have to.*

CHAPTER 22

Michaela watched for Patrick to appear from the newsroom door. She waited in the studio with her headset on, standing next to one of two studio cameras trained on a news set flooded with light in an otherwise darkened studio.

"Where's Patrick?" Stan asked through her headset. "There's only a couple of minutes till we go on the air."

She swiveled down the small microphone attached to the headset to a point next to her mouth. "He said something about the ending to the fracking story. I think he changed his mind on how to end it."

"Well, he'd better get a move on or we'll be coming live to the studio on an empty chair."

"He'll make it. A person doesn't do this job for as long as he has and not have a sixth sense about timing."

Suddenly Patrick burst through the door into the studio.

"About a minute out," Michaela called out. "Get a move on, Patrick. Sit down and get your mike on."

Patrick hurried to Michaela, hand extended with a sheet of paper. "Here, give this to the teleprompter operator and tell him that it replaces the last page of the lead story."

"Got it." She stripped off the headset, hung it on the camera's pedestal steering ring and rushed into the director's booth. She glanced through the large, soundproof viewing window back into the studio. She saw Patrick bounding up onto the foot-high stage platform of the news set, taking his position in the anchor chair. He clipped on his microphone.

Michaela handed the script sheet to the teleprompter operator and quickly explained. She then spun on her heels and raced out of the booth. She heard Stan growl.

"Nothin' like forcing blood pressure up unnecessarily just to get a stinkin' six-o'clock news sequence aired," Stan said to her back. And, yeah, you're welcome to pass that word along to Mister Indecision out there."

Not slowing, she said over her shoulder. "You got that right... and I will."

While Michaela raced to her position near the cameras, Stan hit the studio PA and announced over the loud speaker, "Intro's next, Patrick. Ready or not, here we come."

When Michaela put on her headset, Stan was already counting down. "... Eight... seven... six... Standby..."

She continued on audibly for Patrick's benefit. "Five seconds, Patrick. Here we come," she announced. She lifted her arm high in the air just as the intro music's stinger finished the intro. With a stiff finger, she brought her arm down. The red telly lights on the camera came on. They were on the air. Michaela breathed a deep sigh of relief.

Patrick spoke calmly, deliberately, as if he were the calmest and coolest man on the planet. He was a true professional. He began with the usual welcoming pleasantries and then simply ceased talking. Stan went directly to Patrick's pre-taped opening of the story put together especially for this broadcast. It opened with Patrick's announcement of Barrett's body being found

Friday morning in his home, dead of an apparent heart attack, followed by information concerning Tuesday morning's funeral services, and then he went back on point about Barrett's contribution to the fracking story, and the old guy's fear of what might happen by speaking out as he did. That part of the interview was then cut in so the audience could hear it directly from the rancher's mouth. After Barrett spoke, Patrick went back on the air live in the studio.

After cueing him, Michaela stepped out from behind the camera to better hear how Patrick had revised the end of the report.

Patrick sat silent for a full second before he spoke. "Ned Barrett, lifelong rancher and owner of the Cattle Trails Ranch, dead at the age of sixty-eight..."

Again, he fell silent. He stared into the camera lens, expressionless. The pause was long and awkward.

Michaela urged him to continue speaking with a fast finger roll.

He looked down at the script he had just written and slid it to the side. As if the long, cumbersome silence had been planned, he then spoke. "Shortly before airtime, I called the Comanche Falls police department to see if results of Barrett's autopsy had come back from the forensics lab in Dallas. They had. I was informed Barrett indeed died of a heart attack, but it was artificially induced."

Michaela's breath hitched as Stan said into her headset, "What the hell is he doing? He's off-script. That's *not* what's on the teleprompter."

"Oh crap," Michaela hissed.

Patrick continued, "After a thorough examination of the body, an almost imperceptible needle mark was discovered, prompting tests for specific markers.

Unusually high levels of potassium chloride were found in the blood, enough to stop a heart. A murder investigation has been opened." He looked down and then back up into the camera. "There is more, much more, that needs to be said about this, but it will be reserved until an investigation can performed. The day is coming soon that we will be asking hard questions about the dark world of big corporate money and its influence on government decisions and people's willingness to speak against questionable actions...people like Ned Barrett. Powerful entities within monolithic companies sometimes seem to operate with impunity in this country. At some point this has to be addressed at the highest levels of government and not scapegoated to hired bureaucrats." He paused for another awkward length of time. "Other news of interest after this break."

Audio came up and blared in the studio—a commercial spot for Buick.

Harry Alexander burst through the door from the newsroom into the studio. "What the hell, Daniels! We don't editorialize news stories here!"

"Sorry, Harry, but I was compelled to say it."

"Damn it, man! Keep your compulsive opinions *off-camera*! I want you in my office right after the broadcast."

After Harry stormed out of the studio, Michaela said, "Patrick...are you *trying* to get yourself killed?" almost whining.

"It's not part of the plan," he replied.

"You're out of your mind, but no time to get into it now. Back in five." She raised her arm for the coming cue and brought it down. Patrick was back on the air.

The remainder of the newscast was uneventful, the usual scary stories about warring factions in the Middle

East and American politicians commenting on what this country's part should be in it. Of course no one agreed. There were stories of bombings in London and other reports touching on terrorism. Patrick wound down the sequence with local updates on burglaries, car wrecks, water main breaks and goings-on at City Hall. He finally concluded, "... And that's News Central 12's *News at Six.*"

Studio lights went down and backlights came up for Patrick's silhouette shot during the musical close to the program. Although Patrick was centered in the shot, Michaela still thought the final shot was off balance without Danica sitting in the chair next to him.

As soon as the commercial began, Patrick was on his feet removing his microphone. "Well, I'd better get to Harry's office and take my ass-chewing like a man."

"What were you thinking?" Michaela asked, following on his heels through the newsroom door.

"I was angry. Unfortunately, anger doesn't require, nor is it usually ever accompanied by, analytical thought." He stopped at the news director's office door, his hand on the knob.

"I may be young, but I know enough to realize that a news reporter should never allow personal feelings to play out on the air, unless designated as an op-ed. Your news report was certainly never meant to be an editorial on hydraulic fracturing. If Barrett's heart attack did happen to be the result of a Landers Energy Company order, you've just stepped squarely in front of a runaway train. You do realize that, don't you?"

"I do now... didn't think about it at the time... all part of that 'anger over analytical thought' scenario."

Michaela saw that Harry watched them through the glass door. "You'd better get in there. Don't make him angrier than he already is." Patrick opened the door to the boss's office.

Harry called out, "You'd better come on in, too, Michaela."

A twinge of panic set in. *Wait a minute! I didn't do anything wrong.*

In short, nervous steps she followed Patrick into Harry's office and remained as near to the door as possible while still allowing it to close behind her. "I hope I haven't done anything to offend or anger you."

Harry waved her off. "No, no... not at all. That's not why I wanted you in here." He shifted focus to Patrick. "As angry as I am about that ill-timed editorializing, I've had a few minutes to think it through and have decided I'm more concerned than angry. We *have* to run those next four reports. The future of this news department hinges on viewer success. Those stories will assure that, at least until the next sweeps period." He glared at Patrick and rolled his hand into a tight fist. He clenched his teeth and worked the muscles in his jaws as he raised the fist and extended a finger. "But, as God is my witness, if I ever hear you toss out an opinion on a news story on the air again, Daniels, you're toast. Got that!"

"Yes, sir," Patrick said, barely above a whisper while looking to his feet.

"I didn't hear the commitment in your voice, Daniels," Harry snapped.

Patrick looked up. "Yes, sir," he said much louder. "It was a stupid, impulsive thing. I'm sorry. Won't happen again."

"You sure as hell have that right." He paused and scratched his neck beneath his chin with the backs of two fingers and in a lower tone, said, "I have to say, though, there could not have been a better promotion to entice the

public to watch the next four reports than that comment."
He again spoke up. "Still, it was a stupid thing to do."

Harry took a breath and looked to Michaela. "Look, kid, I wanted you in here to give you an opportunity to opt out of any obligation to this story," he said much more conversationally. "It was a dicey undertaking in the first place. But now, it could actually go from dicey to flat-out dangerous."

Michaela's jaw slackened. A montage of scenarios spiraled through her mind, topped by the one that mattered; she had come too far working on this thing with Patrick in this short time to back out now. She had to see where it led.

Harry seemed to notice her surprise. "I simply figured you might want to distance yourself from it. Of course, there would be absolutely no negative job consequences or poor reviews as a result. You're an excellent videographer and I'm sure we can find plenty of other meaty stories for you to work on."

Hesitatingly, Michaela asked, "Is this a nice way of *insisting* that I back out of my partnership with Patrick on this story?"

Harry's mouth curled into a faint smile. "I don't play games. Whatever I say, I mean...straight up. I leave all that manipulative, mind-bending, political posturing to upper management."

Michaela glanced to Patrick. It was obvious by his stiff posture that he waited and wondered what her answer might be. "Mister Alexander..."

"Please, not so formal, it's Harry."

"Uh, Harry, I've not hidden the fact that I'm ambitious and want to move up the ladder in the news business as rapidly as possible. I can't see that happening if I cower from tough stories. And I have lucked into one of the toughest as my very first assignment." She looked to Patrick and smiled.

His shoulders wilted forward as that stiffened posture relaxed. He sighed and returned the smile. "If it is truly all the same to you, Harry, I want to follow through on the hydraulic fracturing story with Patrick. I see this thing making its way to Washington real soon. And I want to be associated with its genesis right here in Comanche Falls. I foresee strong follow-up stories as that shit, already in the air, finally hits the fan. Pardon the coarse language."

Harry laughed. "I've been around Brister too long for language like that to bother me. Go ahead."

"The only other thing I wanted to say is that I want a front-row seat when accountability is assessed. And I want to watch groveling oil companies and their lackey politicians whine when that day comes."

"I admire your tenacity," Harry said. He turned to Patrick. "If you can hold that opinionated tongue of yours, Daniels, the remainder of those reports should damage no one else's safety. It will all be on Barrett. And, God bless him, it doesn't matter for him any longer. That is, and I repeat, if I can keep you from tossing out inflammatory opinions on the air."

"You got it, boss."

Harry looked away. "I've sort of grown accustomed to having you around. Don't want anything bad to happen to you," he said in a gruff, but humble way. He looked back and flipped a finger toward Michaela. "Keep a close eye on her, Patrick. You are now more than her journalism partner, you're her protector."

Hey, I can take care of myself.

Patrick nodded affirmation of Harry's remark. "I'll have her back." She raised her eyebrows slightly. "And I will have yours."

When he grinned, she remembered what he had said about her "tell," realizing he read her face. She did not, could not, hide her fiercely independent streak.

"Take care of *each other*," Harry said. "Now... both of you... get out of here."

CHAPTER 23

Patrick followed Michaela through the old-west-style saloon doors into the Lazy S Bar in downtown Comanche Falls. He eyed her up and down. She wore large gold hoop earrings and a white shirt with a long tail, form-fitted at the waist. His thoughts were a convolution of admiration, worry and desire. As he watched the gentle roll of slender hips in those tight, faded blue jeans with stylish rips down the legs, desire began taking over, pushing other thoughts about this gorgeous creature aside. A tingle centered in the pit of his stomach forced a ragged draw of air.

Michaela glanced over her shoulder. "Have I ever told you how intuitive I am?"

"No. Why?"

"I feel you staring at me."

"Seriously?"

"Seriously." She stopped at a round table near the bar and faced him. "But that's okay. I have a feeling I know why." A lop-sided grin sprouted but had not yet totally materialized.

"And you're okay with it?"

That hint of a grin now became a slow-developing full smile. "More than okay, actually."

"I can't hear what you guys are talking about," Stan said in that gravelly smoker's enhanced voice as he came up behind Patrick. His eyes darted between them. "Judging by the looks you're giving one another, I have a feeling it's none of my business."

"You do have a death grip on the obvious," Patrick said.

Stan smirked. "Aw shut up, Daniels." He pulled out a chair and dropped onto it at the table. "Enough chit chat. Let's get a beer."

"Stan, why don't you have a girlfriend?" Michaela asked. "What makes you think I don't?"

"You never talk about dating, relationships or anything of the sort."

"Well, young'un, that should tell you everything you need to know about me on the subject. I keep my private life private, unlike some people I know." He flipped an accusing finger toward Patrick.

"Hey, it's not like I work at publicizing those issues," Patrick blurted.

Stan grinned. "I know, buddy, I know." He turned to Michaela and leaned in. He whispered, "I've known you long enough to trust *you*." He flipped a thumb over his shoulder toward the bar behind him. "See that smokin' hot blond waitress with the butterfly tattoo on the back of her hand talking to the bartender?"

Patrick saw the woman. He knew her to be a long-time employee of the Lazy S. She was very attractive—in her mid-forties, perhaps. She wore a tank top cut low enough to expose freckled breasts with a sunburst tattoo on the left one. "Is that your girlfriend?" Patrick asked.

"Hush, I'm not talking to you."

"Sorry."

"Is there a story between you two?" Michaela asked. "If so, I want to hear it."

Stan surreptitiously looked both ways, checking for prying eyes or ears. He then grinned big and nodded, eyes glinting blue light from the neon beer sign next to the men's restroom.

"Well, don't just sit there. Tell me about her," she said.

"Her name is Darlene and... that's enough. You don't need to know any more than that." He turned and waved for Darlene's attention, and then held up three fingers and pointed to everyone at the table.

The seasoned waitress knew exactly what that meant and had three bottles of beer on a tray and was heading to their table in a matter of seconds. "Here ya go, Stan," she said, serving him first.

"So, you're Darlene, right?" Patrick asked.

Stan gave him a you-better-not-say-anything-stupid look. "Yes, I am. Did Stan tell you?"

"Oh, sweet heavenly Jesus, the man has been going on and on about you."

Patrick glanced to see Michaela stifling a snicker.

Darlene put a hand on Stan's back and rubbed tiny circles. "I hope at least some of what he's told you has been good."

Patrick tossed out a limp-wristed dismissive wave at her. "Oh, Sweetheart, this man can't seem to say enough good things about you."

"Good to know... really good," she said, and then focused on Stan. "Later... my place?"

Head hanging lower than the top of his beer bottle from embarrassment, Stan simply nodded quickly.

Darlene moved on to check on the patrons at other nearby tables.

Stan raised his eyes to connect with Patrick. The frown was so deep, it appeared he was glaring through those bushy eyebrows. "I'll get you for this, Daniels."

"Payback's a bitch, ain't it?" Patrick laughed.

Michaela could no longer hold it and laughed as well. She patted the back of Stan's hand. He had been drumming the tabletop with his fingers. "Darlene seems like a lovely woman and regardless what you may think you want, you need a woman in your life."

Stan finally straightened. He watched the waitress scurry from one table to the next, smiling and bantering with customers. That twinkle in his eyes told a bigger story than simply reflecting a lighted beer sign. "'*Need* a woman'," he mumbled. "Interesting concept...to need one, I mean. But, hey, you might be right about that." As he spoke, he stared at Darlene going about her waitressing duties.

Stan had a glimmer in his eyes that Patrick had never seen before. It looked odd on him. He shifted attention to Darlene, and then back again. *Could that woman be the one to finally win this crotchety old man's heart?* He grinned and congratulated himself on a well-played moment with a big gulp of beer.

* * *

Patrick sat on the sofa in his apartment taking off his shoes. Michaela sat at the other end. "I have to say, your apartment seems extraordinarily neat and tidy for a busy single guy." She slid down the sofa to sit nearer to him. "Tell me now, were you *expecting* company this evening?"

"Yeah, but she couldn't make it. So, I invited you," he said without looking away from the task of removing his socks.

She smacked him on the arm with the back of her hand. "Hey!"

"Ow! That hurt."

"Good."

"I was just kidding."

"You had better be, Bucko."

Patrick began to smile. He reached and wrapped his fingers around the back of her neck and pulled her toward him.

She yielded, licking her parted lips and closing her eyes.

He took advantage of this precious second to examine her beautiful face beneath the new very short hairstyle with the sweeping bang partially covering one eye. There was nothing he wanted more than to kiss this gorgeous creature. He closed his eyes and moved in.

His cell phone rang in his jacket pocket, draped over the arm of a nearby chair.

"I wonder who that could be. It's after eleven o'clock," he said. Michaela sighed. "Better get it. The way things have been going lately, it might be an emergency."

As he stood to retrieve the jacket, she sprang up and headed for the kitchen. "This is an excellent time to raid your fridge. I'm hungry."

He retrieved the phone from the inside pocket of his coat, glancing back to Michaela heading for the refrigerator. "Go for it. I think there's leftover fried rice. Good stuff." He hit talk on the phone. "Hello."

A female voice came back. "Patrick Daniels?"

"This is he. Who am I speaking with?"

"Amanda Pine. I'm not sure you know who I am, but…"

"Of course I do. Great article covering Sawyer's city council session on disallowing hydraulic fracturing within the city limits. Kind of risky the way you wrote it though."

He glanced to Michaela standing with the refrigerator door open. She had the cardboard container of fried rice in her hand, but when she heard Patrick's conversation, she immediately returned it to the shelf it came from.

"Risky?" Amanda asked. "You really think so?"

"Yeah. I do."

She paused. "Too risky, you think?"

"Afraid so."

"Hmm. Maybe so. I was just trying to get a response from

Landers Energy Company... which they have not done."

"Actually, I have a feeling they *have* responded...brutally. You have heard about Ned Barrett's heart attack, right? There is solid evidence of foul play."

"Yeah, I heard your report at six. The way you ended it seemed riskier than anything I wrote."

"You might be right. What, exactly, is it I can do for you, Amanda?"

"You and I breaking this story at the same time may have been a coincidence, but I would like to collaborate and share information."

"That's an interesting notion."

"I think it would strengthen it for both of us."

"Excellent point."

"What do you say? Can we work together?"

"If we do this thing, there should be ground rules. Number one:

You can give no shared information to any other television station,

and I will share nothing with competing newspapers."

"Not a problem."

"Number two: You and I should stop editorializing. We need to stick to gathering facts and reporting those."

"My editor at the *Trib* has already reamed me over that."

Patrick grinned. "You, too, huh?"

"So, Mister Alexander didn't like your comments closing the report at six."

"No, he didn't. He chewed my butt out. But he didn't need to. I regretted saying what I did immediately after saying it. It was impulsive and, frankly, dangerous."

"Do you really think we've stirred up something life-threatening?"

"Can't say for sure. But when millions...maybe hundreds of millions of dollars, are at stake, I *do* know that's money worth killing over."

"I can't backpedal now."

"Neither can I."

"So, do we have a deal, Mister Daniels?"

"Sure, I'll share what I find with you. Call me Patrick... please."

"I'll be in touch. Have a good evening." She hung up.

Michaela had returned to the sofa. "Now, where were we?" he asked, sliding nearer to her.

She put a hand in the middle of his chest and held him away.

"You sure were sounding chummy with that newspaper chick toward the end of the conversation."

"What's the matter? Didn't want fried rice?" he asked, ignoring the comment.

"I lost my appetite."

"Do you know Amanda Pine?"

"Yeah, I do...very well. I had her in one of my journalism classes a couple of years ago. She graduated last year and got that job at the *Trib* right out of college."

"What did you think of her?"

"She's a friend. She's smart. She's pretty. She's a go-getter. She's nice. And... I don't like her."

Patrick grinned. "Seriously?"

Michaela's head bobbled. "No... I guess not."

Patrick figured there was nothing he could say that would improve the situation. It was clear Michaela felt a pang of jealousy,

but there was no way he would use the "J" word aloud, especially tonight. He wanted to nurture this relationship and the best way to do that was show, not tell. He came at her without slowing and pressed his lips to hers. He felt her tense but then relax.

This night should be about us, no one else.

She pulled away.

Her eyes darted around his face. He saw desire reflecting his own in those bedroom eyes.

She became the aggressor.

There was nothing left to be said—not tonight.

CHAPTER 24

Michaela sat in class at a desk nearest a window looking out on the beautiful campus beyond this dismal and drab building. She stared out as the professor droned on monotonously while pacing back and forth at the head of the class. Occasional forceful points penetrated the daydream, but randomly and without context. Her mind followed her heart and lay in a different place and time. So much color had been added to her life in the past couple of weeks. It was hard to see a future as she had originally envisioned it. Joy drained from the classroom experience.

Her eyes picked up all movement from this second-floor vantage point. The campus was stunning in the spring. Grass and trees maintained lighter shades of green common to new growth. She heard birds singing somewhere beyond the closed window and the occasional randy squirrel barking a mating call. Students came and went, walking in purposeful stride, milling about, visiting, or in some cases cuddling close. Her eyes darted from one untold campus story to the next that spread before her. She watched it all, chin cradled in a palm on her propped elbow. As her eyes did their thing, her mind and heart were across town, remembering last night. She gently stroked her thigh above the knee as the romance of last evening became a bit too vivid. She abruptly straightened and sat bolt upright at her desk. She swallowed hard and drew a sudden deep breath, realizing heat rose swiftly over her entire body at an alarming rate. Her face flushed, embarrassingly so.

The unexpected move caught the attention of those sitting around her. All eyes fell upon her. So did the professor's. "Did I finally make a point that interests you, Miss Ross?" Scattered snickers salted the room. She drew many stares.

"Uh, yeah. Good lesson... great information," she babbled.

The professor remained focused on her. His head took a thoughtful tilt. "It was brought to my attention that the video, both the shooting and the editing, on the Daniels hydraulic fracturing story at Channel 12 was your work. Good job," he said, while students mumbled approval as well. The professor then added, "I assume lugging that camera around and hours of editing probably saps most of your energy and makes it difficult to get your mind onto class work."

Michaela did not reply, just nodded swiftly and nervously. She might as well have fabricated and recited a much grander story because it would have been no bigger lie than the simple nod.

The smile he bore appeared sincere, but she noticed what could only be describe as a glint of knowing. "I guess I can let you slide this time," he said, as the smile metamorphosed into a smirk. He picked up where he left off, but as his head turned to address the class at large, his eyes lingered on her a second longer. Neither job, nor this class had a thing to do with what was on her mind. The professor seemed to know that. How could he? Or could it be that she simply felt guilty for allowing amorous thoughts and feelings to hit a fever pitch in class? She was thankful he had not quizzed her on what point he made that brought her to attention. The class was half over and she had no clue what had been, or was being discussed, much less the finer points.

Still, she could not get Patrick out of her head. Her thoughts swung from romance to logicality. Her feelings were no longer a question in need of an answer. She was falling in love. The fact that Patrick turned out so different than her initial negative opinions of him accelerated the fall. She thought about her contentious words when Amanda Pine called last night. Her reaction irked her. Becoming jealous over a simple phone call? *What was I thinking? Hell...I wasn't thinking at all, just hit with a flash of jealousy and reacting to it.* Her handling of the situation could not have been any more idiotic. Still, she knew Amanda well enough to realize that the girl would do anything to get what she wanted. She remembered when a poor grade in a key journalism class a couple of years ago had miraculously transformed into a good one after witnessing Amanda flirt with the professor. There was little doubt what she did to earn that grade. On top of that, Amanda had what it took to pull it off. She was a highly intelligent and seductive knock-out, possessing looks and the will to get things done. Whatever it took. The tall, slender, and very well-endowed young woman had a thick head of hair the color of a new penny. How could Michaela think of her as anything other than a nemesis and, possibly, a sexual predator?

Michaela clenched her teeth, suddenly jealous all over again. She reached over and pinched her arm hard enough to cause pain. *Stop it...stop it...stop it! Get your stinkin' head out of this pubescent rut.*

The harder she worked at getting Patrick out of her mind, the more persistent his image became. As much as she wanted to concentrate on the professor's lecture, he might as well have been Charlie Brown's teacher, because none of the information he was teaching was making it through her daydreams. She began to think that if she passed these final two courses necessary to obtain her degree, it would be a miracle, and not of her making.

She wondered if she could get away with doing something like Amanda Pine would do and then skate through the remainder of her classes. She looked to her professor. He continued pacing back and forth making points about something or other. She examined the man. He was short and wide, mostly bald with an unkempt black fringe too curly and too long surrounding a pale head with random liver splotches over his bare pate. The man carried a paunch bulging from beneath his belt. Michaela swallowed rising bile in the back of her throat. Even the thought of having sex with such a man for a better grade repulsed her.

After that disgusting little imagining, Michaela figured she better start listening and taking notes right now. She was no Amanda Pine.

As Michaela put the awkward morning in class behind her, she walked through the door of KBTA, the other world that had become integral to her life. She may have entered the building in a rush, but she stopped so abruptly she almost lost her balance. It occurred to her like a bolt of lightning that she had lost her ability to compartmentalize. School and work had become a mixed-up mess of vague, indecipherable priorities. She felt like a ditzy schoolgirl not knowing which way to turn.

"Something on your mind?" Jeanie Fromme asked.

"Huh?"

"It looked like you abruptly remembered something as you came inside."

"Oh, it's nothing. I was trying to prioritize the rest of the week when it occurred to me I didn't know how. As streaming thoughts will do, that generated another thought about my future goals. And, voila! I was suddenly overwhelmed." Michaela grinned, a little embarrassed. "You just happened to see the precise moment it occurred. Sorry that I seem so out of it."

The pretty young receptionist smiled. "No need to feel bad, not around me. You're looking at a girl living her life never knowing which way to turn next. Gosh, most days I have trouble trying to decide what to have for lunch, much less what I want to be doing later in the week."

Michaela relaxed and smiled. "Have you ever taken the time to make a list of life goals?"

"I'm not sure I know what you mean?"

"Where do you see yourself a year from now? What do you see yourself doing at the end of twelve months, still working here as a receptionist... married... or maybe starting a business of your own?"

"I don't know."

"Tell you what...when you go home this evening get a piece of paper and think hard about it. Write down the next five years and beside each year what you want to be doing by the time each year begins and what you want to accomplish before each year ends. Once you refine it, pin that in a prominent place in your home so that you see it every day. But don't just see it. Take note of it... internalize it."

"Everyday?"

"Everyday. It's amazing how the human mind works. You will automatically begin working toward those future achievements from the moment you pin it to the wall. Read it before you begin each day. Those printed goals will steer decisions you make, consciously or not."

As she spoke, it became clear that what she told Jeanie to do was exactly what she had lost—direction and timing. That goal list she carried pinned to the wall of her mind most of her life had fluttered to the floor of her thoughts, and she had been trampling all over it.

"I sure appreciate it, Mikki. That's good advice. I'll do it."

Thanks to a sweet but ditzy receptionist, Michaela suddenly rediscovered what she should do. Renew a goal list and then make it happen. How hard could that be? And then she thought of Patrick.

CHAPTER 25

"Based on the number of calls we're getting on the Barrett series, our May Nielsen numbers might survive the sudden departure of Danica after all," Patrick told Stan as they stood in the cool, dimly lit studio. He straightened his tie and smoothed his collar.

"Yeah, well, keep your head screwed on straight," Stan replied in that raspy voice, chewing on a small, unlit Swisher Sweet cigar. Ratings aren't the only consideration. I've noticed a few of those messages aren't at all in favor of what Barrett said...some contained threats. Remember, it's not only Landers Energy and the other corporate oil people that can be hurt. This county is full of simple redneck folks that depend on a thriving oil industry for their livelihoods. Who knows what some of those *good ol' boys* would do if they lost work over *your* story." Stan gently poked Patrick on the chest. "And, once energy companies are forced into court to protect their revenue source, those *good ol' boys* might be comin' after you for threatening their jobs."

The quartz halogen studio lights all came on at once, flooding the news set with brilliance. The studio temperature instantly went up a couple of degrees. An electronic click came from the PA speaker mounted near the ceiling and a disembodied voice said, "Hey, guys, it's about ten minutes till airtime. We'd best get things together."

Stan waved to the darkened glass of the director's booth toward the owner of the voice, although he could not see the boy, a new hire.

"Rookie. The boy's nervous as a cat that he's going to screw something up. Little does he know that I'm not going to let that happen." Stan laughed, catty and wheezing.

Patrick snickered. "Still, I'd better cut the chitchat and let you get about your business," Patrick said, putting his jacket on.

"Eh, I'm not concerned. I had the graphics built into the video queue shortly after the producer sent scripts up. I'm ready."

"Stan?"

"Yeah."

"Is it my imagination or has Michaela been avoiding us lately?"

Stan pulled the little cigar from the corner of his mouth, licked his lips and then an incredulous look descended over his face. "You honestly have the audacity to use the word 'us' in that question?"

"I don't understand. Every time you and I are together it seems she avoids us."

"Right there is where your logic falters, buddy. Mikki and I laugh and carry on like school kids...when you're not around." But, when you're in the mix, the girl becomes scarcer than hen's teeth."

"What have I done to deserve that?"

"Beats me, but I can guess. I'll tell you the same thing I told Danica just before she jumped ship. Your love life is very entertaining to watch from a distance. Don't be asking me questions or searching for advice when it's about your women and messed-up relationships. I don't want to be in the middle of that mess."

"Sorry. I didn't mean—"

"Yeah, well... just don't." He backhanded Patrick gently on the stomach. "Come on, let's get a six o'clock sequence under our belts."

As Stan walked back toward the director's booth, Michaela came into the studio. "Aren't you running a little late?" Patrick called out.

She ignored the question. "Take a seat. I need to get the camera shots framed."

Patrick reared his head at the chill coming at him. "Is everything okay?"

"Fine," she said curtly. "Now, sit down and let me do my job." She was not smiling.

As he moved around behind the desk bathed in bright light, his eyes never left Michaela, wondering *what the hell...?* He preferred the chatty sarcasm her first day on the job to this—whatever this was.

His butt was barely in contact with the chair when Michaela began zooming, focusing and framing. She then moved over to
camera two and repeated the set-up procedure. One camera was for
a centered tight shot while the other was offset for the use of graphics. After the shots were set, Patrick expected her to step out to
a position between the cameras so they could chat until time to go on, as usual. Not today. She remained behind the camera, working her position so that very little of her body could be seen.

"Michaela, I don't know what happened or what I might have done, but it's obvious you're angry with me. Why?"

"I'm not angry...with you or anyone else. Get ready. One minute till intro." She held her position out of sight behind the camera.

It was as if she might give in and talk to him if she made eye contact, and she was clearly working hard at not doing that. Why? "Okay, if you're not angry then what's troubling you?"

"Thirty seconds to intro. Nothing is troubling me...nothing I can't manage."

"Aha! So something *is* bothering you." He smiled, believing it was a personal dilemma that had nothing to do with him. He

shielded his mouth with the back of his hand as if sharing secret information. "Is it your monthly visitor?" he asked, smiling, and then gathered news scripts together.

Intro music blared in the studio. "No... shut up... and standby." He leaned sideways trying to glimpse her expression, hoping to see a smile but ran out of time.

"Five seconds," she announced and raised her arm high and out from behind the camera. "Here we come."

Suddenly, all went quiet as his studio microphone was keyed. She brought the arm down.

They were on the air.

As Patrick went through obligatory news teasers of upcoming stories, led by the latest in the Barrett series, he relaxed. He had become confident whatever troubled Michaela was something he could help with. He put it out of his mind for the remainder of the news sequence.

When the six o'clock news ended, studio lights went out and house lights came up. Patrick sprang to his feet and hurriedly removed his microphone, preparing to confront Michaela.

She had already begun leaving the studio, passing Stan coming out of the booth. "Do you mind taking care of wrap-up duties tonight?" she asked. "I'll owe you one."

"Sure. Go on. Looks like you need some alone time."

"Hey, Michaela, wait! I want to talk to you," Patrick said, jogging past Stan.

"Want to meet me later at the Lazy S and get a—"

"Not today, Stan. I have to find out what's bothering her."

Stan sighed. "Okay, go do what ya gotta do."

"See you tomorrow," Patrick called out over his shoulder, now at the exit to the parking lot. He hurried outside. Michaela had already backed out of the parking slot. She accelerated hard, tires screeching as she left the parking lot onto the street heading in the direction of her apartment.

"Oh, no you don't," he mumbled. "You're not getting away from me that easy. I deserve an explanation and I'm going to get it." He hurried to his car, dropped into the driver's seat and was in pursuit in mere seconds.

Although he had lost sight of her car, it didn't matter much. This time of day there were only a few places she might be. The Lazy S was one and, given her mood, that was unlikely. Since she had no evening classes the campus was equally doubtful. That only left her apartment. Since that was the direction she headed, it had to be her destination. He took the shortest route possible.

He pulled into the driveway of her garage apartment just as she opened the door at the top of the stairs. Her head turned. She saw him but did not falter before opening the door, going inside, and closing it behind her.

Patrick came to a fast, hard stop on the simple driveway of double concrete ribbons. He threw open his door, got out and bounded noisily up the rickety external stairs to her apartment door. He knocked, and the door swung open immediately. "Michaela, I..." he said, then cut it off abruptly, shocked by a face he did not expect. "You must be Belinda, the roommate."

The girl stood stiffly—expression rather belligerent. "Yep."

The similarity to Michaela was astonishing. This girl, too, was tall and slender with short, dark hair. She and Michaela could have been sisters. "Can I come in?"

"Nope."

He glanced to the street as a dirty, white and badly dinged dually pickup truck with a mobile welder in the back eased up to the end of the driveway and appeared to be about to pull in behind his car, but it did not...probably a mistaken address. The notice of it was peripheral and quick. "Please, I really need to talk to her."

Over Belinda's shoulder he glimpsed Michaela coming into the living room from the bedroom. "It's okay. Let him in," Michaela told her roommate.

"You sure? I don't mind hanging around to protect you." Michaela bounced a quick smile. "No, it's not that kind of a problem."

Patrick looked past the roommate. "That's just it. I don't know what the problem is," he said, voice shifting into a higher range.

Belinda poked a finger in his chest. "Don't disrespect my girl Michaela. You hear?"

Michaela drew a deep breath and sighed. "Come on in. We need to talk anyway, and I've been unwilling to face it. Might just as well be now, I suppose."

Belinda looked to Michaela, then to Patrick, and then back to her friend. "Okay," she said, then paused. "Tell you what," she said, pulling car keys from a hook on the wall next to the door and then retrieving her purse from the top of a short bookcase beneath the key hooks. "I'm going downtown to O'Reilly's to get a drink and listen to a little jazz by that chick who sounds like Diana Krall. I have a strong feeling I'll be in the way if I hang around."

Michaela kept her eyes locked onto Patrick. "Thanks, Belinda. You're a good friend."

Patrick slipped sideways inside as Belinda made a move to trade places with him, moving out onto the second-story landing.

When she passed close enough for Patrick to feel her breath on his face, she whispered, "Remember what I said. Respect her. She's one of the best people I've ever known."

He nodded. "I know... and I will." He closed the door behind him. Michaela gestured to the dated velveteen sofa, the only seating in the living area. "Come. Sit."

"I'm baffled. I have no clue what's troubling you. Is it something

I can fix or at least help you with?" He sat on the far end of the sofa. Michaela sat at the other end. "Something you can fix? No.

Something you can help with? In a way, I suppose that's possible."

"Please tell me. I don't like this kind of suspense... at all. What is it?" She studied him, her eyes traveling around his face.

"Well?"

She drew a ragged breath as her roving eyes settled on his. She could not seem to pull her thoughts together and simply stared a while longer. It was as if what she had to say troubled her to verbalize. She abruptly heaved a sigh, closed her eyes, and then blurted, "You dumb shit, I've fallen in love with you." Her eyes popped open and she looked away at the same instant her eyes glossed with tears.

Patrick's worry metamorphosed into joy, and he began sliding to Michaela's end of the sofa.

Michaela held out an open palm.

Halted by the stiff-armed hand on his chest, he said, "Michaela, what—"

Suddenly a scream from somewhere outside toward the street invaded the subdued conversation inside the apartment.

"What the hell?" Patrick hissed.

"That sounded like Belinda."

They sprang to their feet in unison and hurried to the nearest window with a view of the street.

Patrick flipped back the curtain to see a burly man in a sleeveless shirt and dirty, short-billed welder's cap on his head holding onto Belinda. She struggled to get away. They were next to a pickup truck— the same one he saw slowly circling the block a few minutes ago.

Patrick ran for the door and flung it open. He stepped out onto the landing to hear Belinda scream, "Get your greasy hands off me, you butt-ugly—"

The big guy backhanded her hard across the face. He swung her around. She stumbled and fell onto the grass holding the side of her face. "Get away from her!" Patrick shouted, running down the stairs. Michaela was close behind him.

The guy in greasy blue jeans pointed a stern finger at Belinda. "Tell your boyfriend what I said or I'll come back and do it again. Next time, it won't be a love tap." He leaped into the idling pickup truck and screeched off down the street.

Patrick ran into the street to get a license number.

Michaela dropped to her knees next to Belinda.

The pickup had already turned at the end of the block, speeding out of sight. He did not get a good look at the license plate, but he had a good description of the vehicle and the man. He turned and walked back to the girls.

Belinda sat up slowly. Blood trickled from her nose down around her mouth to her chin. A deep scratch was centered in a growing lump on her cheekbone.

"Did you know that guy?" he asked.

Belinda sniffed, and then with the back of her hand she swiped at the blood trickling from her nose. "No." She looked to Michaela. "He thought I was you." Her eyes went to Patrick. "He gave me a message meant for you, Mister Daniels. He became royally pissed when I told him you weren't my boyfriend. He reeked of whiskey and accused me of being a lying bitch and then went crazy. Before I had a chance to explain anything else, he hit me." She sniffed and swiped again at blood still slowly oozing from her nose.

"Oh God, I'm so sorry," Michaela said.

"What was the message?" Patrick asked.

"Landers Energy has begun laying off people, saying they need the funds to build a legal defense war chest. That guy lost his job yesterday. True or not, it looks like word is getting around fast among the blue collar crowd that you and that newspaper reporter at the *Trib*, Amanda Pine, are responsible."

Patrick stepped behind Belinda and put his hands under her arms to help her up.

She staggered and Patrick righted her, continuing to support her till she regained her balance.

"Thanks," she said over her shoulder. "I guess I'm a little woozy."

"Let's get you to the emergency room and have you checked out," Michaela said.

Belinda tossed a dismissive hand in her direction. "I'm okay. I just need to shove a tissue up my nose and put a Band-Aid on this scratch. I'll be fine."

"Are you sure?"

"I'm sure. But I think I'll put off that drink for another time," she quipped. "Mind if I encroach on your conversation and go back to the apartment?"

Michaela reached for her hand and led her toward the steps. "I insist on it."

Patrick followed the girls up the stairs, staying close behind them in case Belinda had another dizzy spell. He and Michaela helped her down onto the sofa.

Patrick's cell phone rang. He pulled it out of the side pocket of his pants and hit the talk button. "Patrick," he said.

"It's Loyd Solomon."

The Comanche Falls police detective sounded somber. "Yeah, Loyd, what's up?"

"It's Amanda Pine..."

"What about her?"

"They found her about an hour ago, unconscious in her car in the parking garage at the newspaper, badly beaten and close to death. It appears that it happened right there as she was about to leave work."

The news traveled like a tingling charge of electricity all over his body. "Amanda Pine... in critical condition? Really?"

"What?" Michaela rushed to his side and grabbed his arm.

"Afraid so," the detective continued. "She managed to get in the car before she lost consciousness. The keys were in her hand. Her skull is fractured. She's in extremely critical condition."

"I knew there would be blowback from the fracking story, but I had no idea it would get this violent."

"That's the reason for this call. Until we get this sorted out and arrests made, I suggest you and that young videographer stay off the streets and lay low."

"How long?"

"Can't say, but you and the girl will be at risk anytime you're out in public."

"You think Landers Energy is behind it?"

"I shouldn't be speculating, but I wouldn't be surprised. Timing was suspiciously convenient for lay-offs. Don't you think?"

"What do you mean?"

"All a supervisor would have to tell those guys at the time of discharge is that Channel 12 and *The Falls Tribune* could be thanked for their problems. If planned, you, the Ross girl and Amanda Pine's names could have been thrown in to get the pot boiling. Suddenly, we have unemployed and very unhappy oilfield workers unleashed. All the while, Landers Energy keeps their hands clean. Of course, the motive would be simple: force the television station to dump the remainder of the Barrett interviews and coerce the *Trib* to abandon coverage altogether."

"I see what you mean," Patrick said. He pursed his lips and looked down at Belinda sitting on the sofa, nursing her battered face. "Judging by what just happened here, I'd say if Landers' people were involved, it tracks that our addresses were also made conveniently available."

"Why?"

"It wouldn't take Sherlock Holmes to find Amanda Pine or myself, but there's no way a run-of-the-mill oilfield employee would know the name Michaela Ross, her connection to all this, or where she lives."

"Is the Ross girl hurt?"

"No. It's her roommate. The girl was mistaken for Michaela. Amanda Pine wasn't the only one assaulted today."

CHAPTER 26

Michaela dabbed at the deep scratch on Belinda's face with a damp washcloth while listening to one side of the conversation Patrick was having on the phone with that detective. She leaned in and whispered to her roommate, "I'm sorry for getting you caught up in all this."

"That's enough of that. You've already apologized once. It wasn't your fault that I admired you so much I wanted to look like you," Belinda said and then smiled, but dropped it instantly, grimacing. "Ouch!" She protectively cupped her hand over the injury and drew a breath. "Wow. It hurts to smile." Belinda then added, "Anyhow, just because that comment was intended to be humorous, it doesn't make it less true. Do I sound a little jealous?"

Michaela squeezed her friend's arm. "Maybe a little...but only in the nicest sense. You're a good friend."

Belinda gently poked around the growing bruise with fingertips. "It may be a day or two before I can grin again. This cheek will simply not bunch."

Patrick ended his call. "That was Loyd Solomon, the detective."

Michaela nodded. "So I gathered."

"He's coming over to take a statement since he's the lead detective on the Barrett murder case, and he suspects this attack may be linked, as well as Amanda

Pine's brutal attack. I tossed in my two-cents-worth and told him that I didn't think there was any doubt that it was all connected." He paced away a couple of steps and then spun back. "Michaela, I don't want you leaving this apartment for any reason until the police get a handle on this. It may take a couple of days."

Michaela sprang to her feet. "Are you out of your mind? I can't do that."

Patrick turned away to face the wall, ignoring her comment, clearly lost in thought. "I'll talk to Harry and see if we can work out a paid leave of absence for you. Considering the work-related nature of the problem, it should not be a difficult sell," he said in rapid monotone barely above a whisper. It was information not offered as suggestions for debate; he was simply verbalizing a plan forming. He then added, still mumbling, "Now about those classes of yours, what can I do?" He brought a hand up and tapped his lip with a finger, then turned and reconnected to the moment and Michaela. "Here's a possibility. Maybe I can ask detective Solomon to—"

"Whoa! Stop right there. We *are* partners on this story and, by extension, in this problem *together*. Are we not?"

"Of course we are, but I'm going to do everything in my power to keep you out of harm's—"

"Say no more. I'm a big girl. You don't need to coddle me," she blurted.

"I have to keep you safe. I lo...I care for you too much to let anything happen to you." He glanced down at Belinda. Admitting feelings like that in front of a virtual stranger put the rose of embarrassment in his cheeks. The L-word had almost slipped out.

Michaela calmed and smiled. "I care for you, too." She allowed the reply to hang in the air between them for a moment. Her eyebrows went up slightly. She then offered sarcastically, "Therefore, I think I'll call Harry and see if he will give you a paid leave of absence while—"

"That's absurd! I have to work and make sure the rest of that series airs as scheduled. Otherwise, everything we've worked for and been through will have been for nothing."

Michaela did not respond immediately as her smile broadened. "Right." She reached for his hand. "That's exactly my point. Life goes on. Things still need to be done. Don't you think that holds true for me as well?"

Once the shock of hard truth soaked in, his face softened. He put his hands on her shoulders and pulled her into an embrace. "Besides gorgeous, you're intelligent and one tough chick, ya know that?"

"Of course I do."

He held her a little tighter.

"On a slightly more serious note, I'll accept gorgeous and intelligent, but I'm not tough...not in the slightest. I'm determined. Thanks for saying it though." She pushed him away.

His eyes lost that frantic look and went dreamy, becoming oblivious to his surroundings. He cupped her face between his hands and moved in for a kiss.

She resisted and saw confused wonder on his face. *Why am I resisting? What the hell am I doing?* She suddenly did not want to hold him away. She let it happen.

He kissed her deeply, and her body went limp from his touch. She was losing herself to him.

"Hey, guys," Belinda said, "I know I should close my eyes and make myself as small and quiet as possible so you can have this moment. Unfortunately, I'm nosy. Besides, I love this kind of story." She huffed a noisy, melodramatic sigh.

Patrick pulled away quickly. He wiped his mouth and looked to his feet. "I'm sorry, Belinda. I forgot where I was."

"I noticed. I may not be able to smile right now, but I really, really want to."

Michaela said nothing, just stared at him, enchanted. The presence of her friend and roommate did not bother her in the slightest, but it was an endearing side of Patrick that she witnessed for the first time. He was not totally immodest. It was cute. That alone made this moment worthwhile.

"How about y'all take it to the bedroom and I'll shove cotton in my ears, in case noises I should not want to hear penetrate the door."

"Oh, no," he stammered, "this is your home. I would never disrespect you like that."

She flipped a dismissive hand toward him. "Oh pooh." She looked to Michaela and shielded her mouth, pretending to whisper, "He really is from a different era, isn't he?"

Michaela continued staring at Patrick, having lost all desire to keep him away. She wanted him closer, much closer. "He's a gentleman that pretends he isn't."

"I have to admit it, Mikki, Mister Daniels is nothing like I thought he would be, certainly nothing like that Walter Peck guy."

Michaela finally ended her gaze at Patrick. "I'm glad you've had a chance to get to know him a little better, even though it happened to be in this odd and painful way for you. Your opinion means a lot to me." She returned her attention to Patrick. "I don't want to debate principles with you. How about we go right on living our lives. I'll watch your back and you watch mine. How's that for a plan?"

"I'd rather do more to keep you safe."

"I know."

He sighed. "Okay, we'll do it your way."

"Good." Michaela briskly stepped away. "Now, let's find something to eat. I'm starving."

Patrick pointed a stern finger at Belinda. "And my name is Patrick, not Mister Daniels."

"So? My daddy's name is Bill, but I still call him, Daddy." Patrick raised one eyebrow and glared at Belinda. "You have quite the sense of humor."

The roommate's eyes grew large and then she snapped a salute. "Aye, Captain. Patrick it is." She started to grin, but didn't get far with it. "Ow!"

"Sarcasm, right?" Michaela asked.

"Well, yeah, it was supposed to have been. I guess without good facial expression; world-class sarcasm falls flat. I'll be back in form in a couple of days. For now, just know that I'm laughing on the inside."

"Good to know you're into it. I hope you can take it as well as you dish it," Patrick said. "Because, I *will* get you back."

"Cool."

Patrick's smile wilted as he addressed them both. "Look, you girls watch out for one another and please... *please* stay home or at least close to it. Michaela, I'm going back to my apartment to draft a story for tomorrow's broadcast that details Amanda Pine's condition and the incident here with Belinda. It has to be worded just so, to infer a connection of these assaults to the hydraulic fracturing story and Landers' involvement without drifting off into libelous editorializing. I've done it once. I'd better not press that button again." He reached for and held both of Michaela's hands. "Tomorrow, when you get to the station, I want you to look it over, edit it and make suggestions to improve it."

"You trust me to do that?"

"Implicitly. If we're going to be partners on this, your involvement has to go beyond shooting the video. The copy has to be a joint endeavor as well. It's all about the story. What do you say to that?"

Michaela was overwhelmed with emotion. "Yes. Yes!" She threw her arms around his neck, pressed her head onto his shoulder and hugged him hard. "Thank you, so much."

"You're worth it." He returned the hug with a quick squeeze and hurriedly pushed away from her. "I'd better get out of here before I do something I probably shouldn't. I'll see you tomorrow afternoon."

He headed for the door but suddenly stopped and turned to Belinda. He studied her face for a couple of seconds. "You know what? When the swelling goes down, you might consider silicone injections. You'd look *great* with fat cheeks."

It was Belinda's turn to glare. She stuck her tongue out and blew, rattling her lower lip."

Patrick offered a big smile. "Gotcha." He winked at Michaela and rushed out the door.

She hurried to the open door and considered asking him to stay, but then slowly closed the door behind him. *It's no use. When I'm around him, I want him. The man has become like an addictive drug. Shouldn't I be fighting these urges?* It miffed her that he felt compelled to leave before something happened. *Maybe I wanted something to happen. I need a fix. Oh, God, what am I thinking?*

* * *

Patrick got in his car and began backing out of the driveway from Michaela and Belinda's apartment, stopping at the street. He wrung his hands over the top of the steering wheel, gazing at the seventy-five-year old garage with living quarters above it. The abrupt need to stare at it had nothing to do with the architecture. His first thought was concern for their safety, but that transformed into visions of Michaela, just Michaela. Even before Michaela's admission of love, he knew he was falling. He struggled with competing mindsets. He could not give in—not now, not yet. *Haven't I created enough trouble for myself, and problems for others? That girl is wonderful. I don't want to screw up her life like I did Margaret's...and Danica's.*

He backed out onto the street, slammed the shifter into drive and accelerated hard, feeling it important to put as much space between Michaela, that apartment, and himself quickly. He had to think.

During the ride home, he considered the difference in maturity levels of the two girls he had just left. Although they were the same age, and apparently similar in many ways including appearance, it seemed as though Belinda was like all other college girls he had ever encountered, wondering where the next party was, or what to wear Saturday night—not goal-setting for the future. He had dated many girls when he was in college. They were all about the same age as Belinda and acted like her, and there was certainly nothing wrong with that. He felt as though he already knew Belinda well enough to see that graduation was an end game, not a beginning; whereas, Michaela's level of development could pass for a thirty-five-year-old woman, envisioning where she would be five years into the future in a resolute way.

He frowned and tipped his head. *Could it be that I want to see it that way, so I do?*

He began to wonder how much thought he would be able to give to the story of Amanda Pine and Belinda... *Hell, I don't know what Belinda's last name is.*

He suddenly felt stupid. A man, fancying himself an investigative reporter, could not even produce the last name of one of the principal victims in an important story. Then he remembered that detective Solomon said after he prepared an arrest warrant for assault against the guy in that old pickup truck who hit Belinda he would drop by and get a statement from her.

He slammed a fist against the steering wheel. "Damn it! I should have stayed. I should be there."

In such a hurry to get away from a snowballing physical attraction to Michaela, he had forgotten about the detective's planned visit. True, he had to go home and work on the story, but that was certainly not the reason he rushed out. Patrick knew himself well enough to realize that if he hung around, Belinda's joke about the bedroom would become reality. Solomon was probably already there. The case for romantic distraction had suddenly become airtight. He could not concentrate on anything but Michaela.

CHAPTER 27

Staring into the mirror, Michaela's thoughts were random and without depth, a blissful diversion from recent nagging decisions that still needed to be made. She prepared to go to the station for her afternoon part-time shift. Makeup pencil in hand, she sketched the perfect line beneath her eyes. Quiet arrogance oozed out when the thought crossed her mind that her eyes did not need improving. The application of eyeliner was little more than a conditioned habit. She almost smiled but then shook it off. It was time to focus, forcing thoughts away from girlie things to important issues. Hopefully, the television station would provide a more challenging use of a highly educated mind.

Now that the truly interesting part of her day was about to unfold, the events of the past few days crowded out randomness. Her view of a perfect existence began occupying her thoughts and fed imaginings more to her liking.

Michaela looked forward to working with Patrick on the story that would likely blow the hydraulic fracturing issue into a mushroom cloud of intrigue that would go national. Of that, she had no doubt.

Once the networks get wind of people getting hurt by this, it will snowball beyond debate over pros and cons of the process. The focus will quickly shift to the cover up. All the major news organizations will pick it up and swarm into Comanche Falls.

She fidgeted with the long, sweeping bang on her new, short hairstyle—not entirely comfortable with it yet. Finally, she determined that no matter how many times she shoved it up and out of the way it would hang across her right eye. Turning her head this way then that, she studied it. *Okay it's sexy. I can handle sexy.* She tossed her head to the side and grinned provocatively at her reflection. *Don't even attempt to deny my allure, Patrick Daniels.* She kissed the air.

She whirled around with renewed confidence and walked out of the bathroom. On her way through the kitchen, she checked the clock on wall—1:32. She did not have to be at the station until three o'clock, but a chance to work closely with Patrick on the script was worth being early for, even if unpaid for the extra hour.

When she pulled into the parking lot of KBTA, she noticed movement in her rearview mirror. It was Patrick. He had come from the direction of downtown and turned into the parking lot behind her. They pulled into side-by-side spaces.

She got out of her car and looked back over the roof to his, waiting for him to get out. When she saw him emerge, she asked, "Are you just now getting to work?"

He closed the door behind him and appeared distraught. "No, I left the station about an hour ago and went to Comanche Falls Medical Center to check on Amanda."

"And...?"

"She's conscious but in bad shape in ICU. They let me visit with her, but for only a couple of minutes. Since we were aware of one another's coverage of Landers Energy, it became emotional. I'm having trouble with it. Amanda cried and begged me to back off the story before something happened to us. Can you believe that? She's close to death and she's concerned for *our* safety. It touched me, considering we've never actually met before. Hell, the girl has a life and death struggle ahead of her, and she was worried about us..." His voice sank into a lower range. "... about *us*." He shook his head, frowned and dropped his chin, apparently having trouble understanding Amanda's big-hearted display while in dire pain.

Patrick was right to wonder. Michaela thought it odd as well, and she knew Amanda much better than he did. It went against Amanda's arrogantly flippant personality she remembered so well, to be so deeply sincere about anything. "I wish I had known. I would've gone with you. We were never close, but I did know her pretty well."

"Sorry, it was an impulse. I just got in my car and went." He began walking toward the front door of the station and mumbled something.

She caught up to him. "What'd you say?"

"She's a redhead... Amanda is a redhead."

"So?"

"Before today, I had not known her as anything other than a name on a byline or a voice on the phone. I had not given it a moment's consideration what she looked like. I never considered the living, breathing person behind the name and the voice. Standing there looking down at her, I hated myself for my intolerable lack of humanity. Even beyond the black eyes and bandages, the woman is beautiful. I did not expect it."

An ill-timed pang of jealousy sharpened an edge in Michaela. The reaction shocked her. It was worrisome. Amanda lay badly injured and this was the emotion she felt? It was neither right nor appropriate. Still, she knew how Amanda had been, how she had gotten what she wanted from men. Although jealousy had no place in this conversation, nor should it have entered her mind, there it was, barreling in like a freight train rolling over all other reactions. *Is it even possible that Amanda is still as manipulative as I remember? How could she be while in that kind of pain?* Michaela followed Patrick closely as he walked across the parking lot, searching for the strength and wisdom to respond to his distress objectively, compassionately. It seemed clear enough, his concern for Amanda was genuine. She attempted coming to grips with the possibility that Amanda was indeed sincere in her concern for their safety. Try as she might, each time she reached out to the cosmos for empathy and wisdom, all she drew back was jealousy. *How could he be so concerned for a woman he didn't even know existed before this story blew up?* She grabbed his arm and stopped him, pulling him around to face her. "Are you going back?"

"To the hospital?"

"Yeah."

He put a hand on her arm and then let it slide down to hold her hand, his face disheartened. "Did you know that she has no parents?"

"Well, if you... uh, what did you say?"

"She had no parents. She was raised by an elderly, widowed aunt." The question took her by surprise. "No, I didn't."

Patrick nodded. "The aunt is in her eighties with health problems of her own, almost bedridden, and there's no way she can get down here from Chicago to be with her niece. That old lady is her only living family. Judging by what Amanda told me, she has no close friends around here either." His reddened eyes shimmered in the bright sunlight with fresh tears. "I was the only one that had been to see her. Can you believe that, Michaela, I was the *only one* to give a flying flip about her?" A tear spilled, tracking down his cheek and around his mouth. "Her editor at the *Trib* and a few co-workers called and inquired about her condition, but no one took the time to go see her." He then mumbled, "Those sons o' bitches."

His tears became her tears. "How about we both go see her after the six o'clock broadcast?" she asked.

"Sure. I think she would appreciate that."

Together, they walked toward the lobby door of the television station. Michaela's jealousy had transformed into extreme self-loathing in two blinks and a heartbeat. She felt horrible for thinking Patrick's thoughts had somehow been romantic or sexual toward Amanda. The man had been touched by Amanda's unpretentious fear for his safety and by extension, hers. Amanda must have fashioned an emotional connection akin to family based solely on the fracking story. Someday, to soothe her conscience, Michaela vowed to apologize to Amanda for thoughts horribly unbecoming a friend.

Stan met them coming through the door. "Hey, guys, have that story ready for the six yet?"

"Not completed, just a draft," Patrick said. He then looked to Michaela and smiled. "I want her to go over and edit it for me. I need her input."

"Harry wanted me to let him know as soon as you came in. How about you go on back and stick your head in the door so I don't have to explain to him why I didn't tell him you were here?"

"Both of us?"

"Mikki's your partner, right?"

"Of course."

"Then yeah, both of you."

Patrick walked by Stan. As Michaela passed, she mouthed to Stan, "Thank you."

Stan grabbed her arm and whispered into her ear, "Beer... seven-thirty... Lazy S."

She patted the hand that clutched her arm and winked at him before moving on.

As it turned out, all Harry wanted was to insure that Patrick would not be editorializing the report, and rightfully so. As Harry lectured Patrick, Michaela read the draft Patrick handed her. His personal feelings were all over it. When Patrick asked her to edit it, she thought it would be a simple matter of giving it her blessing. She had no idea it would need such extensive whittling of opinions to get it down to pure fact with only carefully considered speculation— much more carefully considered.

When they walked out of the News Director's office and achieved a semblance of privacy, she waved the script at him and whispered, "What is this? What are you trying to do, get us killed and the station sued into bankruptcy?"

"I was a little distracted last night. So, I wrote what I felt. Not very objective, is it?"

She looked to the big clock extending out from the wall in the corridor. "We have a couple of hours. Let's pare it down to get most of the assumptions and *all* of the opinions out of it."

"I can't seem to stop thinking about Ned Barrett, Amanda Pine and your roommate. Those people and situations are swirling in my head and drawing me in deeper. It's becoming far too personal and distracting."

He gently palmed her cheek—his gaze clearly affectionate. "For other reasons, too." He smiled.

As she read his eyes, it did not take a crystal ball to see that, due to Amanda's situation, Patrick's thoughts about the fracking story were overlaid and tainted by his concern for the critically injured girl. What she saw in his eyes was relatable to her own feelings toward him. "I know what you mean. I really do," she said and then thought, *God, what am I saying? I should be encouraging him to press on.*

It was as clear as the eyeliner she had so carefully applied just for him. Things were heading for a change that she might be powerless to control. She felt as though her life had sailed out of a sunny ocean directly into an uncharted, dark, tropical tributary. Her life was taking a questionable turn.

CHAPTER 28

Patrick was proud of Michaela. She took his disastrous script attempt and turned it into an admirable work of unbiased journalism that still retained enough questions to infer a connection between the violence and the news series on fracking. It would not take a genius to connect a few more dots that would take it all the way to Robert Landers' doorstep, but the script contained not a single libelous word.

After the six o'clock sequence, he and Michaela got in his car and headed for Comanche Falls Medical Center. "You did great," he said. "Thanks."

"If I would have presented that story as I had written it, I would have been fired." He looked sideways at her, and then again. His pride in, and affection for, this woman half his age strengthened. Still he worried, wanting to protect her as if she were a fragile porcelain figurine. She stared, unblinking, at the highway ahead. "You look deep in thought," he said.

She smiled, as if fearing exposing true thoughts. "I— I guess I am."

"Care to share?"

"Just thinking about our conversation in the parking lot earlier."

"Yeah, me too."

Patrick glanced to her often as she stared down the highway. His overactive imagination pumped out a montage of disturbing images. Topping those visions was one of Michaela lying in a hospital bed clinging to life like Amanda Pine. Each time mental snapshots threatened to reel out of control he shuddered, but he could not prevent them. As this total feminine package sitting next to him neared absolute irresistibility, so did the distraction she represented. Important things needed to be done. But his head was crowded with a jumble of competing thoughts. That vow of getting it all done, no matter what, did not seem so intransigent at the moment. Ignoring her, or her safety, was not an option.

Patrick wanted to say something to ease the tension. After considering several different approaches, nothing seemed appropriate or helpful. He loosed a long, slow sigh, finally choosing to say nothing. A gulf of quiet deepened between them and thickened the air inside the car. *I suppose I'm not the only one that needs to think things through.* There was no other conversation during the fifteen-minute ride from the television station to the hospital.

Walking side by side down the corridor of the hospital toward the elevators, Patrick noticed Michaela looking at him. He smiled at her and she bounced a mirthless smile in reply. That was all it took for negative possibilities to spin in a tornadic whirl through his head.

On the elevator, she finally spoke her first words since getting out of the car. "Are we ready for this?"

"I suppose we'd better be," he said as the elevator stopped and the doors parted, exposing a view of the fourth floor nurses' station. He saw a red placard with white lettering suspended from the ceiling straight ahead over it: INTENSIVE CARE UNIT. An arrow pointed the way.

As he approached, a nurse looked up from her paperwork and asked, "May I help you?"

"We're here to see Amanda Pine."

"We sedated her. She's asleep. Sorry, you can't go in, but you're welcome to look in on her through that observation window over there. It's the second one." She pointed to a specific rectangular window in a series of four.

Patrick nodded as he put a hand against Michaela's lower back and ushered her forward. "Thank you," he said over his shoulder to the night nurse who had just come on duty as they moved in that direction.

When they came to stand before the window, Patrick cringed at the sight.

Michaela drew a sharp breath. "Oh my God," she muttered. The exposed part of Amanda's face was battered and swollen—the remainder of her head heavily bandaged. "I had no idea she looked this bad." Her lip quivered.

"When I first saw her, neither did I." He stepped laterally until their bodies touched. He circled her limp arms with his own and pulled her into a side-by-side embrace. "Now you understand why her concern for our safety touched me like it did, especially after learning of her family situation...or lack of it. I had a heck of a time not crying while talking to her."

They stared through the window without speaking.

Images of Michaela's face superimposed on Amanda's body would not go away. Patrick surreptitiously attempted shaking them away to no avail. "I can't help but feel cornered," he said.

"What do you mean?"

"People are getting hurt and killed over a story I insisted on doing. Now, I'm contemplating options and one of them is to walk away before more people get hurt.

Unfortunately, too many people are depending on the success of it. I'm trapped."

"You can't think like that," she blurted. Michaela finally offered him full attention. "The story you're doing may *save* lives and millions of dollars in property damage. You said it yourself; we've come too far to back up now. I *believed* it when you said it. Now, *you* believe it!"

"Don't be angry... please," he said, calmly and deliberately. He pointed to Amanda. "That could be you. Just the thought of that possibility scares the hell out o' me."

She appeared about to explode, preparing to aggressively argue or, maybe, hurl a string of obscenities. She leaned into him, pushing her angry face nearer to his. She wore the appearance of violent intention like a rubicund mask. But she said nothing; she just shook all over. Whatever thoughts prevented a detonation also softened the hard lines. The expression transformed into one of resolve. The argumentative head of steam lessened. Was she as conflicted as he was about the whole thing—the safety and danger of it all? She turned and again looked through the viewing window at Amanda Pine lying helpless in that hospital bed, unconscious, appearing ghoulish from swelling and bruises. After a moment, a nod was the only answer Michaela offered. Whatever propelled the explosive moment dissipated. She drew a breath. "Stan invited us to the Lazy S for a beer," she said. "I'm not in the mood for the bar scene. I don't want to be around people, but a beer and quiet time would be okay. How about we buy a six-pack or two and drive out to the lake?"

He offered a contrived appearance of thinking over the offer, but there was nothing to consider. He would do whatever she wanted. "Sure." He wondered where her anger and frustration went, but chose not to question it and smiled. "I don't think Stan will be upset over our absence if that waitress, Darlene, is working tonight. In fact, I don't think he'll care at all, as long as she's doting on him."

"I think you're right." She grabbed his hand. "Come on, let's go before this funk we're in gets deeper."

As Michaela pulled him in tow down the hall, youthful exuberance and willingness to take charge sent a tingle through him. It was electric. *What have I done to deserve you?* He swallowed, forcing a rising lump down before it choked him.

* * *

Lake Comanche was located within the city limits of Comanche Falls. It was an old impound, silted and shallow. There was a place on the north side near the dam, a finger of land covered in tall reeds and cattails that extended out for several hundred yards that, many years ago, had been submerged. A narrow, rutted road extended the length of the peninsula, ending at the water lapping against rocks. Fishermen and high school couples looking for privacy were the only people to ever use it. Even among locals, it was not common knowledge where it was located and, for that reason, never maintained—the perfect place for beer and quiet time with Michaela.

Patrick drove to the very end and parked. He scanned the area and saw no other cars around. He grabbed one of the cold six-packs. "Come on, let's sit on the hood."

When Michaela came to sit next to him, he had already removed the cap from a beer bottle and handed it to her.

"Thanks." She swept condensation from the chilled bottle and took a drink. "Um, good. I needed that." She propped her feet on the front bumper and took a breath of the cooling early evening air. "Beautiful night."

Patrick looked to the sky. There was no moon, but bright stars overlaid God's silver brush stroke, the Milky Way. The lights of Comanche Falls created a glowing orange arc on the horizon that did not reach the stars, but the combination proved a beautifully serene sight. The orange glow danced on rippling water as it rhythmically lapped at the shore, creating its own music.

Michaela took another drink. "This is too good. I'm afraid I'll drink it faster than I should. What if it goes to my head?"

He grinned. "I'll take my chances," he said and then drank from his own bottle.

She pushed back, sliding on the hood until the windshield stopped her. She leaned back and rested her head on it.

Patrick joined her. "I don't want to talk about television, news stories, or anything else related to work. As a matter of pure fact, I don't want to discuss anything that requires deep thought." He lolled his head toward Michaela, staring, studying her in the dim light.

She said nothing but reciprocated the analytical, admiring look, noses only inches apart.

With the fingertips of his free hand, Patrick traced the features of her face. He drew a ragged breath. "I'm not sure how I got to this point, but I'm so deeply into you that I can't see through, over, or around you. You are the end game."

Michaela sighed. The glow of her smile dimmed. "I know." She took a drink of beer, a big one.

Patrick noticed the sudden demeanor shift. "Am I crazy for feeling this way?"

"No crazier than I am." Michaela turned and stared into the night. "Then we both must be out of our minds for doing this."

"Doing what?" Michaela asked as she moved her head closer to his. "This." Patrick slid his head across the windshield toward hers.

She rolled her head to face him again.

Their lips met. As soft as a down feather, he grazed his lips over hers, savoring the sensation. An intense depth of feeling warmed him—a feeling he did not want to end.

Michaela did not seem to want a slow-moving game and pressed her mouth to his for a passionate kiss as she draped a leg over his. She clenched his lip between hers and explored his mouth, circling his lips with the tip of her tongue.

Suddenly, bright light flooded the area.

"Damn," Patrick muttered. He reluctantly lifted his head and looked back over the car top. He saw a pair of headlights. "Probably some high school couple looking for a place to...well, do what we're doing."

Michaela did not take her eyes off him. "I'll never snitch on them if they don't bother us." She snickered.

Patrick smiled and moved in for another kiss, but the headlights of the approaching vehicle were obnoxiously bright and seemed to be coming in fast. It was a noisy vehicle. If the goal was to remain unnoticed, the oncoming vehicle was going about it all wrong. He raised his head again for another look. "Those headlights are high off the ground and coming at us fast." He squinted, looking for detail. "That's no car. It's a big pickup truck with a bad muffler."

Clearly curious now, Michaela looked back as well. "I don't think that's a couple of love-struck teens."

The vehicle abruptly slammed on the brakes and slid to within inches of Patrick's rear bumper. A bar of lights snapped on above the cab of the truck, flooding the area with even harsher light than the high-beam headlights alone. A large, young, bearded man stuck his head out the driver's side window. "You assholes don't deserve a moment's peace as long as I'm without a job!" he shouted, slurring his speech in a slobbery drawl. He was twenty-something and intoxicated. Patrick didn't need to read the results of a Breathalyzer test to know it. "All of us out o' work oil patch guys shouldn't be the only ones havin' to suffer!"

How did this guy know we were out here? Even I didn't know where we were going until a few minutes ago. My car must be known by every laid-off roughneck in Comanche Falls, and there must be more of them than I thought.

The large pickup truck with oversized tires and bumper guard contacted his rear bumper and accelerated.

"Wait a minute!" Patrick shouted.

The big truck began pushing his car toward the water.

"Stop!" Patrick shrieked.

His car could not resist the huge, prominently treaded, all-weather tires of the pickup truck. Even with locked wheels, his car began to turn parallel to the water once the front wheels were shoved into the slick mud at the water's edge.

The pickup stopped. The drunken man again stuck his head out the window. "I have two kids and a wife at home. I think that fancy car o' yours shoved off in the lake is a fair trade for taking their happiness!" He accelerated again. The truck roared.

Patrick rolled off the hood.

Michaela rolled off the other side.

Patrick raced back to the truck, leaped up onto the running board and reached through the open window. He grabbed the man by his jacket collar. "Stop! Think about what you're doing! I am not your enemy!"

The guy stared drunkenly through heavily veined and glazed eyes, but said nothing.

"When you sober up, I hope you realize that. One way or the other, you will certainly regret this in the morning."

Patrick saw a glimmer of lucidity in the guy's face, so he pressed on. "Come on, man, don't complicate your situation by doing this while in a drunken fit of rage. Your conscience will eat you alive when you sober up, and your family will be in a worse predicament than they already are. I'm certain of that. You could get jail time over a stunt like this. Can't you understand that?"

The man stared, bleary-eyes set in a head that drifted fluidly atop a rubber neck, but he seemed to understand, even offering a loose-lipped nod.

Getting a tighter grip on the man's collar, Patrick yanked his face nearer to his. "Landers Energy is not your friend. You are the marionette and they are the ones pulling your strings, making you do things like this. You're a pawn in a much larger game. You're out here acting on their behalf and didn't even have to be told, while their hands remain clean. Can't you see that? You and all the other laid-off oil patch guys are doing exactly what they want you to do, and they can deny any responsibility while getting exactly what they want. Come on, man, go home. Stop this foolishness. You'll thank me in the morning. I promise."

The guy abruptly reared his head, as if a flash bulb went off in his face. He placed a big, square palm in the middle of Patrick's face and shoved.

Patrick catapulted backwards off the truck's running board and onto his butt in the grassless, muddy fringe of the lake.

The pickup truck reversed and, with all four tires spinning, it spewed mud and rocks all over Patrick's car as it shot backwards. The bright lights above the cab went off. The headlights receded as the truck drove backwards, bouncing the hundred or so yards to the main road. Patrick wondered how the guy could drive so fast in reverse and be as drunk as he obviously was. The truck came to the end of the rutted road, turned toward town, and then raced away.

Patrick jumped to his feet and hurried in the dark to where Michaela should be. "Where are you?"

"Over here."

His eyes followed the sound and finally picked up her silhouette backed up against a patch of cattail reeds. "Are you okay? Are you hurt?"

Michaela sat on the ground—knees up, arms encircling them. "I'm fine. How about you?"

"I landed on a rock when he shoved me backwards. My ass hurts." She snickered in a humorless way. "Well, now, that's a bit of justice."

"How do you mean?" Patrick asked as he helped her to her feet. "You dragged me over a threshold into an old house while I was

unconscious, bruising my butt. Remember?" She brushed grass and twigs from the seat of her jeans. "It's still sore."

"Oh... that." Patrick looked to his car, awkwardly askew at the water's edge. "I hope he didn't shove us so far that I can't back out of the mud. Come on, let's take the positive approach. Let's get in the car and believe— deeply believe—that I'll drive us right out of here."

"Sure you will." She looked around. "Where's the beer?"

"Are you serious? After the scary thing that just happened, your thought is on the safety of the beer?"

"Well... yeah. I came out here for quiet time and a beer. We sure as hell did not get the quiet, so I want my beer. What's so odd about that?"

"Nothing, I guess." He reversed direction and walked back to Michaela, stopping in front of her. He put his hand on the back of her neck and touched his forehead to hers. "Yes, my queen, the quest for your beer shall not be interrupted by raving rednecks."

In a self-important way, she glided toward the car. "That's better. Your liege will eagerly await your return in the coach."

Patrick retrieved the remainder of the six-pack. One had broken and the two they had been drinking spilled out on the ground and were mostly empty. He approached the car where Michaela sat on the passenger side. He presented three unopened bottles.

She let down her window.

"The nectar of the gods, milady." He handed her the beer, still in the cardboard carrier.

She took it from him and smiled. "That's better. With the six-pack on the backseat, this ought to last us. You may enter now." He bowed and backed away a couple of steps.

Patrick worked his way around the car, slogging through mud to the driver's side—the car virtually parallel to the waterline. "That mud is like overcooked chocolate pudding."

Michaela twisted the cap off a bottle and took a long swig. She let out a loud and long belch, then wiped her mouth like a sailor. "I bet that gooey mud doesn't *taste* like chocolate pudding. I have a ten-dollar bill in my pocket that says you won't try to prove my theory on that."

He looked at her firmly fixed smirk and shook his head. "I've never seen this side of you. Where did this come from?"

She shrugged. "Thought you knew me, didn't ya?" She guzzled more beer.

"I guess I don't know you as well as I thought." He started the car. "Let's go back to my place. It's not as serene as this setting, or the way it was before that drunken yahoo showed up anyhow, but safer."

"Sure." She took another couple of gulps. "Get this overpriced puppy turned around and let's get out of here."

He put it into gear and as soon as the transmission engaged, the front wheels began to spin. He accelerated slightly and the wheels spun freely. The car went nowhere, except deeper into the mud. "Okay," he said. He pulled out his cell phone and dialed.

"Now what?" she asked.

"A wrecker. Hope you don't mind waiting a while." She looked down at the beer. "If it doesn't show up by the time all this is consumed, then yeah, I'll mind."

Patrick got through to Red River Wrecker Service and gave them a location. As he hung up, he said, "Well, they said it might be up to half an hour before they get here. They only have two trucks. One of them responded to a wreck on the Interstate north of town, and the other is towing an abandoned car to police impound."

"Like I said, as long as they get here before the beer is gone, I'm good." She took another man-size swallow from her bottle.

"You seem to have a sudden desire for inebriation."

She sighed. "Not really. I just want to be mellow and unencumbered by serious thoughts."

"I suppose that *was* the plan before redneck hell broke loose, wasn't it?"

"Yep. And now its importance has taken an abrupt upward turn."

"You're right. Hand me a bottle."

He twisted the cap off the bottle she handed him and took a couple of big gulps. "It would seem I have a little catching up to do." She let her head fall back against the seat. "Ya know somethin'?"

"What?"

"We really *don't* know much about each other, do we?"

He thought about that. He knew nothing about her life before he met her. They had exchanged a few tidbits in the old house on the Cattle Trails Ranch, but nothing substantial. He could not even measure their relationship in months, just days. It had suddenly become an issue, an important one. "You're right. So, tell me about Michaela Ross."

Head still resting back against the seat, she let it roll sideways to face him. "Nothing much to tell, really. I was a beautiful baby, obedient child and loving daughter. Cheers!" She held out the beer bottle in the manner of a toast and then put it to her lips. Her eyebrows went up slightly.

"Aha!"

"Aha... what?"

"Those eyebrows... that's your 'tell.' Without admitting it, you just let me know what you said was bullshit for my benefit."

"Seriously, did I really *need* to give you a tell?"

He grinned. "Not really."

"What do you want to know? I'm an open book."

"How about your parents?"

"Dad is a professor of literature at the University of Texas. Mom was one of his students about twenty-four years ago. Remind you of anyone?" She sipped her beer.

"I refuse to answer that. Besides, you're not my student."

"In a way I am." She took another drink. "I was a love child. What they had was real and they got married. I was born seven months later. They're still married and very happy. I love them both very much."

"Any siblings?"

"Nah. They achieved perfection with the first one and stopped trying." She grinned.

"Funny girl." He took a sip. "You're intelligent. Why are you not following in your father's footsteps and becoming a teacher?"

"Good question. I have a great answer. I'll tell you the same thing I told him. I don't want to spend countless hours gaining

knowledge from books and then pass it on to the next generation of students without ever experiencing or applying it. I wanted to gain the knowledge, go out in the world, use the information, and then after having actually lived the life that I studied so hard for, maybe then and only then could I feel comfortable passing the knowledge on. Regurgitating information from books just doesn't cut it for me."

"I sure do like your style."

She stared at him for a moment. "Drink your beer... but not too fast. It may have to last a while."

"How about the earlier years, your childhood?" Patrick asked. "It was fairly uneventful until high school. I loved basketball. I was most valuable player in the region and made all-state my senior year."

"That's wonderful. But, somehow, it doesn't surprise me. You're a winner. I knew that from the get-go."

"If I weren't so averse to syrupy sentimentality, I'd say that was a sweet thing to say."

He took a drink. "You don't have to say it." He grinned. "I'll just know it."

She downed the final two swallows from her bottle and opened

another. "That's all I'm going to say about me. What's your backstory?"

"I'm the seventh son of a seventh son and cursed for all eternity." Michaela reached across and slapped him hard on the stomach.

"Don't pull that crap on me. I want the truth."

"I grew up on a cotton farm on the Texas South Plains—that part of the state above the Caprock where there's nothing to impede a view of sunsets except the ears of a few jackrabbits and occasional fence posts."

She frowned. "I almost believe the seventh son thing as much as I believe that."

"It's true. The first nineteen years of my life was on the home place, a cotton farm in the flattest country you'll ever see, but the people are also the finest folks you'll ever meet. My life went little farther than the schoolhouse or the cotton patch. I played a little football, a little basketball, ran track and participated in academic competitions, although I wasn't particularly good at any of them."

"If you weren't good, how'd you make it on all those teams?"

"Small school. Every student had to participate in multiple programs to justify offering them every year. I was even on the golf team without ever having played a single round of golf. They needed an extra member, and when I found out I could ditch school for a day, I was quick to volunteer."

"Ha! I bet that was a hoot to watch."

"Yep. Lost all my coach's golf balls and bent one of his clubs. Needless to say, he wasn't too happy with me." Patrick took another drink.

"Your parents? What about them?" Michaela asked.

"Good people. Hard workers and loving. They spent a lot of time with my sister and me, instilling values."

"Sister? You have a sister?"

"Have I failed to mention that?"

"Well... yeah! Don't just sit there. Tell me about her."

"Her name is Meagan. She's three years younger than I am. She's married to a really nice guy, Terry Donnelly, and they have three kids, two girls at home and a son in the Army. They live in Woodville, a town in southeast Texas. She helps Terry run a small hardware store."

"You have a *younger* sister old enough to have a son in the Army?"

Suddenly, Patrick felt old. He had no choice but to confirm what she already knew. "Yep." This hard truth that had gone unspoken until now had suddenly moved to center stage. The inevitable time had come to confront it head-on. "The fact is, Devon Donnelly, my nephew, is only a year younger than you are." He turned up his beer bottle and gulped twice. He let his head fall back against the seat top and stared through the windshield into the night sky, hoping this line of questioning would end.

"I'm sorry," she said, "I wasn't thinking of us when I asked that about your nephew. Please, don't be sensitive about it." She reached for his hand and held it tight. "I have no delusions about our age difference. I know it's substantial and I don't care. All I do care about are my goals, your goals, and our compatibility."

He smiled. "The way you talk and see the world astounds me."

"Why?"

"You don't talk like any twenty-three-old I've ever known before. You're young, Michaela, but you are definitely an old soul."

"It's strange that you said that."

"Why?"

"That's what my daddy always told me, and still does."

"Yeah. You told me that already."

"Oh." She took a quick drink. "Of course, I will reserve our age difference as a wonderful source of jokes and sarcasm."

He sneered at her. "Drink your beer. You're still too sober."

"Not as sober as you might think." She laughed. "Alcohol affects me faster than anyone I know." She then gulped again from the bottle. She pulled it away from her lips, wiped her mouth and asked, "How much longer do you think we have until the wrecker gets here?"

He checked his wristwatch. "I figure more than ten minutes but less than fifteen. Or so they promised when I called."

"I have one last question."

"Shoot."

She glanced back. "You think if I set that other six-pack on the floor that the backseat would be big enough for both of us?"

Although dark inside the car, Patrick distinctly saw a sexually charged look on Michaela's face that seemed to provide its own light. He did not attempt to answer the question, just reached back and set the reserve six-pack off onto the floor, and then began moving to the backseat.

CHAPTER 29

Stan watched as Darlene glided from table to table doing what she did best—flirting, serving drinks and then offering to bring more. For a fifty-something woman, she knew how to manipulate men to get what she wanted. He should know, it worked on him—a man who spent a lifetime avoiding entanglements that might lead to a relationship, something he never thought much about; therefore, never prepared for. And then, one day, wham— blindsided. This woman he watched going about her business had swooped in and yanked out a piece of his heart before he knew what hit him. The lifelong rule of no romantic entanglements no longer ruled, although he continued to pay it lip service. His mindset was in the throes of transfiguration.

He continued watching her. Sitting alone made it easy, no distractions. He was set free to follow his fantasies wherever they happened to lead. Darlene stopped at a nearby table of three men and worked it. They wanted her to stay and visit. She didn't. Nonetheless, a new drink order was the end result again. She was good. No, not simply good—extremely talented. She earned every dime of her tips. It was not only men. She could endear herself to a table full of women out for an evening. Stan had seen all her moves time after time. One of the numerous reasons he admired her with such intensity. Her talent deserved admiration. She had a way of putting people under her spell, and we were definitely not immune. He was smitten but had not considered the depth of his infatuation.

Darlene worked her way to his table and stopped. "How about you, Sugar, need another beer?"

Stan sat alone, elbow on table, chin on palm. He lifted only his eyes and grinned. The twinkle in them was hard to miss. "Sure." The look he offered was designed to let her know that his desire went beyond beer. He grabbed her wrist, pulled her close and whispered, "What I really want is you to drop that tray, take off that apron and join me...just you, me, and our mutual friend, this long, long night." His grin grew wider. "Whaddaya say?"

She looked both ways and then put her lips to his ear. "I'm miles ahead of you, babe. It was supposed to have been a surprise, but what the hell, I'll tell you now. Heather is covering the remainder of my shift, but you'll have to wait another five minutes. Can you do it?"

He jerked his head off his palm. "Hey, that *is* a surprise... and a nice one." He babbled, "Can I take you to dinner, to a movie or...well, just about anything you want?"

"Don't try so hard. As long as I'm with you, we can sit right here, if that's what you want." She gave him a peck on the cheek, but then surreptitiously looked around. "For now, I'd better act a little more detached, though." She grinned and winked. "You know how this business works. It's all about tips, you know. I need to appear available, true or not."

"Yeah." He patted her hand that lay upon the table, remaining intimately close for a few more seconds. "I understand. I really do."

"I'll be back with your beer and then a few minutes later without this apron." She stared for a silent second into his eyes. "Of course, when I do, I'll be expecting your full attention."

He smiled so big that he showed dimples that had not made an appearance on his face in years, knowing what that entailed. "You got it, kid." He watched her as only a staunchly heterosexual man would as she walked away. He sighed and let his imagination run wild with visions of where the remainder of this night might lead.

He had five minutes to kill and only a cold, sweating bottle of beer to keep him company. His fantasies shifted to something that had clouded his thoughts for several days—the hydraulic fracturing story. A nanosecond later, Patrick Daniels and Michaela Ross became the focus of his introspection. *Damn. I hope those two are careful. That story has pissed off every roughneck in Comanche Falls, directly affected or not.* It was not something he cared to dwell on, not tonight. But he and Patrick had grown close over the years. Michaela may have only recently popped onto the scene but she, too, had carved a place in his heart. Those two, he knew, were a winning combination in love and in business. A man could not live upon this earth as long as he had and not see it. They might as well have had a flashing neon sign with a giant heart-shaped arrow pointed at them. They were born to find one another. As a couple, Patrick and Mikki were diamonds in a sandstone world.

The worst case scenario crossed his mind. *Crap! If something should happen to them, I'm not sure I could stay on at that television station. They fill a void in me I did not know existed until they found one another.*

Stan's eyes picked up Darlene as she went about her job. *And my feelings toward that woman are the result of those two and they don't even know the role they played. I'm not sure I do either. I just know I woke up one morning wanting what they have.* "Humph." He shrugged his shoulders and, with a fingertip, swiped condensation from his beer bottle, snatched it up and took a drink. He stalked Darlene with his eyes. *Now I need her. I'm not sure I can see beyond the here and now without that woman in it.* He grimaced. *Crap!* He was hooked.

A deep voice rose above the general din of barroom banter, stealing away concentration. "This is the place. I wonder if that prick is here."

Stan turned to see a man holding the entry door open. He wore a red plaid flannel shirt with the sleeves cut off to the shoulder. He had to have been six-five and about two-sixty, red beard, kinky red hair to his shoulders and freckles over every exposed part of his body. His arms were substantial in size, not fat, but rippling muscle. Two smaller men dressed in similar fashion followed him into the Lazy S. It was sort of an odd sight. Those types of guys usually clustered at the bars out on the highway near welding shops and pipe yards on the outskirts of Comanche Falls.

The big, bushy-haired, red-headed one surveyed surroundings. "You boys see anyone familiar?"

One of his minions muttered something with a negative headshake. The other one seemed to agree.

"Well hell. It looks like this trip is a bust," the big one said, pointing to an empty table. "Let's sit. Might as well have another beer while we're here."

Stan figured that they knew this was a local gathering place for media people and were looking for Patrick. He studied them. They were already inebriated. It wasn't difficult to surmise they were oilfield trash, as he called them. Like media people had a certain look, so did those guys. It was clear they worked in the oil patch.

After a stint overseas in the military and combat experience under his belt, Stan did not intimidate. In fact, that button was totally unreachable, always had been. It may have been dangerous for someone with a short temper, but Stan was slow to anger. Those rare times that he did hit the boiling point, someone, not him, would be stretched out on the ground, unconscious. He considered himself lucky to be alive, considering the scrapes he'd gotten himself into over the years. Plus, years of rubbing shoulders with inquisitive news people gave him a curious nature. Compelled by his thoughts and this opportunity, he rose and sauntered toward the restroom, which just happened to take him by their table.

As he approached, the big one hunkered over, with elbows supporting those massive arms upon the table. Stan slowed to hear better. The red-headed giant said, "That dick of a reporter will get his, I swear. It may not be tonight, but I won't quit until I have the satisfaction of bruising his face."

Stan gave in to his compulsion and stopped next to the table. "Who is that 'dick of a reporter' you're referring to? He allowed his head to sink sideways into a curious puppy-dog tilt."

"Daniels...Patrick Daniels," the man said before looking up. He then raised his head slowly to meet Stan's gaze. "I understand he has a little college cheerleader that's always with him."

Ignoring the comment about Michaela, Stan said, "Patrick Daniels, huh? Why should he be a dick and you're not?"

The big guy sprang up so fast that the chair slammed to the floor and slid away behind him.

Stan smiled. "Wow. I must've said something you found interesting."

Darlene rushed to Stan's side. "What are you doing?" she hissed.

"Just having a conversation with my new friend..." He looked back to the big guy. "Uh, sorry, but I didn't get your name. What do you go by?"

The man glared at him through a drunken haze.

"Seriously," Stan said, "I'd like to get to know you. Please, don't choose this point in our budding relationship to forget your name, for God's sake." He gave the man a look meant to antagonize.

"Asshole."

"Oh, okay. Got it." He turned to Darlene. "I'd like you to meet Mister Asshole, my new best friend." He winked at her and then pushed her away.

He looked back just in time to see a calloused and massive square fist heading for his head.

He ducked, sprang back up, plowing a fist into the point of the big man's chin—all before the guy had finished the follow-through on his swing.

The guy reeled and went down, then rolled onto his back, clearly surprised by the strength and quickness of Stan, an old guy with a wiry, wrinkled face, white flattop hair and squinty eyes. The man's expression went from surprise to anger. He began to get up.

Stan dropped a knee onto the man's neck. "How about you just lay there and cool off for a minute, bud. I don't want to fight you." The big guy's friends came around the table.

The Lazy S bouncer, an overweight guy with the nickname Bear, came to Stan's side. "Ya okay, Stan?"

The two friends suddenly didn't see the need to intervene and backed away.

"Aw, yeah," Stan said. "My new friend here misunderstood what I said is all." He looked down at the guy, now turning red-faced from the knee on his throat. "Ain't that right?"

The guy managed to squeak, "Yeah...misunderstood."

Stan eased off but was slow to stand, gauging the man's intent. Once he saw that the guy did not appear eager to resume, he stood and extended a helping hand down to the man. "Come on, I'll buy you and your friends a beer."

The man took Stan's hand, rolled to his side, then pushed off the floor. Once the man was standing, Stan continued holding the man's hand, which was twice the size of his, "Are we good?"

The man rubbed his chin with the back of his hand. A tiny smile came up. "Yeah... we're good, as long as you've got the next round."

Stan looked to Darlene. He pointed at the guy and his friends and then to himself.

She nodded understanding.

"You're covered, friend. Enjoy the beer," Stan said, and then added. "By the way I assume you lost your job over the fracking story."

"Yeah."

"Sorry, man. But you gotta know, Patrick Daniels and Michaela Ross had nothing to do with that. They just reported a story, a factual series of events. Your employer, Robert Landers, is the real asshole in all this. He's stirring the pot by unnecessarily laying you boys off and blaming them for it. He figured y'all could do his dirty work without him lifting a finger. It seems to be working...and he doesn't even have to pay you anymore to get it done."

"Seriously?"

"Yeah... seriously."

The big guy ran a palm over his scruffy cheek. "I never thought about it that way."

"It's not your fault. You were just trying to make a living and support your family. Landers knew that's where your focus would be and exploited it. He's the dick... guaranteed."

The man nodded slowly. "You may be right."

Stan held out a cordial hand. "I'm hoping you'll spread that word to your laid-off friends."

"I will." The man took Stan's hand and shook it.

"Enjoy your beer and have a great evening." He turned and walked back toward Darlene.

She took off her apron, tossed it onto the bar, followed Stan back to his table and sat across from him. "You didn't really need to use the restroom, did you?"

He grinned. "Nah. I'd need at least two more bottles of beer before that urge becomes a problem."

"How in the world is it possible that you smashed the guy's chin with a fist and he ends up being a friend?"

He shrugged and then downed the last swallows of his beer, a smug expression fixed on his face.

"Well? Say something."

"You have your talents, I have mine. We're quite a pair." He smiled and turned to look at the three guys just as Heather, the other waitress, delivered the beer to them. He offered them a salute.

All three of them smiled and waved.

"I'm not sure I can believe what I'm seeing," Darlene said.

CHAPTER 30

Michaela woke. She felt the warmth of Patrick at her back, his arm draped over her. As she opened her eyes, the abundant light and angle of it filtering through closed blinds over the window made it clear that it was well past sun-up, possibly around mid-morning.

Gently, she lifted his arm and slid from beneath it, scooting to the side of the bed and easing up onto her feet. She turned to see that he still slept. She felt at ease with her nakedness. That gave her pause. Looking down at herself, she realized that even if he should wake, there was no desire to be other than what she was, naked and all his. It was a disquieting feeling, not a cozy one. Her comfort level with this situation contradicted everything she had wanted for herself before she met him.

But then, remembering comical events of the night before at the lake, she smiled and snickered softly. The wrecker arrived while they were in the throes of passion in the backseat of Patrick's car. She was certainly embarrassed then and definitely in a rush to cover her body.

Once the wrecker pulled Patrick's car up onto dry ground, they drove back to his apartment, laughing all the way about giving that truck driver something to remember, wondering just how much they did reveal to him. Patrick had the audacity to suggest they find him and demand payment for the show.

With eyes locked on his sleeping form, she continued smiling, not wanting to break the spell of this moment or of that sweet memory. She watched him sleep, allowing her mind to take wings and soar into a possible future, their future as a couple.

A couple? The fantasy shattered as her thoughts snapped back to the present.

Serious things flooded her mind—the dangers of what they faced as partners, the videographer and the reporter. It was real and in the moment. Suddenly, she became hyper-aware that she was unclothed, naked before this man, and to a truth that had to be addressed soon. It meant his career and hers, whether they be together or not in that future time.

She turned away, gathered her clothes and hurried to the bathroom, now hoping she could get out of his apartment before he woke. Delusions melted away. If he woke while she was still there, she would not be able to resist and would lie at his side until he chose to end it. She must get out while he slept.

Once her jeans and top were on, she tiptoed to the front door of his apartment, slowly opened it and slipped out. She attempted to close the door quietly. The only sound was the click of the latch snapping into the jamb receiver. She hurried away, shoes in hand.

Once she reached the end of the block, she leaned against a street light pole and put her shoes on. She retrieved her cell phone from her hip pocket and called a taxi. She craved bacon and eggs. Other people around town probably had burgers and chicken fried steaks on their minds. It was almost eleven.

While waiting for a ride, Michaela attempted formulating a plan. First, she had to consider the situation. She was at the genesis of a promising journalism career, even before having a college degree in that chosen field.

She had fallen in love with her co-worker and partner while working on a story that could catapult him into a network television position. Additionally, she realized her presence might be too much of a distraction, hindering his ability to take the story all the way to an award-winning conclusion. He worried about her safety. It wasn't just the concern of a co-worker, but the potentially debilitating fear for a loved one, weighing heavily upon him. This was an indelible truth that carried its own weight meant for her. If Patrick allowed it to rule, his chance of fulfilling that network dream would vaporize. Like falling dominoes, if that should happen, her coat-tail adventure would be for naught anyhow. She had plenty of time to make her bones in the business. Time was her ally, but not so for Patrick. It might not be his last chance, but he could not have that many more.

Her eyes filled with tears. The truth saddened her. She had power over him—undeserved manipulative control, but hers nonetheless. She wanted to use it wisely. But what, exactly, was wise—for her, for him, for them both? She slammed a fist into her palm as her face tightened. She cried. Why hold back? There was no one around. Tears streamed. Truth hovered in front of her, yet she clenched her eyes and sobbed. She had too much love and not enough courage to face it.

The familiar yellow taxi approached. She swiped away tears as he pulled to the curb and let down the passenger side window. "You call for a taxi?"

She turned her face away, nodding vigorously as she did. She quickly got into the backseat.

The driver glanced back over his shoulder but never made eye contact. "Where to?"

She gave him the address to the studios of KBTA and then added, "I have to pick up my car, and then all I want is to go home."

* * *

"Patrick and I are just taking up one another's space right now, and not in a healthy way. Can't you see that?"

Stan said nothing. He looked to his feet and then back up into Michaela's eyes with a sympathetic gaze.

"Come on, Stan, you're supposed to be my friend. Say something."

Stan looked both ways, up and down the hall of KBTA. He took a step closer and placed an affectionate hand upon her shoulder. In a low, even tone, he said, "I *am* your friend. Don't ever doubt that. But I'm also Patrick's friend. I know what you want and I know what you think you want. The trouble is, I'm not sure which is which. And, as far as Patrick is concerned, it's the same dilemma. There is a stew of wants and desires between you two that I see so clearly, but I will not...hell, I cannot figure out what's most important. That's for you two to figure out. If I attempted to intervene, it would piss one or both of you off and I'd likely lose both of you as friends. Aint' gonna do it, girl... ain't gonna do it."

Michaela attempted a stone face, but then her lower lip began to quiver. "Please, Stan, I don't know what to do. And there's no one else who understands like you do. Even my roommate is no use. She only sees the problem from the relationship side of the equation. She's never understood the depth of my career passion."

He quietly stared into her brown eyes. With the gentlest touch, he pushed that long, sweeping bang away from her eye. "Have I told you yet how much I like your new short hair style?"

She punched him on the shoulder. "Shut up. I need advice, not compliments."

Stan drew a breath and then huffed it out. "Look, you are as close to a daughter as I'll ever have. Patrick is as close to a brother as I'll ever have. You two were made for each other. I see it clearly, as if posted on a flashing neon billboard on the Interstate, for Christ's sake." He paused, looked down and then back into her eyes. "But...your career is barely off the ground. I do understand your passion on that count. Patrick is as close as he may ever be to national prominence with this fracking story, and that is his passion. All these things are nosediving right now and need to be sorted before they hit the ground and explode in an unwanted conclusion that might... no, not might; it would likely destroy you both on one front or the other." He stroked her cheek with the flat of his palm. "Hon, I can't tell you which way to turn. I would be an arrogant jerk if I pretended to know what you should do...either of you."

Michaela could not prevent a spasmodic draw of air that propelled more tears. "I'm confused and lost, Stan! Tell me something... anything!"

"Shh." He gently cupped her chin and squeezed her cheeks together so she had to look him in the eyes. He glanced around for unwanted interest. "This problem is between you and Patrick. Don't feed the gossip mill."

She nodded and then whispered, "I'm so lost right now."

"I know, Mikki... I know."

CHAPTER 31

After Michaela walked away, down the hall of the television station crying, Stan stood unmoving, thinking, worrying. He had told her he was a friend and to never doubt it. He told her she was the closest thing to a daughter he'd likely ever have. So, why was he now standing like a slack-jawed dullard? Was what he told her the best thing that could have been said to a friend—to a daughter? Surely there was something else he could do or, at the least, something he could say that might comfort her. But what? For God's sake, what?

He turned and rushed back into master control, tossing the production work order in his hand onto the console in front of the switcher on duty.

"Hey, Stan," the young girl operating the video switcher said. "Aren't we going to do this rental store spot now? It airs tomorrow morning."

"Give me a minute," Stan said over his shoulder without slowing. "I have a call to make." He rushed to his small office next to the restrooms just off the back hall. He closed the door securely behind him and snatched his cell phone from the cluttered desk. He dialed and waited.

It rang several times and was interrupted by a click on the fourth. "Hello."

"Darlene?"

"Of course," came the reply. "Who did you expect to get at this number?" She snickered.

"Sorry. I'm a little rattled."

"Oh?" she asked, her voice suddenly serious.

"I'm afraid for Mikki."

"Why? What's the problem?"

"She has fallen hard for Patrick but is very afraid she might be a dangerous distraction for him. I talked to her, but I'm not at all sure it was the right thing to say. I'm afraid she'll make a decision she'll regret the rest of her life. I don't know anything about relationships. I need your input."

"What did you tell her?"

Stan detailed the conversation.

"Oh, babe, this is why I like you so much."

"I don't understand."

"Stan, you told her everything a good friend could have. You can't dictate a course of action. All you can do is be a port in her storm, a shoulder when she needs it. The decision she makes has to be hers. After she makes it, *whatever* it is, then you be a cheerleader that she is doing the right thing. That's all you can do. You did exactly what I would have done or anyone else that truly has love for someone. But remember, be close enough to reach out when she implements a plan, because, Babe, whatever course of action she chooses is going to be difficult on her. You need to be there as her strength, friend enough to help ensure her decision works and was the right one."

He breathed a sigh of relief. "Thank you. I needed to hear that. I'm such a loner that these things baffle me... you know... relationships and such."

There was a long pause. "Can I tell you something, Stan Brister, even if it means risking that you run screaming in fear?"

"Sure."

"I think I love you."

"Uh... okay."

"'Uh, okay,'" she mimicked, but in deep, moronic style. "Is that all you have to say?" The shock leveled out. He smiled. "No. That's not all, just... not here, not over the phone. I need to show you."

"My shift ends at ten."

"Then I'll see you one minute after." A second later he heard a click when she hung up. He tossed the cell phone back onto the heap of papers on his desk. He thought about Darlene, about Mikki and about Patrick. *Damn! Life sure has gotten complicated.*

Suddenly his legs seemed to turn to jelly and his knees shook. *What the hell?* He thought he might be about to collapse onto the floor and sent out a groping hand for the corner of his desk. It wasn't his imagination, or the fault of his legs; the desk was vibrating. Once he realized that, the unadorned free-hanging light fixture over his head swayed to and fro, pushing light and shadows from one side of his office to the other.

He heard someone yell from beyond the closed office door, "Earthquake!"

Stan sprinted for the door, threw it open and raced back into master control.

The assistant chief engineer and the young switcher on duty stood huddling in the middle of the room.

"Don't just stand there," he shouted, "Get out of here into the parking lot. Hurry!"

As the three rushed toward the full glass door that opened into the main corridor, Stan saw employees spilling into the hall from every office along its length. Once he joined them, he herded them toward the front door. "Everyone get out into the parking lot!" The dazed pack of people did not move fast enough to suit Stan. The drill sergeant in him came out. "Move it, move it, move it!"

The floor of the building jerked side-to-side several inches, enough to cause some to lose balance and stumble. Everyone helped each other to stay on their feet and keep moving. Girders supporting the roof above the drop ceiling over their heads creaked as the seismic event escalated.

Stan was the last to exit the front door of the building behind the group of employees. As he came out into the bright sunshine of midafternoon, his first thought was of everyone at the newsroom end of the building. He began to run awkwardly on the shaking pavement toward the far end of the television station. The asphalt on the surface of the parking lot had begun cracking and separating, several inches in places. Before he made it halfway, people began streaming around the corner of the building into the parking lot.

He frantically searched faces. "Where's Patrick and Mikki... and Harry? I don't see them."

One of the reporters coming at him said, "The last time I looked, the three of them were in Mister Alexander's office." The young professional looked around to his co-workers, searching for confirmation. Some nodded. Some shook their heads. Others just shrugged shoulders.

Stan clenched his jaws, becoming supremely angry. "You mean not one of you cared to check?"

He received the same response—shakes, nods and shrugs.

"Goddamn it, people!" He ran, heading for the newsroom door at the end of the building. As he did, he looked up to the thousand-plus feet tower in the open field behind the television station. It swayed noticeably. *Damn! I hope those guy-wires hold.* The securing cables undulated like slack ropes.

He slung the newsroom door open and raced inside. Archived files, old video cassettes and reels, even older sixteen-millimeter film reels stored on floor to ceiling shelves attached to the side wall spilled in fits and starts from shelving to the floor in noisy crashes.

As he turned the corner, he saw the glass wall and full glass door of Harry Alexander's office. Patrick and Harry were tugging on the door but could not budge it. The building had wracked enough to jam it shut. Mikki danced nervously behind them with an eye toward the ceiling. One of the fibrous panels from the suspended drop ceiling fell to the floor.

Harry noticed him and yelled through the closed door, "It's jammed!"

Stan spun in a circle, scanning nearby desks. He grabbed a desktop CPU and yelled, "Back away to the other side of the office!"

He ripped the wires from the backside of the computer unit, hoisted it over his head and charged the glass wall next to the door that Harry and Patrick had no success with. He tried to stop and began sliding across the tile floor. But before he lost forward momentum, he heaved the computer into the glass.

The tempered glass exploded into thousands of nickel-size pieces. "Come on! Let's get the hell out of here!"

Harry stepped over the frame of what had been a full glass wall. Patrick took Michaela's hand and guided her over a pile of glass to Stan's waiting hand and he led her the rest of the way out. Patrick followed.

Harry had already made it and waited outside the building as the three rushed through the door to join him.

Tremors continued for a few more seconds and then stopped as suddenly as they had begun. The four stared at one another, none taking for granted that it was truly over.

Stan was the first to look away and to the tower. It had not settled yet, still swaying, guide cables moving. He drew a breath and let it out in a huff. "An earthquake...a freakin' earthquake... in Comanche Falls, Texas? This can't seriously be happening."

"It did," Patrick said.

"Has there ever been an earthquake here?" Michaela asked.

"I haven't lived here all my life," Stan said, "but I can definitely say not within the past twenty-seven years."

"Well," Harry said, "I've lived here all my life and have never experienced one. In fact, I don't think one has ever happened within recorded history around here. If there is a fault line within fifty miles in any direction, I'm unaware of it."

Radio scanners of police, fire and sheriff's office radios began squawking non-stop through the open door of the newsroom.

"Sounds like there might have been some significant damage around town," Mikki said. "I sure hope no one was hurt."

Again squelch broke on the scanner and a dispatcher from the sheriff's office reported, "We have an emergency call from Webber. Tremors opened a sinkhole; one house is in it and a second one has broken off and tumbled onto the other, crushing part of it. Injuries are likely... no fatalities reported as of this call. People are trapped. Fire and rescue urgently requested."

Patrick took Michaela's hand. "Come on. We're five minutes closer to Webber than any first responders. Robert Landers is a fool if he thinks he can absolve his company of complicity in this... sinkhole *and* earthquake."

The two ran for the news van at the edge of the parking lot, hopped in and were racing down the driveway toward the highway in a matter of seconds. As Stan watched, his body twitched, wanting to join them. But it was a workday and he was not a news reporter.

There was plenty of work to be done right here, beginning with overseeing cleanup of his area of the building and commercial spots that still had to be produced, earthquake or not. Still, he stood rigid, rubbing his arm as if his skin crawled.

"Don't just stand there dancing like you're walking on hot coals. Go after them," Harry said.

"Damn it all, I can't," Stan hissed in frustration. "The brass would hand me my head on a platter if I left right now."

"Bullshit." Harry reached into Stan's shirt pocket and retrieved one of his sweet cigars he so loved to chew on. "Here, stick this in your mouth. That ought to calm you down. Now, go on. I'll clear it with the front office. If y'all aren't back in time for the six o'clock sequence, I'll get one of the engineers to direct and call in our noon news anchor to take Patrick's place. Besides, you might be able to set up a live shot from out there and we can do the entire six o'clock sequence from Webber. This is a big event for Comanche Falls and too big of a story for you to be sitting on the sidelines with a broom and a dust pan in your hands."

Stan began to smile as he removed the cellophane from the cigar. "You'd better be careful, old man. You're dangerously close to becoming a good man."

"Aw shut up and get out of here."

CHAPTER 32

"Do you remember where to turn up ahead?" Patrick asked as Michaela sped toward the Webber cut-off.

"Sort of hard to forget, considering all the crap we went through in this neck of the woods just a few days ago."

As she spoke, he noticed her puffy red eyes and was reminded that she had had something to say to him a few minutes before the tremors hit. "I almost forgot. You had something you wanted to talk to me about earlier before all hell broke loose. What was it?"

Michaela stared down the highway in silence. Finally, she glanced sideways. "We can talk later. Right now we need to focus on the job at hand."

The look on her expressionless face and the monotone lilt of reply troubled him. "Are you sure?"

"I'm sure."

Patrick's ringtone sounded off. He pulled the phone from his jacket pocket. "Daniels here."

"Patrick... Harry. Moments ago, I received a call from the Dallas bureau of NBC news. Apparently, they already had a reporter and cameraman headed this way. The plan was to do their own fracking story. Then the earthquake hit. They're only about fifteen minutes behind you."

"I'll see if we can get a live shot set up for us... and the NBC guys, if they should need it. I'm certainly no engineer and Michaela has never done it before but..." He pulled the phone away from his mouth and looked to Michaela. "Do you think that between the two of us we can get the mast on the van up and align a live shot?" Harry interrupted. "Patrick."

Patrick signaled Michaela to hold her answer. "What?"

"If you see a beat-up old red Ford pickup racing up behind you, it's Stan. He's headed your way. He can get that set up for you. You don't need to worry about that; just get the damn story."

"You got it, boss. Have you heard any sirens racing by the television station yet?"

"No, but I can hear a symphony of them near downtown. They're on the way."

That worried Patrick. "We might be there as much as ten minutes before first responders arrive. We're coming up on the cutoff to Webber now. I have no idea what we might find when we get there."

It was clear that Harry heard the concern in his voice. "If you have to pitch in and help, then do what you have to until the pros arrive."

"Yeah... yeah, I will." Patrick ended the call and dropped the phone back into his pocket.

"Well?" Michaela asked as she steered off the highway onto the small, paved road leading into the isolated residential housing addition known as Webber.

Before Patrick could utter a word, the van began to vibrate. Michaela slammed her foot on the brake and came to a complete stop. It was another tremor.

Patrick held a gaze on Michaela as she stared back at him in silence.

Ground movement lasted a few seconds and then stopped. "Ya think it's over?" she asked.

"Don't know, but let's move on and check out the damage."

She accelerated cautiously, as if apprehensive the street would shift beneath the news van or, worse yet, drop them into a new sinkhole. The street curved toward the west side of the addition, which ended at the high fence of the Cattle Trails Ranch.

The last row of houses that backed up to the ranch's property line and fence came into view. There was a conspicuous gap in the line of homes. Next to that was a house that had been torn away, leaving part of a living room exposed beyond bared and broken framework.

People were still streaming out of their homes into the street. It was all women, children and the elderly. It was the middle of a workday and, as populous as this community was, few were at home at this particular time on a weekday. As they came nearer, Patrick saw a woman climbing out of the gaping hole where the house had been devoured. She was disheveled and dirty, and her shirt and jeans were ripped. She began running toward them, panicked. A neighbor lady grabbed her by the arm and made her stop running.

Michaela brought the van to a stop.

Patrick hurried out and jogged toward a group encircling the lady. As he approached, every one of them was speaking at once, sounding more like cackling hens than language. He could not understand any of what they said. "Is she all right?" he called out.

"Her three-year-old daughter is trapped inside the house!" a woman shouted above the chatter.

He shouted back to Michaela some distance behind him but heading his direction. "Start unloading equipment and then help Stan get set up for a live shot when he gets here. I've got to help if I can."

Michaela reversed direction to do as told.

Patrick pushed his way between an elderly man and his wife to stand before the hysterical woman. "Where's your daughter?"

She grabbed his shirtsleeve and pulled him to the ragged edge of the sink hole. "There, in there!" She pointed spastically down at a house totally swallowed by the hole. She sobbed and wailed. The peak of the intact end of the roof was just below street level. "We've got to get her out of there!" she shrieked. "You've got to help me! Please! Please!"

"Where inside the house did you last see her?"

She wailed. Her body shuddered violently as she attempted to form words that were apparently not forthcoming.

Patrick put his hands on her shoulders and forced her to turn away from the hole and face him. "Look at me." All he saw in her eyes was loss of reason. "You have to be strong for your daughter."

Her eyes ceased darting side-to-side and settled on his. She nodded but continued to sob uncontrollably.

He stared into her eyes quietly for a few seconds and then calmly said, "Now, tell me where you last saw her."

"In her bedroom." She pointed to the back corner of the house that had been crushed by a portion of the neighbor's broken house when it collapsed into the hole.

Patrick waved to the neighbor lady who had first spoken to him standing a few feet away, summoning her to his side. "You keep an eye on her. Don't let her follow me."

The lady nodded confirmation, and then put her arm around the panic-stricken woman, holding her tight. "Shh, it'll be all right. More help is on its way," she told the young mother.

Seeing that the neighbor had this situation temporarily in hand, Patrick ran to the end of the depression where the roof was intact and accessible. As he prepared to jump over onto it, the ground shook beneath his feet.

A woman screamed.

More debris from the broken house tumbled into the sunken house. It happened to be exactly where he needed to get to. *Damn! If this ground doesn't stop shaking, that entire back corner will be crushed. God help that little girl if it should happen.* He did not attempt to get over onto the roof while the ground shook. After a few seconds, it stopped.

Patrick glanced back toward the news van. He saw that Stan had arrived and was rushing toward him. Michaela was on Stan's heels, camera shouldered.

Patrick leaped onto the roof of the sunken house.

"Wait," Stan shouted, "I'll help."

Patrick didn't wait and picked his way down and over an unstable rubble pile at the crushed end of the house. Already breathless, he saw that the reinforced framework of a front bedroom window seemed to be the only thing supporting that end of the heavily damaged roof. He figured that he might be able to enter the house at that point and, with luck, make his way to the back corner bedroom where the young mother said the three-year-old should be.

Patrick saw that Stan was on his way down to lend a hand. "No use both of us taking the same risk. Why don't you stay out here?"

He offered Stan a weak smile. "I may need you to rescue *me* if this doesn't go well."

"I hardly ever give you credit for making sense, but I'm afraid that does." He held a stern warning finger on Patrick. "Okay, but don't take any stupid chances... in and out. Got it? And, for God's sake, if the ground starts shaking again, get the hell out. You can try again after the earth quits moving."

"Sorry, buddy, but that depends entirely on having that little girl in my arms when it starts shaking. If I don't, well..." He had no intention of continuing the conversation and contorted his body to fit through the racked window frame.

Once inside, the only way he could move about was down on hands and knees crawling, or on his belly slithering like a snake. It was an obstacle course of collapsed ceiling joists, splintered walls, and exposed nails everywhere. There was no straight path or easy way to get to the other bedroom, a mere fifteen to twenty feet away. He persevered, picking his path slowly, carefully.

Finally, he heard a whimper.

CHAPTER 33

Viewfinder to her eye, the electronic sound of the camera hummed in Michaela's ear, assuring that video was being captured as the scene down inside the sinkhole unfolded. Her breathing hitched as Patrick disappeared through the partially crushed window at the front corner of the house. She shut off the camera and dropped it from her shoulder to look at what was going on without the aid of the tiny screen, as if what she saw reproduced electronically might not be real.

Stan remained down on his knees offering words of encouragement through the mangled window, as Patrick obviously worked his way through the debris out of sight. Michaela swallowed hard, understanding how delicate and dangerous this rescue effort had to be. She could not hide personal feelings and was losing objectivity at alarming speed. Fear for Patrick's safety obliterated thoughts of why she stood on the precipice of a sinkhole with a camera in her hand in the first place. She stood frozen, staring at Stan and the crushed window frame. She had told Patrick that she loved him. Yet, at this moment, this precise flash in time, she realized how deep that love had become in such a short time. Fear for his safety pulled her stomach into a tight knot. She would not, possibly could not, move until she could see that he made it out unharmed. Thinking the worst, her hands shook. A strong image of his bloody corpse pulled from the rubble sent a tingling charge down her spine. She shuddered violently.

"Are you okay, dear?"

The question snapped her out of the sordid mind's eye image and back to the moment. She whipped her head around to see an elderly woman leaving her husband's side and approaching. "I'm fine... really."

The lady lifted Michaela's free hand and patted the back of it. "It's not difficult to see the concern on your face. Don't worry. Your partner will find the little girl. We must have faith that she will be alive and well."

Michaela thought about that. "You're right. I just need to do my job and trust things will turn out okay."

The elderly lady offered a warm smile and then returned to stand next to her husband.

Shame descended over Michaela like a dark veil. The safety and well-being of the child had not even crossed her mind. Her ears became tuned to the buzz of conversation coming from the small group of huddled neighbors. It was all about the youngster. She suddenly felt selfish and silly.

She heard something overtaking the chatter. She turned an ear to the highway a few hundred feet away. It was the wail of sirens getting louder. She drew a deep breath and sighed—her relief palpable. Help was almost here. A caravan of emergency vehicles turned into this detached but heavily populated community surrounded by open ranchland. A fire truck and an emergency med tech truck followed a string of cars from the Department of Public Safety and County Sheriff's office. Trailing behind was a large news truck emblazoned with a colorful peacock on its side. *Has to be NBC.* As they came nearer, that became clear. It appeared they were arriving with everything needed to set up their own live shot. The sight was sufficient to re-establish at least a smidgen of detachment as she forced her head away from personal feelings back onto the story.

As she brought the camera to again rest on her shoulder, she heard Stan's voice move into a higher range. She caught sight of him just as he rocked back to sit on his heels. "That's it, buddy. You've got it made. Come this way, Patrick, this way." She quickly hit the play button and put the viewfinder to her eye, recording the scene.

The ground trembled, and the house emitted a cacophony of groaning lumber along with the squawk of wrenching nails.

Michaela clamped her jaws tightly together but kept the camera to her eye, recording the scene as the ground vibration intensified into side-to-side movement.

Michaela widened her stance for stability. The image in the viewfinder swayed as she did.

The noise coming from the house made it clear that a collapse was imminent.

The sound of crying and whimpering could also be heard once Stan's encouragement paused, and Michaela lost control of her emotions. She dropped the camera to her side and screamed, "Get out of there, Patrick!"

The neighbors stood in a huddled group, supporting one another against the quake.

The damaged roof at the back corner of the house collapsed. Dust belched from the partially crushed window frame. It appeared poised to come down as well. If so, it would block Patrick's only escape route.

Michaela ran the final three steps to the edge of the hole. "He'll be trapped!" she screamed. "Get him out of there, Stan!"

The ground movement stopped as suddenly as it had begun. Michaela could not relax. The house voiced its intention to finish coming down with squawks and groans.

Stan, now on his belly reaching through the opening, began backing out.

Michaela saw that he had Patrick's free hand in his. "Yes...yes!" she squealed in a crescendo of excitement. She snapped the camera back up onto her shoulder and hit record almost simultaneously. *Patrick would kill me if I missed this shot.*

The neighbors re-animated and moved as a group nearer to the edge. They all yelled encouragement at the same time. It was obvious that hope had suddenly transformed into anticipation of a good outcome.

With Patrick's hand still in his, Stan stood and pulled her favorite anchorman and the child clear of the debris.

Patrick did not have time to even attempt standing. The roof finished coming down and that window collapsed less than a second after he cleared it. It would have been like a guillotine on his body had it happened while he was coming through it.

Patrick wrapped up the clinging three-year-old's head with an arm, covering her head against possible flying debris and choking white dust.

The neighbors cheered.

Michaela felt a presence next to her. She continued recording, but pulled her eye away from the viewfinder to see two men standing next to her. "Hi," she said. "You fellas must be from NBC." She went back to focusing on her camera work. Still, she glanced frequently in their direction.

"That's right. I'm George Sparks, the Dallas news division bureau chief and this is Lance Hughes, my cameraman, engineer, and general know-it-all." He grinned at the younger man holding a camera down to his side.

Hughes, the younger and considerably more rugged appearing man with long unruly hair, rolled his eyes. He wore about a week-old beard and faded jeans topped by a blue t-shirt sporting a picture of Donald Duck. "Don't listen to him. I'm here to do a job, just like he is. Of course...he wouldn't get it done without me." He returned a Cheshire cat grin.

"Touché," Sparks said. He turned his attention back to her. "Fill me in, what's happening?"

Michaela spent a few seconds detailing the situation at hand, plus adding back-story about the location of the oil and gas wells on the Cattle Trails Ranch a few hundred feet west behind the row of houses where they now stood, just out of sight over the hill.

Suddenly, nearby conversations became a din of joyous chatter, and she abruptly stopped her explanation to the network boys.

Three of the first responders had already made it to the bottom of the hole and one took the girl from Stan. Michaela made sure to get that shot framed perfectly.

Stan pulled Patrick up onto his feet. It was clear at a glance that Patrick relished the sight of the bright afternoon sunshine. Patrick and the girl were coated in white dust, presumably from crushed drywall. The high-priced suit pants and shirt he wore were ripped in several places. The little girl appeared to be in remarkably good condition, just dirty and scared.

The small group of huddled neighbors cheered and clapped, trailing the excited young mother to the other end of the hole.

"Wow," Sparks said, "who is our super hero down there?"

Without pulling the camera away from her eye, Michaela replied, "Patrick Daniels. My partner and best damn reporter and anchorman in the entire state of Texas, likely the best in the nation at this moment."

"That's certainly a glowing assessment. He must be a good friend."

The word "friend" hit her like a cold slap. She may have told Patrick that she loved him, but she had not yet called him one. She glanced yet again toward Sparks. "Yeah...yeah he is, a really good friend...and mentor."

Sparks turned his attention back to the goings-on down in the hole. "So, that's Patrick Daniels?"

"You ask that like you know him," she said, still recording.

"I'm aware of him. Your news director, Harry Alexander, apparently called the Vice President of News at the network and put in a good word on his behalf. In turn, the VP called me and asked if I had seen any of Daniels' work. Of course I had, thanks to all this. His hydraulic fracturing series is why we're here. But we certainly did not expect this kind of action."

Michaela saw streaks of blood on Patrick's face and spots of it on his shirt. The brutal assault by splintered lumber and exposed nails had taken a toll. He stood for a moment, exhausted and breathing hard, hands resting loosely on his hips, appearing as though he had just sprinted through a combat zone.

The mother had begun screaming the young girl's name when she first appeared through the broken and splintered window frame. She continued to do so as rescuers passed the child one to the other, until the last one took the child and walked across to the highest point of the broken roof. The mother sprinted to the edge of the hole nearest them.

"Sorry," Michaela told the network boys, "we need to stop talking for a couple of minutes. I need to make sure I get some natural sound of the child and mother reunion."

"You got it," Sparks said.

Michaela wanted to stay focused on Patrick but dutifully followed the child in the arms of the rescuers until the last one handed the frightened child across into the eager arms of the woman. Mother and child could not hold one another tight enough. Tears of joy and relief streamed from their eyes.

After a couple of minutes, Sparks told Hughes, "Come on. We need to interview Daniels as soon as he climbs out of that hole." As they hurried away, Sparks called out over his shoulder, "Would you mind sharing that sound-on footage for our B-roll?"

"Not at all. I'll have to clear it first, but I believe it will be okay. We'll make it available." With that question, it struck Michaela that Patrick had become the story, not simply a reporter of it. Objectivity again waned, becoming a near-debilitating nuisance. With the camera so close to her face, hiding an overt show of emotion became a non-issue. She did not attempt to stop the tears snaking down her cheeks. If she had to explain, it could be an expression of shared joy for the mother and child reunion.

She was proud of Patrick. Her heart swelled. He was a man, a real man, who thought first of others, willing to set personal desires and ambitions aside. *Karma is real and it's coming around soon to kiss you, Patrick.*

She kept the camera trained on him as he followed the rescuers up and over the rubble to take his place next to George Sparks, The NBC reporter. She saw the news team from their local competition, KFAL, the CBS affiliate, careening down the street and coming to a hard stop in their news van. She smiled when she saw that lecherous Walter Peck, microphone in hand, scurrying to get into the action. *You don't look so arrogant now, do ya, Wally?* Satisfaction at his tardiness put a smile upon her face. No doubt they would be uploading the story to their network, and she was supremely confident that before this day ended, every major network news organization would know the name Patrick Daniels, as a hero and the reporter that broke this story. His star was not simply shining brighter. It was streaking.

It also galvanized her intention. She knew what she had to do.

CHAPTER 34

"That was quite an afternoon you had yesterday. Now that you have the world's attention, what are you going to do with it?" Harry Alexander asked Patrick.

"Yeah," parroted Stan, "what *are* you going to do with it?"

Patrick shrugged his shoulders. "At the moment I can't answer that question. I don't have a clue."

A number of employees stood surrounding Patrick in the cool, darkened studio, congratulating him for courage and for the touching response to the NBC reporter's questions on his rescue of the three-year-old girl. "No news story on the planet is important enough to risk the life of a precious child. There was no heroism involved, only reaction to what had to be done," he told Sparks. "Any person with a heart would have done the same thing."

The package story he and Michaela put together afterward for their own newscast, the six o'clock sequence, had been equally emotional but went further, touching on strong circumstantial evidence tying the drilling process to the tremors and sinkholes.

As co-workers clamored to shake his hand, Patrick smiled and thanked each in turn, but as important as the series of events had been yesterday, that was not what occupied his mind. While he and Michaela worked closely and feverishly in the editing bay yesterday putting it all together, she had behaved oddly—unusually quiet, detached, as if the importance of what they did was overshadowed by something else on her mind. Something weighed on her and he wanted to know what it was. Repeated questions netted no satisfactory answers. He worried about her. Something was wrong but nothing she wanted to share. "Has anyone seen Michaela yet?" he asked, scanning the studio over the tops of every head encircling him. "She should be here to share in the accolades."

He received negative mumbles and grunts. "She'll be in shortly, I'm sure," Stan said. "Probably had school stuff to tend to."

Patrick nodded. "Yeah... that's probably it."

Harry clapped his hands. "I hate to break up this little party, but I have work to do and I'm sure all of you do, too. So, let's get on with the afternoon."

Before Harry finished the comment, Jeanie announced a page over the public address system, "Patrick Daniels, line four please... Patrick line four." She paused then giggled, and announced for all to hear, "It's CNN."

"And now it begins," Harry said.

Stan slapped the old man on the back. "You knew it would. Don't sound so down."

"I just hate the thought of possibly losing Danica and Patrick within the same year... hell, within the same Nielsen sweeps period." He sighed, slumped and shook his head. "Oh well..."

"Thanks everyone," Patrick said as he hurried away toward the newsroom. He flung the door open, stopped at the nearest cubicle, and snatched up the phone, punching the appropriate line. "This is Patrick Daniels."

"Mister Daniels, this is Arthur Penbrook, vice president of news at CNN, Atlanta."

"Yes, Mister Penbrook, what can I do for you?" he asked as Harry and Stan came through the newsroom door. Patrick turned his back to them, wanting a degree of privacy.

"That was an impressive piece you aired on your station last night, not to mention your heroism and the interview you did for the NBC boys."

"Thank you."

"That said, have you ever considered moving up to a network position?"

"A network job, huh? Interesting thought."

On that reply, Harry and Stan abruptly stopped and walked back to crowd Patrick in the tiny work cubicle. They didn't seem to give a damn about his desire for privacy.

"I have already received consensus from my board, and we're ready to make you an offer to come work for us here in Atlanta. Is a move to the east coast something you would consider if, of course, it's a substantial career advancement?"

"Absolutely," he said with excited flair, and then paused. "But I do want to throw out a caveat."

"Oh? What?"

"I would not have been able to pull all the pieces together if it had not been for the expert videography, editing and copy assistance provided by a very talented Michaela Ross."

"What, exactly, are you asking?"

"Frankly, I want to offer you a package deal, Michaela and me together as a team."

Harry frowned deeply and shook his head, mouthing, "No, no, no."

Stan backhanded Patrick on the arm, offering his own unspoken negative assessment.

Patrick returned a frustrated frown of his own, waving them away. "How would you respond to that counter offer, Mister Penbrook?"

"Uh... if she is as talented as you say, we might take a look at her, but separately from any offer we extend to you. We're just not into packaged employment deals like that."

"Hmm... well..."

"Is that a deal breaker for you?"

Patrick ran a hand through his hair. "No," he drawled, "not necessarily. I wouldn't categorize it as a deal breaker, but I need to hit pause and think about it first. Would you give me time to consider your offer?"

"Sure, but we are looking at another reporter for this position from the Minneapolis market. So, I'd like to have an answer before the close of business Friday. Is that doable?"

"Oh yes, and quite fair. Thanks. I guarantee I'll call before that deadline." After exchanging more cordial banter for a few seconds, Patrick hung up.

"Are you out of your ever lovin' mind?" Stan bellowed.

Harry grinned. "It looks like I'll be hanging onto my number one news anchor a while longer after all. But I've got to say, that is the stupidest career blunder in the making that I've ever seen or heard about."

"It may seem like a mistake to you guys, but it's important to me."

The exchange of opinions that followed turned into an argument. Patrick ceased attempting to convince his two longtime friends and coworkers. He stopped talking altogether as they piled on a barrage of indelicate comments.

Michaela followed one of the other reporters through the door into the newsroom from the studio and noticed the chatter. "Hey, why are y'all ganging up on Patrick?"

Her question elicited three abrupt stares and an equally sudden end to their conversation.

"Oops... must be none of my business."

Stan rolled his eyes. "Oh, it's very much your business," he said with no hesitation.

"Well, it's not this yahoo's business to be telling you about it, nor mine. That's Patrick's job," Harry said. "Come on, Stan, let's put in a few minutes at the chess board and let them talk."

As Harry and Stan walked away, Michaela turned to Patrick. "What are they talking about? What is it you should be telling me?"

Patrick relaxed, now that his detractors had walked away. He smiled and placed his hands on her shoulders. "I got my first network offer a few minutes ago."

A broad grin stretched Michaela's face. "Really? That's wonderful! What network?"

"CNN."

"Would you be going to Atlanta?"

"Yep."

"Did you get at least a ball park figure on salary?"

"No. We hadn't gotten to that point."

"Oh. Does that mean you have to fly out to Atlanta for an interview first?"

"We didn't talk about that either. The guy became hesitant when I told him that any deal would have to include you."

Michaela's face soured. "What?" She stepped back from under his hands. "You actually told someone in the CNN hierarchy that?"

His smile wilted away. "Well...yeah. Don't you remember discussing it? I thought we agreed on it, if I got an offer."

"For God's sake, Patrick, that was a perfect world fantasy. I never expected you to follow through on it! No freakin' way!"

"It's okay... really. If that offer falls through, there'll be others."

She back-stepped yet again. "Oh, hell no! I will not be your excuse to not follow your dream. Nor do I want you to be the albatross around my neck!" Her anger ratcheted up.

"Excuse? Albatross? Where is this coming from?"

She did not answer the question and said nothing more, suddenly uncertain—maybe afraid she might explode into a fit of rage.

Patrick glanced toward Harry and Stan at the other end of the long room and saw that they were watching. Clearly, that chess game was not holding the attention of either man. Patrick leaned toward Michaela and whispered, "I love you. I just wanted a way for us to stay together."

Her chin fell to her chest. "I know," she replied, buried within a sigh. He thought he might be cracking a hastily improvised defensive barrier. He again smiled. "Look, if we can—"

"Stop talking." Her lip began to quiver. She planted a hand on his chest. "Whatever you're about to say, don't." She turned and headed for the door at a hurried pace.

Shock swarmed over him. He was speechless.

She opened the door into the studio but stopped and looked back at him, eyes filling with tears. She bore an odd expression, as if she studied him and took several seconds to do it. When she turned to leave, her pace slowed, body slumped. It did not take a psychologist to see that profound sadness clouded her movements.

CHAPTER 35

Michaela drove as she thought, circling the city of
Comanche Falls at least five times, maybe six. She didn't
know and didn't care. It was needed time to think things
through before deciding anything. She checked the clock
on her car radio. An hour had elapsed since she walked
out of KBTA. In that time, her resolve hardened. A firm
decision was coming together.

She suddenly made a dangerous and illegal U-turn in
the middle of a busy street. The move earned honks and
angry stares from motorists forced to slam on brakes, and
squealing tires to prevent ramming her car. She had
become so committed to what she needed to do, the honks
and squeals barely registered. Courteous driving would
have to wait for another day. What she did care about was
putting a plan into action before her resolve faded.

Michaela took the nearest onramp up onto a cross-
town expressway, heading for her apartment. She was in
a race with weakening will to follow through. Arriving,
she steered into the driveway, clipping the curb and
bouncing over it. The front of the car dipped as she
tromped the brakes to a squealing stop.

Her roommate, Belinda, apparently heard the
commotion and came out the apartment door to stand on
the second-floor landing above the double garage.

Michaela marched toward her but paused at the bottom of the rickety wooden stairs.

"Something wrong?" Belinda asked.

"Yeah," she said as she began rapidly up the stairs, "and I need to stop it before it reels totally out of my control."

"Anything I can do to help?"

Michaela slowed long enough to examine the bruise on Belinda's cheek where the angry roughneck had slapped her below her eye, knocking her to the ground. It was an attack meant for her, not Belinda. She touched it gently. "I'd say you've already been through quite enough on my behalf."

She stepped into the apartment and began turning in a circle, suddenly feeling lost. "Where's the stationery?"

"On the table at the end of the sofa, where it always is. God, Mikki, you *are* addled, aren't you?"

"Yeah, sorry. Not thinking straight. But I've got to get past it and get this done," Michaela answered as she snatched up a number of sheets of paper and the ballpoint pen next to the stack. She moved to the table in the small dining area and dropped heavily onto a chair. She stared out the window toward the street, twiddling the pen between her fingers. She glanced back and saw Belinda watching her. "Sorry to ignore you, but I've got to concentrate on the best way to get this said."

"I'll leave you alone," her friend said, briskly walking away to her bedroom, closing the door behind her.

The weight of what she needed to write pressed against Michaela's determination. Tears welled as she put pen to paper and began to write.

After half an hour and a dozen wadded sheets of paper, she slowly put the pen down, wondering if there still might be a better way of saying it. After some thought, she came to believe, finally, it could not be improved upon.

She pulled her cell phone from the hip pocket of her jeans and dialed Harry Alexander's private number at the television station. After a couple of rings, "Hello," came a reply.

"Harry, this is Michaela. Sorry for running off like I did."

"Well, since I saw the reason first-hand, I'm not surprised."

"Can you ask Stan to have someone cover the six o'clock sequence for me?"

"Not a problem."

"One other favor, will you meet me somewhere outside the station for a few minutes when you get off work?"

"I can do that. How about the Lazy S at...let's say... six forty-five?"

"I'd rather not. How about that little jazz club downtown?"

"Sure, but why?"

"It's a place I'm confident Patrick won't show up. That's his ex-wife's new favorite hangout."

"Ah, got it."

Michaela said no more, ending the call.

"Belinda?"

"Yeah," her roommate replied, coming out of the bedroom to stand at her side.

"You offered your help and, as it turns out, I may need a favor after all."

"Whatever I can do, I will."

"Can you find another roommate?"

Belinda stared down at her. "What? Why?"

"I'm quitting school and my job. I'm leaving town, maybe as early as tomorrow."

"Are you serious?"

"Very." Michaela came to her feet and embraced Belinda. "You have been a good friend and confidant. You always will be. I promise you, dear heart, I'll always be there for you, no matter where I am or what I'm doing." She then snickered while sweeping a trickling tear from her cheek. "God knows; we've had some serious fun over the past couple of years." She sniffed and drew a breath. "I'm sorry to do this to you, but I have to put distance between myself and the situation I find myself in. Or, I should say, the situation that I put myself in."

"Don't worry about me. I'll find another roommate, but I'll miss you. Are you sure about this? Where are you going?"

"I think I'll go home to Mom and Dad until I can get it figured out. All I can be sure of is that I can't stay in Comanche Falls right now."

"Patrick Daniels?" Belinda asked.

Michaela nodded.

CHAPTER 36

"I bet I tried twenty times after the six o'clock broadcast Friday to contact Michaela, and then off and on all day Saturday and again on Sunday," Patrick said.

"I tried a couple of times myself," Stan replied. "I wanted to invite her to meet me at the Lazy S. When she left Friday, she was wound tighter'n a dollar pocket watch. I thought she might like someone to talk to that didn't want anything from her."

"I don't like how you said that, or what I'm sure you're implying by saying it."

Stan pulled a half-grin. "I really didn't mean it the way you heard it. I simply wanted to offer her a non-judgmental ear to bend, if she needed one." He paused and with dramatic flair put a finger to his lips, and then waggled it. "*Although*, the implication of her possibly not wanting to talk to you does fit nicely." His demeanor shifted. "Aside from her roommate, she doesn't have anyone other than me to confide in. And, in this case, you don't count."

Patrick squinted disapproval of Stan's stab at humor, or that off-the-cuff comment but chose not to address it. "It's after two o'clock. Michaela is usually at the station by two. I'm worried."

"Don't be. It's clear enough to me, if not to you, the girl needs space and time to figure out her immediate future. Buddy, you did sort of send a hard curve ball right across the plate that she chose not to swing at."

"Maybe."

"Aw, I'm sure she's all right. Probably sitting somewhere right now with a tablet and pen listing pros and cons of y'all's conversation Friday. Have you talked to Harry since you came in?"

"Nah, I've been going over raw footage that Michaela shot Thursday and the video the NBC crew shared with us."

"You might ask him about Mikki. He is her boss, ya know. If she made contact with anyone around here, it would have to be him... by necessity I'd think."

"You're right. I'll go back and ask him."

"Let me know what you find out."

Patrick nodded. "A little worried yourself, aren't you?" A wry smile sprouted.

Stan spun around to go back to work. "Don't turn into a wise ass on me. Just go talk to Harry."

Patrick needed an answer. He knew he could get no more work done until satisfied that Michaela was all right and not twisted into a bloody knot by an angry roughneck in an alley somewhere. He hurried across the studio and flung open the newsroom door.

Although the archived footage and glass littering the newsroom as a result of the earthquake had been cleaned up, the glass wall of Harry's office at the far end of the double row of cubicles had not yet been replaced. The glass had provided at least a modicum of privacy. Now, even that didn't exist. "Get in here, Daniels," he barked through the opening. He stood in front of his desk holding an overused and curling yellow tablet covered in scribbles in one hand and a pen in the other.

Patrick didn't attempt to use the glass door, which remained intact. He stepped over the aluminum frame where the glass wall had been, into Harry's office. "Yeah, boss."

"I thought you might be back here when curiosity got the best of you. You're in here about Michaela, right?"

"Sounds like you're expecting me?"

"Sure am."

"Is she okay?"

"Not exactly."

His eyes grew large. He took a fast step toward Harry. "Is she hurt or sick?" he fired back.

"Calm down. It's nothing like that." Harry paused and put a finger to his lips. "Well...not exactly anyhow."

"Then what? Something I did?"

Harry allowed his head to wilt forward, and then let out a sardonic laugh. "Isn't it always when it comes to you and attractive women?"

"I don't think I like the direction this conversation appears headed."

"And you shouldn't. Let me start by saying that, as long as you are employed at KBTA, I might as well stop hiring attractive women in the newsroom unless you suddenly come out as gay."

"Oh crap. What did she do?"

Harry tossed the pen and pad onto his desk and then vigorously rubbed his face as if washing away frustration. "She quit."

"Just like that?"

"Just like that."

Patrick pulled out his cell phone. "That can't be. I've got to talk to her." He punched a quick dial code. "I'll get this straightened out. Things will be back to normal by news time."

"Good luck with that."

This time the call did not even go to voice mail. Instead, he received a pre-recorded message that her phone was no longer in service. He ended the call and returned the phone to his pocket. But he did so slowly, reluctantly, disbelieving she would go so far as to change her number. He stabbed the air with his finger. "Okay, I'll drive to her apartment and talk to her there."

"No you won't."

Patrick grew angry. "Are you telling me I can't leave the station?"

"Stay calm. It's not that at all. You can leave if you like. I could not care less if you do or you don't. But what you'll find is a sweet girl by the name of Belinda... something or other, don't remember her last name, and no Michaela. She's gone."

"How do you know Belinda?"

"I don't. Never met her. But I had a drink with Michaela after work yesterday." The old guy sat on the front of his desk, crossed his arms over his chest and sighed. The pose was one of resignation—at the same time, defensive.

Convinced that he was now about to get the whole truth without having to continue this game of interrogation for carefully doled out nuggets of information, Patrick felt a chill. Suddenly, he wasn't at all sure he wanted to hear it. His body weight seemed to double as he moped to a nearby chair. He lowered himself onto it and then, in a measured way, looked up at Harry. He couldn't remember ever having felt so low, so small, so insignificant.

"Patrick, Michaela shared with me that you two had grown too close, too fast and that her goals for her future had become clouded. It worried her. No, let me re-phrase that; I think it scared the hell out of her."

"I suppose that's the reason she has been acting stand-offish lately."

"Probably. Anyhow, she jokingly referred to herself as an addict and you were the heroin. As it turned out, your attempt at a package deal with CNN was the slap of sobriety she needed to break the addiction."

"I screwed up," Patrick affirmed.

"Yep. You're a real dummy."

"Gosh, thanks for that rousing ego boost."

"This might help. You may have screwed up, but her reaction to it was not at all for the reason I'm sure you're thinking right now."

"Oh?"

"Michaela saw what she needed to do as an act of love and respect for you."

"She wasn't ranting or angry?"

"Not in the slightest, just something she felt she needed to do for both your sakes. She offered to stay on for a week until we found a replacement. But we have a couple of people on staff in the newsroom who could be trained rather rapidly. It seemed logical that if she didn't want to meet me at the station for that conversation last evening, she would have a huge problem working off notice, having to be around you for another week. I told her it was okay and to just go ahead and leave. She's gone, Patrick."

Patrick could not lift his head again to meet Harry's gaze.

"One last thing; she asked that I not tell you where she went. Sorry, my friend, but I will honor that request. She needs time." Harry slid from his perch on the front corner of the desk and stepped toward Patrick, patting him on the shoulder in a consoling manner, and then dropped a sealed envelope in Patrick's lap. "She asked that I give you that."

"Thanks," he mumbled. He picked up the envelope and slid fingers across its surface and then sandwiched it between his palms, knowing it was a final connection to Michaela, a communication that would be the last for a long time, maybe forever. The weight on his heart was heavy. He felt lifeless, muddled and queasy, uncertain about his ability to muster enough courage to read Michaela's farewell. He lifted himself from the chair and, with great care, folded the unopened envelope and placed it in his hip pocket. "I better get to work," he muttered.

"Are you sure you can function?"

"No, but I have to try," he said, as he walked away.

As he crossed the expansive studio, he saw Stan watching him. "You knew what Michaela had done, didn't you?" Patrick asked.

Stan slowly shook his head. "Not specifically, but I suspected that she might have left town. Did she?"

"Afraid so. It appears I'm damn toxic to women employees here."

"I shouldn't be kicking a man when he's down, but since you brought it up...yeah...you are."

Patrick began walking past him without responding or changing expression at all.

Stan put a hand on his shoulder as he came alongside of him. "Can you make it through the six o'clock broadcast?"

"I think so," Patrick said and attempted to walk on by again. Stan did not release his hold. "Meet me at the Lazy S afterwards. We'll drink until the world looks better."

Patrick feigned a slight smile and continued trekking across the studio.

* * *

Patrick and Stan arrived at the Lazy S at the same time and went inside together. Darlene, Stan's favorite waitress and girlfriend, tossed a friendly hand high into the air. She waved from the far side of the bar.

"It would appear you've made an impression," Patrick said.

Stan blushed. "She's a good girl... better than any I've ever known. And, Lord knows, she treats me better than I deserve."

She threaded her way around and between tables to their side of the bar and guided them to a booth in the back corner. "Beer?" she asked.

Stan plopped down and nodded. "That'd be great."

Patrick watched the unspoken part of that exchange. Darlene stood next to Stan, rubbing tiny circles on his back, while he grinned up at her like a kid on Christmas morning seeing a bicycle with a bow on it. *Stan may be too shy to say it, but he loves that woman. And, it appears mutual.* Stan watched her walk away.

"She does seem like a really nice person," Patrick said. "I've known her for years but have never had a conversation with her."

"So, what do you think?" Stan asked.

"About what?"

Stan flashed frustration. "Darlene. Is she a keeper?"

"All I'll say is that if you think so, don't waste time asking me. Make a move. Advice on women from stupid people like me won't get it done. You probably know me well enough to realize that I sure as hell don't have the right answers for myself, much less anyone else."

Darlene sashayed over and placed cold, sweating bottles of beer in front of them. She never took her eyes off Stan.

Patrick snatched up his bottle and gulped it. When he pulled it from his lips, it was half empty.

"Don't beat yourself up," Stan said. "You have a good one in Mikki."

"I think you meant to say *had* a good one."

"I said it the way I meant it. Don't throw in the towel, just give the girl some space. She's at a very different stage of her life than you are. Let the girl have time to get it done her way. I don't see her as the type to latch on to a new guy. Frankly, I think she took her eyes off the road and careened off in a ditch when she met you. I bet she won't do that again, not anytime soon."

"Colorful," Patrick replied as he pulled his lips away from an empty beer bottle and signaled Darlene for another.

"The point is, Mikki had no intention of becoming involved with you, but she did. She's a driven kid and, I believe, back up on the road to her goals. I think she'll finish school somewhere...but not here. And then I wouldn't be surprised to see her as a field reporter at a local station in a large metropolitan market somewhere, or even for a network. With her looks and talent, she'll be on a short list for an anchor position in no time."

"Do you think I'll ever see her again?"

"I have a strong feeling that will be up to you, not her. She made a hard decision, knowing there might be negative, permanent consequences, but she took the chance. She was deeply in to you, buddy. Something like that doesn't go away quickly."

Patrick thumbed condensation from his beer, took a couple of gulps and then fixed his eyes on a blue neon beer sign over and behind Stan's head.

"That's a dangerous look for you," Stan said. "What's on that conniving mind of yours?"

"I was thinking I should be apologizing to people... not just apologizing but down on my knees groveling for forgiveness."

"You need to drink faster. Sounds like a pity party coming on."

"I'm serious, Stan. There's a hell of a lot that I need to atone for. And I say this while still mostly sober. I should be begging Margaret's forgiveness. She never did anything other than try to make me happy. What did I do? I gave her an airtight reason to divorce me. And what about Danica? I strung her along for months, knowing that I did not love her but telling her that I did whenever she asked. I could have really damaged that girl's career and her life. I'm such an idiot."

"Well, yeah, you are for sure. But if you follow through on that apology/atonement thing, you do realize what will likely happen, don't you?"

"What are you talking about?"

"Margaret and Danica would take your grand gesture as throwing the door wide open to resuming the relationship, and voila! You're right back in the mess you created."

Patrick ran a hand through his hair. "Don't do anything. Is that your advice?"

"Not necessarily. I'm simply saying back away from that notion long enough to let your mind settle. You'll see the situation more clearly in a week, or two, or a month."

"You might be right."

"Yep... pretty sure I am."

"It's just that I turned my marriage to Margaret and what could have been a beautiful friendship with Danica into parenthetical asides in my life. I sure as hell don't want Michaela to become a one-line parenthesis in my life's story."

Darlene glided over from a nearby table she had been waiting on and asked, "You boys still doin' all right?"

"I'm just dandy. But go ahead and bring Patrick another round. He's not quite where he needs to be yet."

Patrick smirked at the sarcasm. Still, he nodded approval to Darlene as he finished off the bottle he had been working on and wiped his mouth with the back of his hand. "Okay my gruff, silver-haired guru; where do I go from here?"

"That seems like a no-brainer. Call the guy from CNN, tell him you're interested in that position in Atlanta without stipulation and then get on with your life."

As Stan spoke, detective Loyd Solomon came through the door of the bar with another guy. Solomon noticed him, smiled and gave a quick two-finger salute.

Patrick waved him over.

"How's it going, Patrick?"

"Could be better. Tell me, has the pathology report on Ned Barrett come back from Dallas yet?"

"A couple of days ago. It was murder. He had a heart attack all right, but it was induced. The real work on the case has begun. I need to figure out to whom the blame should fall and come up with the proof."

"I think we both know the answer to that."

"Yeah. I don't think a laid-off roughneck would have the wherewithal to pull it off. It was too clean, too professional looking. And that throws attention right back on Lander's Energy. Who knows? Culpability might go all the way to the top."

"What about those responsible for Amanda Pine's assault? Anything new there?"

"We made arrests just this morning. An eyewitness identified two guys. When we found them, the morons still had bloody baseball bats in the bed of the pickup truck." Solomon began walking away.

"Don't mean to be rude but the wife is expecting me for dinner and I sure want to work in a couple of beers first."

"Thanks for the info, Loyd."

"Ya see," Stan said, "it's not all bad news today."

"Yeah, but as good as it is, it's not fixing this gaping hole in my heart," Patrick said as he shoved his chair back and rose. He picked up the nearly full bottle of beer and downed about half. "I'm going home. If I stay any longer, inebriation won't make me feel better, only make it easier to cry. I have enough ego to not want people to see their number one television news anchor in Comanche Falls blubbering in his beer."

"Can you drive?"

"Sure. I don't even have a buzz on yet."

Stan stared for a moment, clearly judging sobriety. "Okay. See ya tomorrow?"

"Always, my friend, always."

Patrick stepped out into the early evening air, drew a big breath, and walked to his car. As he slid in beneath the steering wheel, he heard and felt the crinkle of paper in his hip pocket.

He removed the envelope Michaela had left for him and held it up to the fading light of day. He questioned whether he really wanted to know what was in it. He considered tossing it out the window and going on home, realizing that no matter the words Michaela had chosen, it would boil down to goodbye.

But, as sad as he was, a long career molded by curiosity and learning facts could not easily be dismissed. He cared less about what it said than how. He had to know. He swallowed hard, building courage to tear it open. After a couple of false starts, he tore away the envelope and, with considerable trepidation, unfolded the single sheet of paper. He angled it toward fading daylight and read:

Dear Patrick,

I read in a novel once, "Life is simply a series of moments strung together and all we can hope for is that they remain within our control." It happened to be a gem in a bad novel. I lived by that rule.

Sometimes, we get caught up in someone else's moments. I did. I slipped into yours. It was easy and wonderful. I have no regrets. Each moment will forever be locked in a cherished place in my heart.

The desire to package you and me to a network to keep us together is the sweetest thing anyone has ever attempted for me, but it's wrong—so wrong. It's an obstacle to your career and I will not allow myself the luxury of furthering my goals at the expense of yours.

I love you, Patrick Daniels, with all my heart. If I stayed locked in your arms, I know I would be happy forever, but in that happy lifetime, I would have wondered if I could have succeeded by my own hand. I have to know. I have to try.

The tear stains on this paper are real. The decision I'm making terrifies me. I won't know if what I'm doing is the right decision until I take the leap. I hope you understand.

I am confident a day will come that our paths will cross again. When they do, maybe we can begin a series of moments to exceed all others— not yours, not mine, but ours. I'm not saying goodbye and as long as there is breath in my lungs, I never will.

He must have consumed more beer than he realized because tears rolled down his face out of control. But within every tear was hope.

We fell in love before we had a chance to become friends first. You are my mentor, my love and, I'm now proud to say, my best friend. When I see you again, call me Mikki. In that moment, I'll know what we have at this moment is real.
I'll see you someday, somewhere, down the road.
I love you.
Michaela

CHAPTER 37

"Where'd Patrick go?" Darlene asked as she walked up to Stan, now sitting alone.

"He's missing Mikki and kind of sad about it, now that she's gone. It's something he'll have to work out on his own."

"That is sad."

"Yep, it's a helluva way to start a week. That's for sure." Stan looked up into her eyes as she hovered over him. "I told him that the only thing wrong was that he and Mikki were at different places in their lives. But you know what?"

"Uh-uh. What?"

"You and I are at exactly the same place in our lives. Pretty cool, huh?"

A smile began to curl her lips. "What, exactly, are you saying, Stan?"

"I'm saying that I'm tired of being who I am and what I have been my whole life. And I really need to cut down on my beer consumption. But it looks kind of silly to come into a bar and not drink. You're the reason I come in night after night."

"Oh, Stan..."

"I'm tired of living alone, too. I can't think of anyone I'd rather share the rest of my life with than you."

Darlene's eyes moistened. "Are... you saying you love me?"

"I guess I am. What am I talking about? I *know* I am. What do you think about the name Darlene Brister?"

"Yes," she said, and then shouted for all to hear, "Yes!" She leaned over and kissed him.

The entire clientele of the Lazy S Bar stood and cheered.